…mith's

IN THE COMPANY OF CHEERFUL LADIES

"Un[…] […]illed with good humor, a
hea[…] […]rality […] and characters who are
eas[…] to know and love. . . . These books offer a
sun[…] window into another world. . . . A few hours
spent with Precious Ramotswe and her friends is always
time well spent." —*St. Louis Post-Dispatch*

"McCall Smith's sixth book in the series . . . may be the
best yet. . . . We continue to be grateful for Mma
Ramotswe, her family, her friends, her wisdom, her
approach to life."
—*The Times-Picayune* (New Orleans)

"Sweet, soothing. . . . McCall Smith can still bring a
smile. . . . He is known to any reader seeking respite
from an impolite and unreasonable world. These novels
are poultices, valued for their healing properties. . . .
This book [has] a contagious warmth."
—*The New York Times*

"Like the first five mysteries in McCall Smith's charming
series, *Ladies* examines the mystery of human relationships and the power of goodness in our lives. . . . [Mma
Ramotswe] is a captivating character, and McCall
Smith's Africa, land of mopipi trees and lebolobolo
snakes, feels both exotic and deeply familiar."
—*People*

"The world of the No. 1 Ladies' Detective Agency is holding firm, its proprietress a full-bodied bulwark against the storm and a comfort to us all."

—*Boston Herald*

"Like its predecessors, this sweet, sage novel will leave you feeling calmer and more centered by the time you're through." —*Entertainment Weekly*

"Charming. . . . Life-affirming. . . . It's a mark of McCall Smith's talent that these books retain their freshness." —*The Plain Dealer*

"McCall Smith gives his readers the distinct pleasure of discovering an exotic yet unfettered world, one that is, in many ways, not so different from their own. That is a great gift, and for that reason, *In the Company of Cheerful Ladies* is worth savoring." —*The Oregonian*

"Thoroughly original. . . . Vivid, affectionately rendered details of everyday Botswana life. . . . A pleasure." —*Pittsburgh Post-Gazette*

"Rewarding. . . . Irresistibly charming." —*The Seattle Times*

"Wonderful. . . . A satisfying, endearing tale of the mysteries of life." —*Detroit Free Press*

"As usual, McCall Smith has created some delightful difficulties with which to test the wits of his charming, sympathetic characters." —*New York Post*

Alexander McCall Smith

IN THE COMPANY OF CHEERFUL LADIES

Alexander McCall Smith is the author of the huge international phenomenon, The No. 1 Ladies' Detective Agency series, The Sunday Philosophy Club series, the 44 Scotland Street series, and the Portuguese Irregular Verbs series. He was born in what is now known as Zimbabwe, and he was a law professor at the University of Botswana and at Edinburgh University. He lives in Scotland.

BOOKS BY
ALEXANDER McCALL SMITH

IN THE NO. 1 LADIES' DETECTIVE AGENCY SERIES

The No. 1 Ladies' Detective Agency

Tears of the Giraffe

Morality for Beautiful Girls

The Kalahari Typing School for Men

The Full Cupboard of Life

In the Company of Cheerful Ladies

Blue Shoes and Happiness

IN THE SUNDAY PHILOSOPHY CLUB SERIES

The Sunday Philosophy Club

Friends, Lovers, Chocolate

IN THE PORTUGUESE IRREGULAR VERBS SERIES

Portuguese Irregular Verbs

The Finer Points of Sausage Dogs

At the Villa of Reduced Circumstances

IN THE 44 SCOTLAND STREET SERIES

44 Scotland Street

Espresso Tales

The Girl Who Married a Lion and Other Tales from Africa

IN THE COMPANY OF CHEERFUL LADIES

IN THE COMPANY OF CHEERFUL LADIES

Alexander McCall Smith

ANCHOR BOOKS

A Division of Random House, Inc.

New York

FIRST ANCHOR BOOKS EDITION, MARCH 2006

The Library of Congress has cataloged the Pantheon edition as follows:
McCall Smith, Alexander, 1948–
In the company of cheerful ladies / Alexander McCall Smith.
p. cm.
1. No. 1 Ladies' Detective Agency (Imaginary organization)—Fiction.
2. Ramotswe, Precious (Fictitious character)—Fiction. 3. Women private
investigators—Botswana—Fiction. 4. Botswana—Fiction. I. Title.
PR6063.C32615 2005   823'.914—dc22   2004056827

Anchor ISBN-10: 1-4000-7570-X
Anchor ISBN-13: 978-1-4000-7570-6

www.anchorbooks.com

Printed in the United States of America
10   9   8   7   6   5   4   3   2   1

This book is for
Helena Kennedy

IN THE COMPANY OF CHEERFUL LADIES

CHAPTER ONE

HONESTY, TEA, AND THINGS
IN THE KITCHEN

MMA RAMOTSWE was sitting alone in her favourite café, on the edge of the shopping centre at the Gaborone end of the Tlokweng Road. It was a Saturday, the day that she preferred above all others, a day on which one might do as much or as little as one liked, a day to have lunch with a friend at the President Hotel, or, as on that day, to sit by oneself and think about the events of the week and the state of the world. This café was a good place to be, for several reasons. Firstly, there was the view, that of a stand of eucalyptus trees with foliage of a comforting dark green which made a sound like the sea when the wind blew through the leaves. Or that, at least, was the sound which Mma Ramotswe imagined the sea to make. She had never seen the ocean, which was far away from land-locked Botswana; far away across the deserts of Namibia, across the red sands and the dry mountains. But she could imagine it when she listened to the eucalyptus trees in the wind and closed her eyes. Perhaps one day she would see it, and would stand on the shore and let the waves wash over her feet. Perhaps.

The other advantage which this café had was the fact that the tables were out on an open verandah, and there was always something to watch. That morning, for instance, she had seen a minor dispute between a teenage girl and her boyfriend—an exchange of words which she did not catch but which was clear enough in its meaning—and she had witnessed a woman scrape the side of a neighbouring car while she tried to park. The woman had stopped, quickly inspected the damage, and had then driven off. Mma Ramotswe had watched this incredulously, and had half-risen to her feet to protest, but was too late: the woman's car had by then turned the corner and disappeared and she did not even have time to see its number-plate.

She had sat down again and poured herself another cup of tea. It was not true that such a thing could not have happened in the old Botswana—it could—but it was undoubtedly true that this was much more likely to happen today. There were many selfish people about these days, people who seemed not to care if they scraped the cars of others or bumped into people while walking on the street. Mma Ramotswe knew that this was what happened when towns became bigger and people became strangers to one another; she knew too that this was a consequence of increasing prosperity, which, curiously enough, just seemed to bring out greed and selfishness. But even if she knew why all this happened, it did not make it any easier to bear. The rest of the world might become as rude as it wished, but this was not the way of things in Botswana and she would always defend the old Botswana way of doing things.

Life was far better, thought Mma Ramotswe, if we knew who we were. In the days when she was a schoolgirl in Mochudi, the village in which she had been born, everybody had known exactly who you were, and they often knew exactly who your parents, and your parents' parents, had been. Today when she went back to Mochudi, people would greet her as if she had barely been away; her presence needed no explanation. And even here in Gaborone, where things had grown so much, people still knew precisely who she was. They would know that she was Precious Ramotswe, founder of the No. 1 Ladies' Detective Agency, daughter of the late Obed Ramotswe, and now the wife (after a rather protracted engagement) of that most gracious of mechanics, Mr J.L.B. Matekoni, proprietor of Tlokweng Road Speedy Motors. And some of them at least would also know that she lived in Zebra Drive, that she had a tiny white van, and that she employed one Grace Makutsi as her assistant. And so the ramifications of relationships and ties would spread further outwards, and the number of things that might be known would grow. Some might know that Mma Makutsi had a brother, Richard, who was now late; that she had achieved the previously unheard-of result of ninety-seven per cent in the final examinations of the Botswana Secretarial College; and that following upon the success of the Kalahari Typing School for Men, she had recently moved to a rather better house in Extension Two. Knowledge of this sort—everyday, human knowledge—helped to keep society together and made it difficult to scrape the car of another without feeling guilty about it and without doing something to let the owner know. Not that this appeared to make any difference to that selfish woman in the car, who had left the scrape unreported, who clearly did not care.

But there was no point in throwing up one's hands in despair. People had always done that—the throwing up of hands, the shrug—but one got nowhere in doing so. The world might have changed for the worse in some respects, but in others it was a much better place, and it was important to remember this. Lights went off in some places, but went on in others. Look at Africa—there had been so much to shake one's head over—corruption, civil wars, and the rest—but there was also so much which was now much better. There had been slavery in the past, and all the suffering which that had brought, and there had been all the cruelties of apartheid just those few miles away over the border, but all that was now over. There had been ignorance, but now more and more people were learning to write, and were graduating from universities. Women had been held in such servitude, and now they could vote and express themselves and claim lives for themselves, even if there were still many men who did not want such things to be. These were the good things that happened and one had to remember them.

Mma Ramotswe raised her tea cup to her lips and looked out over the brim. At the edge of the car park, immediately in front of the café, a small market had been set up, with traders' stalls and trays of colourful goods. She watched as a man attempted to persuade a customer to buy a pair of sunglasses. The woman tried on several pairs, but was not satisfied, and moved on to the next stall. There she pointed to a small piece of silver jewellery, a bangle, and the trader, a short man wearing a wide-brimmed felt hat, passed it across to her to try on. Mma Ramotswe watched as the woman held out her wrist to be admired by the trader, who nodded encouragement. But the woman seemed not to agree with his verdict, and handed the bangle back, pointing to another item at the back of the stall. And at that moment, while the trader turned round to stretch for whatever it was that she had singled out, the woman quickly slipped another bangle into the pocket of the jacket she was wearing.

Mma Ramotswe gasped. This time, she could not sit back and allow a crime to be committed before her very eyes. If people did nothing, then no wonder that things were getting worse. So she stood up, and began to walk firmly towards the stall where the woman had now engaged the trader in earnest discussion about the merits of the merchandise which he was showing her.

"Excuse me, Mma."

The voice came from behind her, and Mma Ramotswe turned round to see who had addressed her. It was the waitress, a young woman whom Mma Ramotswe had not seen at the café before.

"Yes, Mma, what is it?"

The waitress pointed an accusing finger at her. "You cannot run away like that," she said. "I saw you. You're trying to go away without paying the bill. I saw you."

For a moment Mma Ramotswe was unable to speak. The accusation was a terrible one, and so unwarranted. Of course she had not been trying to get away without paying the bill— she would never do such a thing; all she was doing was trying to stop a crime being committed before her eyes.

She recovered herself sufficiently to reply. "I am not trying to go away, Mma," she said. "I am just trying to stop that person over there from stealing from that man. Then I would have come back to pay."

The waitress smiled knowingly. "They all find some excuse," she said. "Every day there are people like you. They come and eat our food and then they run away and hide. You people are all the same."

Mma Ramotswe looked over towards the stall. The woman had begun to walk away, presumably with the bangle still firmly in her pocket. It would now be too late to do anything about it, and all because of this silly young woman who had misunderstood what she was doing.

She went back to her table and sat down. "Bring me the bill," she said. "I will pay it straightaway."

The waitress stared at her. "I will bring you the bill," she said. "But I shall have to add something for myself. I will have to add this if you do not want me to call the police and tell them about how you tried to run away."

As the waitress went off to fetch the bill, Mma Ramotswe glanced around her to see if people at the neighbouring tables had witnessed the scene. At the table next to hers, a woman sat with her two young children, who were sipping with evident pleasure at large milkshakes. The woman smiled at Mma Ramotswe, and then turned her attention back to the children. She had not seen anything, thought Mma Ramotswe, but then the woman leaned across the table and addressed a remark to her.

"Bad luck, Mma," she said. "They are too quick in this place. It is easier to run away at the hotels."

FOR A FEW minutes Mma Ramotswe sat in complete silence, reflecting on what she had seen. It was remarkable. Within a very short space of time she had seen an instance of bare-faced theft, had encountered a waitress who thought nothing of extorting money, and then, to bring the whole matter to a shameful conclusion, the woman at the next table had disclosed a thoroughly dishonest view of the world. Mma Ramotswe was frankly astonished. She thought of what her father, the late Obed Ramotswe, a fine judge of cattle but also a man of the utmost propriety, would have thought of this. He had brought her up to be scrupulously honest, and he would have been mortified to see this sort of behaviour. Mma Ramotswe remembered how she had been walking with him in Mochudi when she was a young girl and they had come across a coin on the edge of the road. She had fallen upon it with delight and was polishing it with her handkerchief before he noticed what had happened and had intervened.

"That is not ours," he said. "That money belongs to somebody else."

She had yielded the coin reluctantly, and it had been handed in to a surprised police sergeant at the Mochudi Police Post, but

the lesson had been a vivid one. It was difficult for Mma Ramotswe to imagine how anybody could steal from another, or
do any of the things which one read about in the *Botswana Daily
News* court reports. The only explanation was that people who
did that sort of thing had no understanding of what others felt;
they simply did not understand. If you knew what it was like to be
another person, then how could you possibly do something which
would cause pain?

The problem, though, was that there seemed to be people in
whom that imaginative part was just missing. It could be that
they were born that way—with something missing from their
brains—or it could be that they became like that because they
were never taught by their parents to sympathise with others.
That was the most likely explanation, thought Mma Ramotswe. A
whole generation of people, not only in Africa, but everywhere
else, had not been taught to feel for others because the parents
simply had not bothered to teach them this.

She continued to think of this as she drove in her tiny white
van, back through that part of town known as the Village, back
past the University, with its growing sprawl of buildings, and
finally along Zebra Drive itself, where she lived. She had been so
disturbed by what she had seen that she had quite forgotten to do
the shopping that she had intended to do, with the result that it
was only when she pulled into her driveway and came to a halt
beside the kitchen wall that she remembered that she had none
of the items she needed to make that night's dinner. There were
no beans, for example, which meant that their stew would be
accompanied by no greens; and there would be no custard for the
pudding which she had planned to make for the children. She sat
at the wheel of the van and contemplated retracing her tracks to
the shops, but she just did not have the energy. It was a hot day,
and the house looked cool and inviting. She could go inside,

make herself a pot of bush tea, and retire to her bedroom for a sleep. Mr J.L.B. Matekoni and the children had gone out to Mojadite, a small village off the Lobatse Road, to visit his aunt, and would not be back before six or seven. She would have the house to herself for several hours yet, and this would be a good time for a rest. There was plenty of food in the house—even if it was the wrong sort for the dinner that she had planned. They could have pumpkin with the stew, rather than beans, and the children would be perfectly happy with a tin of peaches in syrup rather than the custard and semolina pudding that she had thought of making. So there was no reason to go out again.

Mma Ramotswe stepped out of the tiny white van and walked round to the kitchen door, unlocking it to let herself in. She could remember the days when nobody locked their doors in Botswana, and indeed when there were many doors that had no locks to lock anyway. But they had to lock their doors now and there were even people who locked their gates too. She thought of what she had seen only a short time before. That woman who had stolen from the trader with the wide-brimmed felt hat; she lived in a room somewhere which she no doubt kept locked, and yet she was prepared to steal from that poor man. Mma Ramotswe sighed. There was much in this world over which one might shake one's head. Indeed, it would be possible to go through life today with one's head in constant motion, like a puppet in the hands of a shaky puppeteer.

The kitchen was cool, and Mma Ramotswe slipped out of her shoes, which had been pinching her recently (could one's feet put on weight?). The polished concrete floor was comfortable underfoot as she moved over to the sink to pour herself a glass of water. Rose, her maid, was away for the weekend, but had tidied the kitchen before she left on Friday evening. Rose was conscientious and kept all the surfaces scrupulously clean. She lived in a small house on the far edge of Tlokweng, which she maintained with the same rigour as she devoted to her work for Mma Ramotswe. She was one of those women, thought Mma Ramotswe, in whom there seemed to be an unending capacity for hard work. She had raised a family—and raised them well—with little help from the fathers of the children. She had provided for these children on the small wages that she had earned as a maid and by the payment, scant though it was, that she received for the sewing work that she undertook. Africa was full of such women, it seemed, and if there was to be any hope for Africa it would surely come from women such as these.

Mma Ramotswe filled the kettle from the kitchen tap and put it on the cooker. She did this automatically, as one performs familiar tasks, and it was only after she had done this that she noticed that the kettle had not been in its accustomed place. Rose always left it on the small wooden chopping block beside the sink, and the children, Motholeli and Puso, knew to leave it there too. That was the kettle's place, and it would not have occurred to anybody to leave it on the low wooden dresser on the other side of the kitchen. Certainly Mr J.L.B. Matekoni would not have done that—and indeed she had never seen Mr J.L.B. Matekoni touch the kettle in all the six months since their marriage and his arrival in the house on Zebra Drive. Mr J.L.B. Matekoni liked tea, of course—it would have been very difficult to marry a man who did not like tea—but he very rarely seemed to make any tea for himself. She had not thought about this before now, but it was rather interesting, was it not, that somebody might believe that tea just happened along? Mr J.L.B. Matekoni was not a lazy man, but it was remarkable to reflect how most men imagined that things like tea and food would simply appear if they waited long enough. There would always be a woman in the background—a mother, a girlfriend, a wife—who would ensure that these needs would be met. This should change, of course, and men should learn how to look after themselves, but very few men seemed to be doing this yet. And there was not much hope for the younger generation, looking at the two apprentices and how they behaved. They still expected women to look after them and, unfortunately, there seemed to be enough young women who were prepared to do this.

It was while she was thinking this that Mma Ramotswe noticed that one of the drawers in the kitchen dresser was not as she had left it. It was not fully open, but had definitely been pulled out and then not closed properly. She frowned. This was very strange. Again, Rose always shut everything after she used it and the only other person who had been in the kitchen since Rose left had been Mma Ramotswe herself. She had been in there early that morning, when she had got out of bed to make breakfast for Mr J.L.B. Matekoni and the children before they went off to Mojadite. Then she had seen them off on their early start and had gone back into the kitchen to tidy up. She had not needed anything from that drawer, which contained string, scissors, and other items that she would only use from time to time. Somebody else must have opened it.

She moved over to that side of the kitchen and opened the drawer further to inspect it. Everything seemed to be there, except . . . and now she noticed the ball of string which was sitting on the top of the dresser. She picked this up and examined it. This was her ball of string, indeed, and it had been taken out of the drawer and left out by the person who had opened the drawer and, she imagined, who had also moved the kettle from its accustomed place.

Mma Ramotswe stood quite still. It now occurred to her that there had been an intruder, and that whoever it was who had come into the house had been disturbed by her return. That person might have run out of the front of the house when she came into the kitchen, but then the front door, which provided the only means of leaving on that side of the house, would have been left firmly locked. This meant that the intruder might still be inside.

For a few moments she wondered what to do. She could telephone the police and tell them that she suspected that somebody was in the house, but what if they came out to investigate and there was nobody? They would hardly be pleased to be called out for no reason at all and they would probably mutter comments about nervous women who should know better than to waste police time while there were real crimes to be looked into. So perhaps it was premature to call the police and she should, instead, go through the house herself, moving from room to room to see if there was anybody there. Of course that was risky. Even in peaceful Botswana there were cases of people being attacked by intruders when they came upon them in the course of a robbery. Some of these people were dangerous. And yet this was Gaborone, on a Saturday afternoon, with the sun riding high in the sky, and people walking along Zebra Drive. This was not a time of shadows and inexplicable noises, a time of darkness. This was not a time to be afraid.

CHAPTER TWO

TROUSERS AND PUMPKINS

MMA RAMOTSWE did not consider herself to be a particularly courageous woman. There were some things of which she was frightened: curtainless windows at night, for example, because one could not see what was outside, in the darkness; and snakes, because there were snakes about which were truly dangerous—puff adders, for example, the lebolobolo, which was fat and lazy and had great curved fangs, or the mokopa, which was long and black and very poisonous and which was well-known to hate humans because of some distant wrong in snake memory. These were things about which one should be frightened; other things could be frightening if one allowed them to be so, but could be faced up to if one were only prepared to look them in the eye.

Yet there was something very strange about thinking that you were alone in the house and then discovering that you were not. Mma Ramotswe found this very frightening, and had to struggle with herself before she began her inspection, walking first through the door which led from the kitchen into the sitting room next door. She glanced about her, and quickly noticed that everything was in its normal place and that nothing seemed to have been disturbed. There was her ornamental plate with its picture of Sir Seretse Khama—a prize possession which she would have been mortified to have lost to a burglar. And there was her Queen Elizabeth II tea cup, with its picture of the Queen looking out in such a dignified way. That was another thing that she would have been very upset to have lost, because it reminded her of duty and of the traditional values in a world that seemed to have less and less time for such things. Not once had Seretse Khama faltered in his duty, nor had the Queen, who admired the Khama family and had always had a feeling for Africa. Mma Ramotswe had read that at the funeral of Sir Garfield Todd, that good man who had stood up for decency and justice in Zimbabwe, a message had been read out from the Queen. And the Queen had insisted that her High Commissioner should go to the graveside in person, to the very graveside, to read out what she had to say about that brave man. And when Lady Khama had died, the Queen had sent a message too, because she understood, and that had made Mma Ramotswe feel proud of being a Motswana, and of all that Seretse and his wife had done.

She looked quickly at the wall to see whether the photograph of her father—her Daddy, as she called him—the late Obed Ramotswe was in place, and it was. And so was the velvet picture of mountains, which they had brought over from Mr J.L.B. Matekoni's house near the old Botswana Defence Force Club. There would have been many people who would have liked to steal that, so that they could run their fingers over it and feel the texture of the velvet, but it was safe too. Mma Ramotswe was not sure about that picture, and perhaps it would not be an altogether bad thing if somebody did steal it, but she corrected herself and suppressed the thought. Mr J.L.B. Matekoni liked that picture, and she would not have wished him to be upset. So the picture would remain. And indeed, if they ever did have a real burglary, when everything was taken, she was sure that the picture would somehow be left, and she would have to look at it while she sat on cushions on the floor, all the chairs having gone.

She moved over to the door between the sitting room and the verandah and checked it. It was securely locked, just as they had left it. And the windows too, although open, had their wrought-iron bars intact. Nobody could have entered by any of those without bending or breaking the bars, and this had not been done. So the intruder, if he existed, could neither have come in nor gone out through that room.

She left the sitting room and walked slowly down the corridor to check the other rooms. There was a large walk-in cupboard a few paces along the corridor, and she stopped before this, peering gingerly past the edge of its door, which was slightly ajar. It was dark in the cupboard, but she could just make out the shapes of the items it contained: the two buckets, the sewing machine, the coats that Mr J.L.B. Matekoni had brought with him and hung on the rail at the back. Nothing seemed out of place, and there was certainly no intruder hiding in the coats. So she closed the door and went on until she came to the first of the three rooms that gave off the corridor. This was Puso's room, which was very much a boy's room, with little in it. She opened the door cautiously, gritting her teeth as the door creaked loudly. She looked at the table, on which a home-made catapult was resting, and the floor, on which a discarded football and a pair of running shoes lay, and she realised that no intruder would come in here anyway. Motholeli's room also was empty, although here Mma Ramotswe thought it necessary to peer into the cupboard. Again there was nothing untoward.

Now she entered the bedroom she shared with Mr J.L.B. Matekoni. This was the largest of the three bedrooms, and it contained things that somebody might well wish to steal. There were her clothes, for instance, which were colourful and well-made.

There would be a keen demand for these from larger ladies looking for dresses, but there was no sign that the hanging rail on
which these garments were suspended had been tampered with.
And nor was there any sign of disturbance on the dressing table
on which Mma Ramotswe kept the few brooches and bangles
that she liked to wear. None of these seemed to have gone.

Mma Ramotswe felt the tension leave her body. The house
was obviously empty and the notion that somebody might be hiding in it was manifestly nonsense. There was probably some perfectly rational explanation for the open drawer and the ball of
string on the dresser, and this explanation would no doubt
emerge when Mr J.L.B. Matekoni and the children returned that
evening. One possibility was that they had set off, forgotten something, and then come back to the house after Mma Ramotswe
had herself left it. Perhaps they had bought a present for Mr
J.L.B. Matekoni's relative and had come back to wrap it up, a task
for which they would have needed the string. That was a perfectly rational explanation.

As Mma Ramotswe made her way back to the kitchen to
make her tea, she thought of how things that appeared to be mysteries were usually no such thing. The unexplained was unexplained not because there was anything beyond explanation, but
simply because the ordinary, day-to-day explanation had not
made itself apparent. Once one began to enquire, so-called mysteries rapidly tended to become something much more prosaic.
Not that people liked this, of course. They liked to think that
there were things beyond explanation—supernatural things—
things like tokoloshes, for example, who roamed at night and
caused fear and mischief. Nobody ever saw a tokolosh for the
simple reason that there was nothing to see. What one thought
was a tokolosh was usually no more than a shadow of a branch in
the moonlight, or the sound of the wind in the trees, or a tiny ani-

mal scurrying through the undergrowth. But people were not attracted by these perfectly straightforward explanations and spoke instead of all sorts of fanciful spirits. Well, she would not be like that when it came to intruders. There had been no intruder in the house at all, and Mma Ramotswe was quite alone, as she had originally thought herself to be.

She made her tea and poured herself a large cup. Then, cup in hand, she returned to her bedroom. It would be a pleasant way of spending what remained of the afternoon, resting on her bed, and falling asleep if she wished. She had a few magazines on her bedside table, and a copy of the *Botswana Daily News*. She would read these until her eyes began to shut and the magazine fell out of her hands. It was a very agreeable way of drifting off to sleep.

She opened wide the window to allow a cooling breeze to circulate. Then, having placed her tea cup on the bedside table, she lowered herself onto the bed, sinking down into the mattress that had served her so well for many years and which was holding up very well with the additional weight of Mr J.L.B. Matekoni. She had bought the bed and its mattress at the same time that she had moved into the house on Zebra Drive, and had resisted the temptation to buy cheaply. In her view a well-made bed was the one thing on which it was worthwhile spending as much money as one could possibly afford. A good bed produced happiness, she was sure of that; a bad, uncomfortable bed produced grumpiness and niggling pains.

She started to read the *Botswana Daily News*. There was a story of a politician who had made a speech urging people to take more care of their cattle. He said that it was a shocking thing to the conscience of a cattle-owning country that there should be cases of mistreated cattle. People who allowed their cattle to go thirsty while they were driving them to the railway siding should be ashamed of themselves, he said. It was well-known, he went on, that the quality of meat was affected by the experience of the cattle in their last days. An animal that had been stressed would always produce beef that tasted less than perfect, and perfection was what Botswana wanted for its meat. After all, Botswana beef was fine, grass-fed beef, and tasted so much better than the meat of those poor cattle which were kept cooped up or which were fed food that cattle should not eat.

Mma Ramotswe found herself agreeing with all of this. Her father had been a great judge of cattle and had always told her that cattle should be treated as members of the family. He knew the names of all his cattle, which was a considerable feat for one who had built up so large a herd, and he would never have tolerated their suffering in any way. It was just as well, she thought, that he was no longer able to hear this news of thirsty cattle, nor to see the sort of things that she had seen that very day while having her tea at the shopping centre.

She finished the article on cattle and had embarked on another one when she heard a sound. It was a rather peculiar sound, rather like moaning. She lowered the newspaper and stared up at the ceiling. It was very strange. The sound was apparently coming from fairly nearby—from just outside her window, it seemed. She listened very hard and there it was again, once more emanating from somewhere not far away.

Mma Ramotswe sat up, and as she did so the sound occurred again—a soft, indistinct groaning, like the sound of a dog in pain. She got up off the bed and crossed to her window to look outside. If there was a dog in the garden, then she would have to go and chase it away. She did not like dogs to come into the garden, and in particular she did not like visits from the malodorous yellow dogs which her neighbour kept. These dogs were always moaning and whining, in a way which was very similar to the sound that she had heard while lying down.

She looked out into the garden. The sun was well down in the sky now, and the shadows from the trees were long. She saw the paw-paw trees and their yellowing leaves; she saw the spray of bougainvillaea and the mopipi tree which grew at the edge of Mr J.L.B. Matekoni's vegetable patch. And she saw the rough patch of grass in which a stray dog might like to hide. But there was no dog in sight, not under her window, nor in the grass, nor at the foot of the mopipi tree.

Mma Ramotswe turned round and went back to bed. Lying down again, her traditional frame sank deep into the mattress, which sagged down towards the floor. Immediately the moaning sound returned, louder this time, and it seemed rather closer. Mma Ramotswe frowned, and shifted her weight on the mattress. Immediately the moaning sound made itself heard again, this time even more loudly.

It was then that she realised that the sound was coming from within the room, and her heart skipped a beat. The sound was in the room, and it seemed as if it was directly under her, under the bed. And at that point, as this frightening realisation was reached, her mattress suddenly heaved beneath her, as if a great subterranean event had propelled it upwards. Then, with a scuffling sound, the figure of a man squirmed out from under the bed, seemed to struggle with some impediment as he emerged, and then shook himself free and dashed out of the room. It happened so quickly that Mma Ramotswe barely had time to see him before he disappeared through the bedroom door. She had no time to see his features, and she only barely took in the fact that although he was wearing a smart red shirt, he was not wearing any trousers.

She shouted out, but the man was already out of the room. And by the time that she struggled to her feet, she heard the kitchen door slamming as he made his exit from the house. She moved over to the window in the hope of seeing him as he ran across her yard, but he had taken another route, over to the side, and must have been heading towards the fence that ran along the side of her property.

Then she looked down at the floor and noticed, just at the side of the bed, where they were still snagged on the sharp end of a spring, a pair of khaki trousers. The man who had been hiding under her bed had become trapped and had been obliged to wriggle out of his trousers to make his getaway. Mma Ramotswe now picked up these trousers, releasing them from the spring, and examined them: an ordinary pair of khaki trousers, in quite good condition, and now separated from their owner. She felt gingerly in the pockets—one never knew what one would find in a man's pockets—but there was nothing other than a piece of string. There was certainly nothing that could identify this man.

Mma Ramotswe carried the trousers through to the kitchen. She had been shocked by what had happened, but the thought of the intruder having to run off without his trousers made her smile. How on earth would he be able to get home, wherever that might be, clad only in a shirt and socks, and without any trousers? The police would probably pick him up if they saw him, and then he would have some explaining to do. Would he say that he had simply forgotten to put on his trousers before he went out? That would be one way of explaining himself, but would anybody ever forget to put on his trousers before he ventured forth? Surely not. Or might he say that his trousers had been stolen? But how could one's trousers possibly be stolen while one was wearing them? It seemed rather difficult to see how this might happen, and she could not imagine the police being convinced by such an explanation.

She poured herself another cup of tea in the kitchen, the cup she had taken through to the bedroom having been knocked over while the man made his escape from under her bed. Then she took this cup of tea, and the trousers, out onto the verandah. She draped the trousers over the rail and sat down on her chair. This was really rather funny, she thought. It had been alarming to discover that there was a man under her bed, but it must have been much more alarming for him, especially when she lay down on the bed and he had been crushed underneath the sagging mattress. That explained the moaning; the poor man was having the breath crushed out of him. Well, that's what came of hiding where one had no business to hide. He would not hide under a bed again, she suspected, which meant that he had perhaps learned a bit of a lesson. However, there were obviously other lessons for that man to learn, and if she ever found out who he was, unlikely though that was, she would have something to say to him and would say it in no uncertain terms.

When Mr J.L.B. Matekoni and the children returned in the evening, Mma Ramotswe said nothing about the incident until both Puso and Motholeli had been settled in bed and were safely off to sleep. Puso had a tendency to nightmares, and she did not want him to start worrying about intruders, and so she would make sure that he did not hear about what had happened. Motholeli was less nervous, and seemed not to be scared of the dark, as her brother was. But if she were to be told, then she might tell him in an unguarded moment, and so it would be better for neither of them to know.

Mr J.L.B. Matekoni listened intently. When she described the man running out of the room without his trousers, he gasped, and put his hand to his mouth.

"That is very bad," he said. "I do not like the thought that there was this strange man in our bedroom without any trousers."

"Yes," said Mma Ramotswe. "But you must remember that he did not take them off himself. They came off when he was trying to escape. That is different."

Mr J.L.B. Matekoni looked doubtful. "I still don't like it. Why was he there? What mischief was he planning?"

"I suspect that he was just a thief who passed by and saw that nobody was in," suggested Mma Ramotswe. "Then he was disturbed when I came back and he had no way of getting out. I suspect that he was a very frightened man."

They did not discuss the matter further. The trousers were left out on the verandah, where Mma Ramotswe had hung them. Mr J.L.B. Matekoni had suggested that they might fit one of the apprentices and he could give them to him. If they did not, then he would pass them on to one of the second-hand clothes traders who would surely find a good pair of legs to fit into them; honest legs this time.

But the next morning, when Mma Ramotswe went out onto the verandah for her morning cup of bush tea, the trousers had gone. And directly below the place where they had been left, there was a large, yellow pumpkin, luscious and ready to eat.

CHAPTER THREE

FURTHER THOUGHTS ON PUMPKINS

MMA RAMOTSWE inspected the pumpkin from all angles. There was nothing about pumpkins in Clovis Andersen's *Principles of Private Detection,* but Mma Ramotswe was perfectly capable of investigating a pumpkin herself without the need of guidance from others. She did not touch it at first, but peered at the pumpkin itself, and then at the ground around it. The pumpkin had been placed in what was nominally a flower bed, but which had not been cultivated very much since Mma Ramotswe had moved into the house. She devoted herself to vegetables and shrubs, holding the view that flowers required too much effort and gave too little reward. In the hot air of Botswana flowers tended to open briefly and then shut and wilt away, as if surprised, unless, of course, one protected them with shade netting and coaxed them daily with precious water. It was far better, thought Mma Ramotswe, to allow native plants to establish themselves. These plants knew the soil of Botswana and could cope with the sun. They knew when it was time to blossom and when it was time to hide away; they knew how to make the most of every little drop of moisture that came their way.

The bed in which the pumpkin sat ran along the low front wall of the verandah. It was mostly sand, but there were a few plants, small aloes and the like, which had taken root, and it was alongside one of these that the pumpkin had been deposited. Mma Ramotswe looked at the sand around the pumpkin: for the most part it was undisturbed, save for the tiny tracks made by ants, but there, clearly visible, a few feet away from the pumpkin was the print of a shoe—that was all; just the indentations of a shoe-sole, which told one nothing, other than that the person who put the pumpkin there was a man, judging from the size, and that he possessed a pair of shoes.

She stood above the pumpkin and contemplated its promising roundness. This would do for three meals, she thought, with perhaps a little left over to make some soup afterwards. It was exactly ready—with just that degree of ripeness which gives the flesh some sweetness without making it too soft. This was a fine pumpkin, and the person who had left it there must have been a good judge of pumpkins.

Mma Ramotswe bent forward and began to lift the pumpkin, gingerly at first but then more firmly. With the large yellow burden up against her chest, she smelled the sweet pumpkin smell, and she closed her eyes for a moment, imagining how it would be once it was cut up, cooked and gracing the plates on her table. Grasping the pumpkin, which was heavy, she made her way back to the kitchen and deposited it on the table.

"That is a very fine pumpkin," observed Mr J.L.B. Matekoni as he entered the kitchen a few minutes later.

Mma Ramotswe was about to tell him what had happened when she noticed that the children were directly behind him— Motholeli in her wheelchair and Puso neatly dressed in freshly ironed khaki shorts (Rose's ironing) and a short-sleeved white shirt.

"A pumpkin!" shouted Puso. "A very big pumpkin!"

Mr J.L.B. Matekoni raised an eyebrow. "You have been to the shops already, Mma Ramotswe?"

"No," said Mma Ramotswe. "Somebody left this pumpkin for us. I found it out at the front. It is a very fine present." That, at least, was true. Somebody had left the pumpkin outside the house, and it was quite reasonable to assume that it was a present.

"Who was the kind person?" asked Mr J.L.B. Matekoni. "Mrs Moffat said that she would give me a present for fixing the doctor's car. Do you think that she has left us a pumpkin?"

"It may be her," said Mma Ramotswe. "But I am not sure." She looked at Mr J.L.B. Matekoni, trying to signal to him that there was more to this pumpkin than met the eye, but that it was not something that should be discussed in front of the children. He caught her eye, and realised.

"Well, I shall put that pumpkin away in the cupboard," he said, "then we shall be able to take it out later today and cook it. Do you not think that a good idea?"

"I do," said Mma Ramotswe. "You put the pumpkin away and I can make some porridge for the children's breakfast. Then we can all go to church before it gets too hot."

THEY DROVE the short distance to the Anglican Cathedral, parking Mr J.L.B. Matekoni's van round the side, near the Dean's house. Mma Ramotswe helped Motholeli into her wheelchair and Puso pushed it round to the front, where a ramp allowed for entrance. Mma Ramotswe and Mr J.L.B. Matekoni made their way in through the side door, collected their hymn books from the table near the door, and walked to their favourite pew. A few minutes later the children arrived. Motholeli's wheelchair was parked at the end of the pew, and Puso sat between Mma Ramotswe and Mr J.L.B. Matekoni, where he could be watched. He had a tendency to fidget, and would usually be sent out, after fifteen minutes or so, to play on the Cathedral swing.

Mma Ramotswe read through the service sheet. She did not approve of the day's choice of hymns, none of which was known to her, and she quickly moved on to read the parish notes. There was a list of the sick, and she ran her eye down this, noting, with sorrow, that many of those who had been on the list last week were still named. It was a time of sickness, and charity was sorely tested. There were mothers here, mothers who would leave children behind them if they were called. There were poor people and rich people too, all equal in their human vulnerability. *Remember these brothers and sisters* it said at the bottom of the list. Yes, she would. She would remember these brothers and sisters. How could one forget?

The choir entered and the service began. As she stood there, unenthusiastically mouthing the words of the unfamiliar hymns chosen for that day, Mma Ramotswe's thoughts kept returning to the extraordinary finding of the pumpkin. One possible explanation of the mystery, she thought, was that the intruder had come back for some reason—perhaps to break in again—and had discovered his trousers hung out on the verandah. He had been carrying a pumpkin, which he had probably stolen from somewhere else, and had put this down on the ground while he put the trousers back on. Then perhaps he had been disturbed—again—and had run away without picking up the pumpkin.

That was certainly possible, but was it at all likely? Mma Ramotswe looked up to the ceiling of the Cathedral, watching the blades of the great white fans as they cut slowly at the air. No, it was unlikely that the intruder would have returned, and even if he had, would he have had the time to steal a pumpkin from somewhere else? Surely his most pressing concern, without his trousers, would have been to get home or to find some other trousers.

What seemed much more likely was that the disappearance of the trousers and the appearance of the pumpkin were completely unconnected. The garment had been removed by a passer-by, who had spotted the opportunity to acquire a perfectly good pair of khaki trousers. Then, earlier that morning, a friend had dropped off a pumpkin as a present and had merely left it there, not wishing to wake people too early on a Sunday. That was much more probable, and indeed was the solution that Clovis Andersen himself would have identified. *Never go for the excessively compli-cated solution,* he had written. *Always assume that the simplest explanation is the most likely one. Nine times out of ten, you'll be right.*

Mma Ramotswe jolted herself back from these realms of speculation. The service was proceeding, and now the Reverend Trevor Mwamba was ascending the pulpit. She put from her mind all thoughts of pumpkins and listened to what Trevor Mwamba had to say. He had married them, under that tree at the orphan farm, barely six months ago, on that day of which every minute was etched into her memory: the voices of the children, who sang; the canopy of leaves above their heads; the smiles of those present; and those echoing words which had marked the beginning of her married life to that kind man, Mr J.L.B. Matekoni, that great mechanic, who was now her husband.

The Reverend Trevor Mwamba now looked out over the con-gregation, and smiled. "We have visitors," he said, smiling. "Please stand up and tell us who you are."

They looked about them. Five people stood up, scattered amongst the regular congregation. One by one, to a turning of heads, they announced who they were.

"I am John Ngwenya, from Mbabane in Swaziland," said a stout man in a pearl-grey suit. He bowed slightly, and this was acknowledged by a burst of applause from the congregation, who then turned to look at the next visitor. In turn the others revealed who they were—a man from Francistown, a man from Brisbane, a woman from Concord, Massachusetts, and a woman from Johannesburg. Each was welcomed, solemnly but warmly. No distinction was made between those who were from Africa and those who were not. The American woman, Mma Ramotswe observed, was wearing a pumpkin-coloured dress. She noted that, but immediately corrected herself. This was a time of fellowship, and not a time to be thinking of pumpkins.

Trevor Mwamba adjusted his glasses. "My brothers and sisters," he began, "you are welcome here with us. Wherever you may come from, you are welcome."

He looked at his notes before him. "I am sometimes asked," he said, "why there is so much suffering in this world and how we can reconcile it with the faith which we have in a benevolent creator. This is not a new objection. Many people have made this point to those who hold to a faith, and they have often rejected the answers they have received. It is not good enough, they say. Your answers do not convince. Yet why should they imagine that we can explain every mystery? There are some mysteries that lie beyond our understanding. Such mysteries reveal themselves every day."

Yes, thought Mma Ramotswe. *There is one such mystery which has revealed itself in Zebra Drive this very morning. How does one explain a missing pair of trousers and a pumpkin that comes from nowhere?* She stopped herself. This was not the way to listen to Trevor Mwamba.

"There are many other mysteries in this world that we cannot explain and which we must accept. I think of the mystery of life, for instance. The scientists know a great deal about life, but they do not know how to make that spark that is the difference between life and no-life. That bit, that current, is a mystery to them, however much they know about how life works and perpetuates itself. And so we have to accept, do we not, that there are some mysteries in this world that we simply cannot understand? These things are simply there. They are beyond us."

The mystery of life! thought Mma Ramotswe. *The mystery of pumpkins. Why are pumpkins the shape they are? Why is the flesh of the pumpkin the colour it is? Can anybody explain that, or is it just something that is?* Again she struggled to stop her train of thought and concentrated on what Trevor Mwamba was saying.

"And so it is with suffering. It may seem a mystery to us that there can be suffering in a world in which we claim to see a divine purpose. But the more we think about that mystery, the more an answer eludes us. We could, then, shrug our shoulders and fall into despair, or we could accept the mystery for what it is, as being something that we simply cannot understand. And that does not mean that we lapse into nihilism, into the philosophy that says that we can do nothing about the suffering and pain of the world. We can do something about it, and all of us in this place today have the chance to do something, even if only a small thing, to diminish the volume of suffering in the world. We can do that by acts of kindness to others; we can do that by relieving their pain.

"If we look about our world today, if we look about this dear home of ours, Africa, then what do we see but tears and sorrow? Yes, we see those. We see those even in Botswana, where we are so fortunate in many ways. We see those in the faces of those who are ill, in their fear and their sorrow at the thought that their lives will be so shortened. This is real suffering, but it is not suffering that we as Christians walk away from. Every day, every moment of every day, there are people who are working to alleviate this suffering. They are working at this task right now as I speak, right across the road in the Princess Marina Hospital. There are doctors and nurses working. There are our own people and generous-hearted people from far away, from America, for example, who are working there to bring relief to those who are very sick from this cruel illness that stalks Africa. Do those people talk about such suffering as proof that there can be no divine presence in this world? They do not. They do not ask that question. And many are sustained by that very faith at which some clever people like to sneer. And that, my friends, is the true mystery at which we should marvel. That is what we should think about in silence for a moment, as we remember the names of those who are ill, those members of this body, this Anglican church, our brothers and sisters. And I read them out now."

CHAPTER FOUR

TEA ISSUES

IN THE MORNINGS everybody arrived at Tlokweng Road
Speedy Motors at different times, and there was no telling who
would be in first. It used to be Mr J.L.B. Matekoni, in the days
when the offices of the No. 1 Ladies' Detective Agency were
housed separately, but since the two businesses began to share
the same premises it was sometimes Mma Ramotswe or Mma
Makutsi, or, very rarely, one of the apprentices. In general, the
apprentices arrived late, as they liked to stay in bed until the last
possible moment before they bolted down a quick breakfast and
rushed to catch the overloaded minibus that would drop them off
at the roundabout at the end of the Tlokweng Road.

After their marriage, of course, Mma Ramotswe and Mr
J.L.B. Matekoni tended to arrive at exactly the same time, even if
they drove in two vehicles, as in a convoy, with Mr J.L.B.
Matekoni's truck leading the way and the tiny white van, at the
wheel of which sat Mma Ramotswe, following valiantly behind.

On that particular morning it was Mma Makutsi, carrying a
brown paper parcel, who was first to arrive. She unlocked the
office of the No. 1 Ladies' Detective Agency, placed the parcel on
her desk, and opened the window to let in some air. It was barely
seven o'clock, and it would be half an hour or so before Mma

Ramotswe and Mr J.L.B. Matekoni arrived. This would give her time to organise her desk, to telephone her cousin's sister-in-law about a family matter, and to write a quick letter to her father in Bobonong. Her father was seventy-one, and he had nothing very much to do, other than to walk to the small post office in the village and check for mail. Usually there was nothing, but at least once a week there would be a letter from Mma Makutsi, containing a few snippets of news from Gaborone and sometimes a fifty-pula note. Her father could not read English very well, and so Mma Makutsi always wrote to him in Kalanga, which gave her pleasure, as she liked to keep her grasp of the language alive.

There was much to tell him that day. She had had a busy weekend, with an invitation to a meal at the house of one of her new neighbours, who was a Malawian lady teaching at one of the schools. This lady had lived in London for a year and knew all about places that Mma Makutsi had only seen in the pages of the *National Geographic* magazine. Yet she carried her experience lightly, and did not make Mma Makutsi feel at all provincial or untravelled. Quite the opposite, in fact. The neighbour had asked probing questions about Bobonong and had listened attentively while Mma Makutsi had told her of Francistown and Maun, and places like that.

"You are lucky to live in this country," said the neighbour. "You have everything. Lots of land, as far as the eye can see, and further. And all those diamonds. And the cattle. There is everything here."

"We are very fortunate," said Mma Makutsi. "We know that."

"And you now have that nice new house," the neighbour went on, "and that interesting job of yours. People must ask you all the time: What is it like to be a private detective?"

Mma Makutsi smiled modestly. "They think it is a very exciting job," she said. "But it is not really. Most of the time we are just helping people to find out things they already know."

"And this Mma Ramotswe people talk about?" asked the neighbour. "What is she like? I have seen her at the shops. She has a very kind face. You would not think she was a detective, just to look at her."

"She is a very kind lady," agreed Mma Makutsi. "But she is also very clever. She can tell when people are lying, just by looking at them. And she also knows how to deal with men."

The neighbour sighed. "That is a very great talent," she said. "I would like to be able to do that."

Mma Makutsi agreed with this. That would be very good; and indeed it would be good to have just one man to deal with. Mma Ramotswe now had Mr J.L.B. Matekoni, and this Malawian woman had a boyfriend, whom Mma Makutsi had seen coming to the house in the evenings. She herself had not yet found a man, apart from that one she had met at the Kalahari Typing School for Men and who had not lasted very long for some reason. After that she had made a rule: *Never become emotionally involved with one of your typing students*—a rule which was a variant on the advice which Mma Ramotswe had quoted from Clovis Andersen: *Always keep your distance from your client; hugs and kisses never solved any cases, and never paid any bills.*

Now the last part of that advice was very interesting, and Mma Makutsi had considered it at some length. She had no doubt that it was true that emotional involvement with a client would not help you to see a problem clearly, and would therefore not assist the solving of the case, but was it true to say that hugs and kisses never paid any bills? Surely one could argue the opposite of that. There were plenty of people who paid their way through life with hugs and kisses—the wives of rich men, for example, or at least some wives of some rich men. Mma Makutsi was in no doubt whatsoever that some of those glamorous girls who had been in her class at the Botswana Secretarial College, those girls who in some cases got scarcely fifty per cent in the College's final examinations (against her own ninety-seven per cent); some of these girls had made a very astute calculation that the way to get on financially was to make sure that their hugs and kisses went to the right sort of man. And that, in their view, was the sort of man who was earning many thousands of pula a month and who drove an expensive car, preferably a Mercedes-Benz.

Mma Makutsi now wrote to her father about the meeting with this neighbour, but said nothing of the discussion about men, or Mma Ramotswe, or being a private detective; rather, she told him what the woman had cooked for her. Then she told him about the trouble she was having with ants in the new house, and that there seemed to be nothing that could be done. He would sympathise with her on that. Everybody in Botswana had experienced trouble with ants, and everybody had a view on what to do. But nobody ever succeeded: the ants always returned. Perhaps it was because they had been there before people had arrived and regarded it as their place. Perhaps the country should be called Botshoswane, rather than Botswana; this meant the Place of the Ants. No doubt that's what the ants called it anyway.

The letter concluded, she attached a twenty-pula note to it with a pin, addressed the envelope and sealed it. That was her daughterly duty done for the week, and she smiled to herself as she imagined her father opening his small metal postal box (which she paid for) and his pleasure in receiving her letter. She had been told that he would read each letter again and again, extracting new significance each time from each phrase and each sentence. Then he would show it to his friends, the other old men, or read it to those who could not read, and they would talk about it for hours.

By the time the letter was finished, and the quick telephone call made, she heard Mr J.L.B. Matekoni's truck arriving outside.

This truck always made more noise than any other vehicle, which was caused by its engine being different from the engines of other trucks. That was what Mr J.L.B. Matekoni had said, and he was undoubtedly right. He explained that the engine had been badly looked after by the previous owner and it had been impossible to undo the damage altogether. But it remained a good truck at heart; like a faithful beast of burden that has been maltreated by an owner but which has never lost its faith in man. And hard on the heels of the truck came the tiny white van, which drew to a halt in its parking place under the acacia tree at the side of the garage.

Mma Ramotswe and Mma Makutsi had already opened the morning mail by the time that the apprentices arrived. The older apprentice, Charlie, sauntered into their office, whistling a tune, and smiling cheekily at the two women.

"You look pleased with yourself," said Mma Ramotswe. "Have you won a big prize or something?"

The apprentice laughed. "Wouldn't you like to know, Mma? Just wouldn't you like to know?"

Mma Ramotswe exchanged glances with Mma Makutsi. "I hope you haven't come to borrow money," she said. "I am happy to help you, but you really should pay me back that fifty pula you borrowed at the beginning of the month."

The apprentice affected injured innocence. "Ow! Why do you think I should need to borrow money, Mma? Do I look like somebody who needs to borrow money? I do not, I think. In fact, I was just coming in to pay you back. Here. Look."

He reached into his pocket and took out a small roll of notes, from which he peeled off fifty pula. "There," he said. "That is fifty pula, is it not? And that is what I owe you. I am giving it back right now."

Mma Ramotswe took the money and slipped it into her drawer. "You seem to have a lot of money there. Where did you get it? Have you robbed a bank?"

The apprentice laughed. "I would never rob a bank. That is just for fools. If you rob a bank, then the police will surely catch you. That is always true. So don't rob a bank, Mma!"

"I have no intention of robbing a bank," said Mma Ramotswe, laughing at the suggestion.

"Just warning you, Mma," he said casually, ostentatiously putting the roll of notes back into the pocket of his overalls. Then he sauntered out again, having resumed his whistling.

Mma Makutsi looked across the room at Mma Ramotswe. "Well!" she exclaimed. "What a performance!"

"He's up to something," said Mma Ramotswe. "Where would he have got hold of that money if he weren't up to something? Do you think he borrowed it from somebody, from some foolish person who doesn't know what those young men are like?"

"I have no idea," said Mma Makutsi. "But did you see the look on his face? Did you see how pleased he was with himself? And did you see that he was wearing one white shoe and one brown shoe? Did you notice that?"

"I'm afraid I didn't," said Mma Ramotswe. "What can that mean, do you think?"

"It means that he has two pairs like that," said Mma Makutsi, laughing. "Or it means that he thinks he looks smart. I think it is because he thinks it looks smart."

"He's a good enough boy at heart," said Mma Ramotswe. "He just needs to grow up a bit, don't you think?"

"No," said Mma Makutsi. She paused before continuing, "Do you know, Mma? I think that he is seeing a rich woman. I think that he has found some lady to give him money. That would explain the money itself, but it would also explain the fancy shoes, the grease on the hair, and the general air of being very pleased with himself. That is what is happening, if you ask me."

Mma Ramotswe laughed. "Poor woman!" she said. "I feel sorry for her."

Mma Makutsi agreed with this, but she felt concerned for the boy too. He was only a young man, and very immature, and if this woman was much older than he was, then she might be taking advantage of him in some way. It did not look good for a young man to be spoilt in this way by some bored, rich woman. He would be the one to be hurt when the whole thing came to an end, as it undoubtedly would. And in spite of everything, she liked the two apprentices, or at least felt some responsibility for them; the responsibility that an older sister feels for a younger brother, perhaps. The younger brother might be foolish and may get into all sorts of difficulties through his foolishness, but he remained the younger brother, and he had to be protected.

"I think we should watch this situation," she said to Mma Ramotswe. And Mma Ramotswe nodded her head in agreement.

"We'll think of something," she said. "But you are right, we do not want that young man to come to any harm. We must think of something."

THEY HAD A GREAT DEAL of work to do that day. A few days previously, they had received a letter from a firm of lawyers in Zambia, asking them to help in the tracing of a Lusaka financier who had disappeared. The circumstances of his disappearance were suspicious: there was a large hole in the company's finances and the natural conclusion was that he had taken the money. This was not the sort of matter with which Mma Ramotswe normally liked to concern herself; the No. 1 Ladies' Detective Agency preferred to deal with more domestic matters, but it was a matter of professional honour that no client would be turned away, unless, of course, they deserved to be. And there was also the question of money. This sort of work paid well, and there were overheads to be taken into account—Mma Makutsi's salary, the cost of running the tiny white van, and postage, to name just a few of the items that seemed to consume so much of the profits each month.

The financier was believed to be in Botswana, where he had relatives. Of course they were the first people who should be approached, but who were they? The lawyers had been unable to provide names, and this would mean that Mma Ramotswe and Mma Makutsi would have to make enquiries amongst Zambians in Gaborone. That sounded simple enough, but it was not always easy to get foreigners to talk about their fellow citizens, especially if one of them was in trouble. They knew that it was wrong to close ranks, especially when it was a question of embezzled funds, but they did it nonetheless. So there were many telephone calls to be made to see if anybody was prepared to throw light on the case. There were also letters to hotels, asking them if they recognised the person in the photograph which they now sent them. All of this was time-consuming, and they worked solidly until ten o'clock, when Mma Ramotswe, having just finished an unsatisfactory telephone call to a rather rude Zambian woman, put down the receiver, stretched her arms wide, and announced that it was time for morning tea.

Mma Makutsi agreed. "I have written letters now to ten hotels," she said, taking a sheet out of her typewriter, "and my head is sore from thinking about missing Zambians. I am looking forward to a cup of tea."

"I will make it," offered Mma Ramotswe. "You have been working very hard, while I have just been talking on the telephone. You deserve a rest."

Mma Makutsi looked embarrassed. "That is very kind, Mma. But I was thinking of making tea in a different way this morning."

Mma Ramotswe looked at her assistant in astonishment. "In a different way? How can you make bush tea in a different way?

Surely there is only one way to make tea—you put the tea leaves in the tea-pot and then you put in the water. What are you going to do? Put the water in first? Is that the different way you have in mind?"

Mma Makutsi rose to her feet, picking up the parcel which she had placed on her desk when she arrived. Mma Ramotswe had not noticed this, as it had been behind a pile of files. Now she looked at it with curiosity.

"What is that, Mma?" Mma Ramotswe asked. "Is it something to do with this new way of making tea?"

Mma Makutsi did not reply, but unwrapped the parcel and exposed a new china tea-pot, which she held up to Mma Ramotswe's gaze.

"Ah!" exclaimed Mma Ramotswe. "That is a very fine tea-pot, Mma! Look at it! Look at the flowers on the side. That is very fine. Our bush tea will taste very good if it is brewed in so handsome a tea-pot!"

Mma Makutsi looked down at her shoes, but there was no help from that quarter; there never was. In tight moments, she had noticed, her shoes tended to say: *You're on your own, Boss!* She had known all along that this would be awkward, but she had decided that sooner or later she would have to take this issue up with Mma Ramotswe and it could not be put off any longer.

"Well, Mma," she began. "Well . . ."

She paused. It was going to be more difficult than she had imagined. She looked at Mma Ramotswe, who stared back at her expectantly.

"I am looking forward to the tea," said Mma Ramotswe helpfully.

Mma Makutsi swallowed. "I will not be making bush tea," she blurted out. "I mean, I will make bush tea for you, as usual, but I want to make my own tea, ordinary tea, in this pot. Just for me. Ordinary tea. You can drink bush tea and I will drink ordinary tea."

After she had finished speaking, there was a complete silence. Mma Ramotswe sat quite still in her chair, her eyes fixed on the china tea-pot. Mma Makutsi, who had been holding the pot up as if it were a battle standard, a standard for the ranks of those who preferred ordinary tea to bush tea, now lowered it and put it down on her desk.

"I'm sorry, Mma," said Mma Makutsi. "I'm very sorry. I do not want you to think that I am a rude person. I am not. But I have tried and tried to like bush tea and now I must speak what is in my heart. And my heart says that I have preferred ordinary tea all along. That is why I bought this special tea-pot."

Mma Ramotswe listened carefully, and then she spoke. "I am the one who should say sorry, Mma. No, it is me. I am the one. I have been the rude person all along. I have never asked you whether you would prefer to drink ordinary tea. I never bothered to ask you, but I have bought bush tea and expected you to like it. I am very sorry, Mma."

"You have not been rude," protested Mma Makutsi. "I should have told you. I am the one who is at fault here."

It was all very complicated. Mma Makutsi had switched from bush tea to ordinary tea some time ago, and then she had gone back to bush tea again. Mma Ramotswe felt confused: What did Mma Makutsi really want when it came to tea?

"No," said Mma Ramotswe. "You have been very patient with me, drinking all that bush tea just for my sake. I should have seen it. I should have seen it in your face. I did not. I am very sorry, Mma."

"But I didn't dislike it *all* that much," said Mma Makutsi. "I did not make a face when I drank it. If I had made a face, then you might have noticed it. But I did not. I was happy enough drinking it—it's just that I shall be even happier when I am drinking ordinary tea."

Mma Ramotswe nodded. "Then we shall have different tea," she said. "Just as we did in the past. I have my tea, and you have yours. That is the solution to this difficult problem."

"Exactly," said Mma Makutsi. She thought for a moment. What about Mr J.L.B. Matekoni and the apprentices? They had all been drinking bush tea, but now that there was a choice, should they be offered ordinary tea? And if they were, then would they want to drink it out of her tea-pot? She would not mind sharing her new tea-pot with Mr J.L.B. Matekoni—nobody would mind that—but sharing with the apprentices was another matter altogether.

She decided to voice her concerns to Mma Ramotswe. "What about Mr J.L.B. Matekoni?" she asked. "Will he drink . . ."

"Bush tea," said Mma Ramotswe quickly. "That is the best tea for a man. It is well-known. He will drink bush tea."

"And the apprentices?"

Mma Ramotswe rolled her eyes towards the ceiling. "Perhaps they should have bush tea too," she said. "Although, heaven knows, it's not doing them much good."

With those decisions made, Mma Makutsi put on the kettle and, watched by Mma Ramotswe, she ladled into the new tea-pot a quantity of her tea, her ordinary tea. Then she fetched Mma Ramotswe's tea-pot, which looked distinctly battered beside the fine new china tea-pot, and into this she put the correct quantity of bush tea. They waited for the kettle to boil, each of them silent, each of them alone with her thoughts. Mma Makutsi was thinking with relief of the generous response that Mma Ramotswe had shown to her confession, which seemed so like an act of disloyalty, of treachery even. Her employer had made it so easy that she felt a flood of gratitude for her. Mma Ramotswe was undoubtedly one of the finest women in all Botswana. Mma Makutsi had always known this, but here was another instance which spoke to those qualities of understanding and sympathy. And for her part, Mma Ramotswe thought of what a loyal, fine woman was Mma Makutsi. Other employees would have complained, or moaned about drinking tea they did not like, but she had said nothing. And more than that, she had given the impression that she was enjoying what was given to her, as a polite guest will eat or drink what is laid upon the host's table. This was further evidence of those very qualities which obviously had been revealed at the Botswana Secretarial College and which had resulted in her astonishingly high marks. Mma Makutsi was surely a gem.

CHAPTER FIVE

AN ENCOUNTER WITH A BICYCLE

FOR THE REST of that day, with the issue of tea tactfully settled, Mma Ramotswe and Mma Makutsi continued with their attempts to find out about the missing Zambian. This was the office stage of the project; they knew that in a day or so they would have to go out and seek people who might give them information, unless, of course, one of the letters which Mma Makutsi wrote or the telephone conversations which Mma Ramotswe conducted yielded results. At a quarter to five, when the afternoon heat had abated and the sky was beginning to redden over the Kalahari, Mma Ramotswe announced that although the working day still technically had fifteen minutes to run, they had achieved so much that they might in good conscience stop.

"I've made so many phone calls," she said. "I cannot speak any more."

"And are we any closer to finding him?" asked Mma Makutsi doubtfully.

Mma Ramotswe was not one to be defeatist. "Yes, we are," she said. "Even if we have not discovered anything concrete, every step along the path is one step closer to the solution. Mr Andersen says, doesn't he, that if there are one hundred questions to be asked in an investigation, you have to go through every one of them, and so you achieve something even if you get no answer. That is what he wrote."

"He must be right," said Mma Makutsi. "But I am not sure that we will ever find this man. He is too smart. He is not a man to be caught all that easily."

"But we are smart too," said Mma Ramotswe. "There are two smart ladies after him, and he is just one man. No man will escape in such circumstances."

Mma Makutsi still looked doubtful. "I hope that you're right, Mma," she said.

"I am," said Mma Ramotswe simply. And with that conclusion she stood up and began to gather her things together. "I can take you home," she said. "I am going that way."

They locked the office behind them and made their way round to the place where the tiny white van awaited them under its acacia tree. Mma Makutsi got into the passenger seat, next to Mma Ramotswe, who strapped herself in and started the engine. As she did so, Mma Makutsi suddenly grabbed her arm and pointed to something that was happening outside the garage.

A large, silver-coloured car, a Mercedes-Benz, had drawn up at the road side. The windows of this vehicle were slightly tinted, but a woman could be made out at the driving wheel. No sooner had she stopped, than Charlie, the older apprentice, appeared from the front of the garage, sauntered across the ground between the garage and the road, and casually climbed into the passenger seat of the expensive car.

Mma Ramotswe looked at Mma Makutsi. They were both clearly thinking the same thing; Charlie had produced a roll of notes that morning, and Mma Makutsi had quite astutely suggested that he was seeing a rich woman. Well, here was a rich woman in a rich woman's car, and there was Charlie setting off with her at the end of work. There was only one interpretation that anybody could put on that.

"Well," exclaimed Mma Makutsi. "That's that then."

Mma Ramotswe stared in fascination. "Who would have thought that that silly boy could take up with a woman like that? Who would have thought it?"

"There are some women like that," said Mma Makutsi, a strong note of disapproval in her voice. "They call them cradle-snatchers. That is because they take young men away from girls of their own age. They steal these boys away."

"So that woman is a cradle-snatcher," said Mma Ramotswe. "That is very interesting." She paused, and then turned to Mma Makutsi. "I think that we shall have to come back on duty right now," she said. "I think that we should follow that car, just to see where they go."

"That's a very good idea," said Mma Makutsi. "I do not mind being back on duty."

The opulent silver car set off towards town, and as it did so the tiny white van swung out from the side of the garage and set off behind the other car, but at a respectable distance. For a powerful car, the Mercedes-Benz was being driven slowly; most Mercedes-Benz drivers, Mma Ramotswe had observed, seemed to be in a hurry to get somewhere, but this one, this woman of whom they had had only the briefest glimpse, seemed to be content to amble along.

"She's in no hurry," said Mma Ramotswe. "They must be talking."

"I can just imagine it," said Mma Makutsi grimly. "He'll be telling her some tale about us, Mma. She'll be laughing and urging him on."

When they reached the old Game Stores, the silver car suddenly turned into the Village and made its way down Odi Drive. The tiny white van, holding back in case the apprentice should turn and see them, proceeded at a safe distance, following the quarry past the school and the new flats until they reached the University gate. Now came a surprise: instead of turning left, which would have led them into town, the silver car went to the right, towards the prison and the old Gaborone Club.

"This is very odd," said Mma Makutsi. "I would have thought that they would be going somewhere like the Sun Hotel. What is there for them along here?"

"Maybe she lives along this way," said Mma Ramotswe. "But we shall see soon enough."

Mma Ramotswe turned to Mma Makutsi and smiled conspiratorially. The two women were enjoying themselves. There was no real reason for them to follow the apprentice and this woman. Indeed, had they stopped to consider what they were doing, they would have had to admit that it was surely no more than idle curiosity—nosiness, indeed, that motivated them. And it was interesting, in a gossipy sort of way. If Charlie was seeing an older woman, then it would be fascinating to see what sort of woman she would be. Not that there was much doubt about that, thought Mma Ramotswe.

"What would Mr J.L.B. Matekoni think of us?" ventured Mma Makutsi, giggling. "Would he approve?"

Mma Ramotswe shook her head. "He would say that we were two nosy women," she said. "And I think he would be more interested in the Mercedes-Benz than the people in it. That is what mechanics are like. They think . . ."

She did not complete her sentence. The silver car was now near the old Botswana Defence Force Club and was slowing down. Then an indicator light started to flash and the car turned into a driveway—into the driveway of Mr J.L.B. Matekoni's house.

When she saw the car turn, Mma Ramotswe swerved the tiny white van so violently that Mma Makutsi shouted out in alarm. A cyclist, who had been coming in the opposite direction, swerved too, wobbling off the road to avoid the van. Mma Ramotswe drew to a halt and climbed out.

"Rra, oh Rra," she shouted, as she ran towards the fallen man. "I'm so sorry, Rra."

The man picked himself up off the ground and then dusted his trousers. He used careful, deliberate gestures, as might be used by one who is dressed in expensive clothes; but his were worn, and crumpled. Then he looked up, and Mma Ramotswe saw that there were tears in his eyes.

"Oh, Rra," she said. "I've hurt you. I'm so sorry. I will take you straight to a doctor."

The man shook his head, and then wiped at his eyes with the back of a hand.

"I am not hurt," he said. "I am shaken, but I am not hurt."

"I was looking at something else," said Mma Ramotswe, reaching out to take the man's hand. "It was very silly of me. I took my eyes off the road, and then suddenly I saw you."

The man said nothing. Turning to his bicycle, he picked it up. The front wheel, which must have been caught in a rut in the ground, was now slightly twisted, and the handlebars were at a strange angle. He looked mutely at the bicycle, before trying, unsuccessfully, to straighten the handlebars.

Mma Ramotswe turned and beckoned to Mma Makutsi to come out of the van. She had been holding back, out of a mixture of tact and embarrassment, but now she appeared and made a sympathetic remark to the man.

"I will take you to where you are going," said Mma Ramotswe. "We can put the bike in the back of the van and then I shall take that to your place, wherever that is."

The man pointed back towards Tlokweng. "I live over that way," he said. "I would prefer to go home now. I do not want to go to the other place."

They lifted up the bicycle together and placed it in the back of the van. Then Mma Ramotswe and Mma Makutsi got into the tiny white van on one side and the man on the other. With the three of them in the cab, there was barely enough room for Mma Ramotswe to change gear, and each time she did it she dug Mma Makutsi in the ribs.

"This is not a big van," Mma Ramotswe said brightly to their passenger. "But it always goes. So it will get us to Tlokweng very easily."

She looked sideways at the man. He looked as if he was in his late forties. He had a good face, she thought; an intelligent face, the face of a teacher, perhaps, or of a senior clerk. And he spoke well too, enunciating each word clearly, as if he meant it. So many people spoke carelessly these days, she thought, running their words together so that it was sometimes quite difficult to make out what they were saying. And as for people on the radio, these so-called disc jockeys, they spoke as if they had hiccups. Presumably they thought that it was fashionable to talk like this; that it made them more alluring, which it probably did if one was star-struck, and with nothing much in one's head, but which only sounded ridiculous to her.

"I will have your bicycle fixed for you," she said to the man. "It will be made as good as new. I promise you that."

The man nodded. "I cannot pay myself," he said. "I have not got the money for that."

Mma Ramotswe nodded. She had thought as much. In spite of all the progress which Botswana had made, and in spite of the prosperity which the diamonds had brought to the country, there were still many, many poor people. They should not be forgotten. But why was this man, who seemed to be educated, not in a job? She knew that there were many people who could not find a job, but usually these were people who had no skills. This man did not seem to be like that.

It was Mma Makutsi who asked the question for her. She had been thinking the same thing as Mma Ramotswe. She had noticed the disparity between the signs of poverty—something that Mma Makutsi knew all about—and the educated voice. She had seen, too, that the man's hands were what she would describe as well-kept. These were not the hands of a manual labourer, nor those of a man who tended the land. She noticed such hands at her part-time typing classes at the Kalahari Typing School for Men. Many of her pupils there, who worked in offices, had hands like this man's.

"Do you work in an office, Rra?" she asked. "And may I ask you: What is your name?"

The man glanced at her, and then turned away.

"My name is Polopetsi," he said. "And no, I have no work. I am looking for work, but there is no place that will take me."

Mma Ramotswe frowned. "It is hard now," she said. "That must be very bad for you." She paused. "What did you do before?"

Mr Polopetsi did not answer directly, and the question seemed to hang in the air for a while. Then he spoke.

"I was in prison for two years. I have been out for six months."

The tiny white van swerved slightly, almost imperceptibly. "And nobody will give you a job?" asked Mma Ramotswe.

"They will not," he answered.

"And you always tell them that you have been in prison?" interjected Mma Makutsi.

"I do," said Mr Polopetsi. "I am an honest man. I cannot lie to them when they say what have you been doing this last year. I cannot tell them that I was in Johannesburg or something like that. I cannot tell them that I have been working."

"So, you are an honest man," said Mma Ramotswe. "But why were you in prison? Are there honest men in prison?" She asked the question before she thought about it and she immediately realised that it sounded very rude; as if she were questioning the man's story.

He did not seem to take objection. "I was not sent to prison for dishonesty," he said. "But there are honest men in prison, by the way. There are some very dishonest men there, and some very bad men. But there are also men who are there because of other things that they did."

They waited for him to continue, but he did not.

"So," said Mma Ramotswe. "What did you do, Rra? Why did they send you to prison?"

Mr Polopetsi looked at his hands. "I was sent to prison because of an accident."

Mma Makutsi turned to look at him. "An accident? They sent you instead of somebody else?"

"No," said the man. "I was sent to prison because there was an accident while I was in charge of something. It was my fault, and a person was killed. It was an accident, but they said that it would not have happened had I been more careful."

They were nearing Tlokweng now, and Mma Ramotswe had to ask for directions to the man's house. He pointed to a dusty side-road, not much more than a bumpy track, and she drove the tiny white van down that, trying to avoid the larger holes in the ground. If there was a grader in Tlokweng, then it must rarely have bothered to come this way.

"Our road is not very good," said Mr Polopetsi. "When it rains all these holes fill up with water and you can go fishing if you like."

Mma Makutsi laughed. "I have lived along a road like this in the past," she said. "I know what it is like."

"Yes," said Mr Polopetsi. "It is not easy." He stopped, and pointed at a house a short way down the road. "That is my place."

It was a simple, two-room house, and Mma Ramotswe could see that it was in need of painting; the lower part of the outside walls was specked with dried red mud, which had been splashed up at the last rains. The yard, which was small, was well-swept, which suggested that there was a conscientious woman in charge of it, and there was a small chicken coop to one side, again well-kept.

"This is a very tidy place," said Mma Ramotswe. "It is good to see a place that is well-kept, as this one is."

"It is my wife," said Mr Polopetsi. "She is the one who keeps this place so clean."

"You must be proud of her, Rra," said Mma Makutsi.

"And she must be proud of you," said Mma Ramotswe.

There was silence for a moment. Then Mr Polopetsi spoke. "Why do you say that, Mma?" he asked.

"Because you are a good man," said Mma Ramotswe quietly. "That is why I said that. You may have been in prison for two years, but I can tell that you are a good man."

THEY LEFT Mr Polopetsi in his house and drove back down the pothole-ridden road. The bicycle was still in the back of the tiny white van and Mma Ramotswe had agreed with Mr Polopetsi that she would take it to be fixed the following day and bring it out to him when it was ready. As he had stepped out of the van, she had offered him money to compensate him for the accident, but he had shaken his head.

"I can tell when something is an accident," he said. "And people are not to blame for accidents. I know that."

She had not pressed the matter. This man had his pride, and it would have been rude for her to persist. So they agreed about the bicycle and left him outside his house. They were largely silent as they drove back. Mma Ramotswe was thinking of Mr Polopetsi, and his house, and the humiliation that he had suffered in his life. That must have been why he was in tears after the accident; it was just one more thing that he had to bear. Of course they had heard only his side of the story of the prison sentence. Surely people were not sent to prison in Botswana for nothing? She knew that they could be proud of their system of justice—of their judges who would not kow-tow to anybody, who were not afraid of criticising the Government. There were so many countries where this was not so, where the judges were browbeaten or chosen from amongst the ranks of the party faithful, but this had never been the case in Botswana. So surely these judges would never have sent a man to prison unless he deserved punishment?

Mma Makutsi was anxious about being late for the typing class she was due to give at seven o'clock, and so they did not linger on their way back, although they did go slightly out of their way in order to drive past Mr J.L.B. Matekoni's house—or, rather, the house which belonged to Mr J.L.B. Matekoni but which was now occupied by a tenant. The silver Mercedes-Benz was still there.

"Does she live in that house?" asked Mma Makutsi. "Did Mr J.L.B. Matekoni let the house to a woman?"

"No," said Mma Ramotswe. "He let it out—without first asking me, mind you—to a man whose car he used to fix. He does not know him very well, but he said that he always used to pay his bills."

"It is very strange," said Mma Makutsi. "We will have to find out more about this."

"We certainly shall," agreed Mma Ramotswe. "There are many mysteries developing in our lives, Mma Makutsi, what with these rich ladies in silver cars, bicycles, pumpkins, and all the rest, and we shall have to sort them all out."

Mma Makutsi looked puzzled. "Pumpkins?" she asked.

"Yes," said Mma Ramotswe. "There is a pumpkin mystery, but we do not have time to talk about it now. I shall tell you about it some other time."

THAT EVENING Mma Makutsi could not get pumpkins out of her mind, and it was one of the words which she got the typing class to type. She held these classes several times a week in a church hall that she rented for the purpose. The Kalahari Typing School for Men, which admitted only men, was based on the supposition that men usually cannot type very well but are afraid to admit this fact. And while it would be perfectly possible for them to register for any of the part-time courses provided by the Botswana Secretarial College, they tended not to do this for reasons of shame. Men would not wish to be outstripped by women in typing, which would be sure to happen. So Mma Makutsi's discreet classes had proved very popular.

She stood now before a class of fifteen men, all eager students of the art of typing, and all making good progress, although at different rates. This class had worked on finger position, had worked its way through the simple words which start every typing career (hat, cat, rat, and the like), and was now ready for more advanced tasks.

"Pumpkin," Mma Makutsi called out, and the keys immediately began to clatter. But she had something to add: "Do not leave out the p. That is very important."

A number of the keys stopped, and then started afresh, on a new line.

CHAPTER SIX

FURTHER DETAILS

MMA RAMOTSWE had intended to ask Mr J.L.B. Matekoni about his new tenant that evening, but it was busy at home, with the children making demands to be taken here and there and Rose staying late to talk to her about her sick child. So by the time that nine o'clock arrived, and the pots and pans had been washed in the kitchen, and sandwiches made and wrapped up for the children to take to school the next day, Mma Ramotswe was too tired to start a new conversation, particularly one which might prove awkward for Mr J.L.B. Matekoni. So they both retired to bed, where she read a magazine for a few minutes before drowsiness forced her to abandon her reading and she switched off the light.

So it was not until the next morning when Mr J.L.B. Matekoni came into the office for his mid-morning cup of tea, that she was able to raise the subject of what she and Mma Makutsi had seen the previous evening. She had told him about the accident, of course, and he had told the apprentices to fix the bicycle that morning.

Mma Ramotswe had expressed doubts about their abilities to fix it properly. "They are very rough with machinery," she said.

"You've told me that yourself. And we've all seen it. I don't want them to make that poor man's bicycle worse."

"It is only a bicycle," said Mr J.L.B. Matekoni, reassuringly. "It's not a Mercedes-Benz."

Now the topic of Mercedes-Benzes came up again, as she passed Mr J.L.B. Matekoni his brimming mug of bush tea.

"Mma Makutsi and I saw a Mercedes-Benz yesterday," she began, glancing at Mma Makutsi for confirmation. "It stopped right outside this place."

"Oh yes," said Mr J.L.B. Matekoni, in a tone which suggested that he was not very interested. "There are many Mercedes-Benzes these days. You see them all the time. What sort was it?"

"It was silver," offered Mma Makutsi.

Mr J.L.B. Matekoni smiled. "That is its colour. There are silver Toyotas too. Many cars are silver. I meant what model was it?"

"It was a Mercedes E class," said Mma Ramotswe.

This remark made Mma Makutsi look up in astonishment, and then look down in shame. Of course that was exactly the sort of detail which a detective should spot, and which Mma Ramotswe had indeed noted. Whereas she, Mma Makutsi, a mere assistant detective, had noticed nothing other than the colour.

"A good car," said Mr J.L.B. Matekoni. "Not that I would ever spend that much money—even if I had that much—on a car like that. There must be a lot of rich people around."

"I think that the driver was a rich lady," said Mma Ramotswe. "I think that she is a rich lady who is seeing Charlie out there. Yes. I believe that."

Mr J.L.B. Matekoni stared down into his tea. He did not like to think of the private life of his apprentices, largely because he imagined that it would be distasteful in the extreme. It would all be girls, he thought, because that is all they had in their minds. Just girls. So he said nothing, and Mma Ramotswe continued.

"Yes. Mma Makutsi and I saw Charlie getting into this Mercedes-Benz with the rich lady who was driving it and then they drove off."

She waited for a reaction from Mr J.L.B. Matekoni, but he merely continued to drink his tea.

"So," she went on, "they drove off towards the old airfield and then they went to a house." She paused before adding, "Your house, in fact."

Mr J.L.B. Matekoni put down his mug of tea. "My house?"

"Yes," said Mma Ramotswe. "They went into your house, and that is what made me swerve and make that poor man fall off his bicycle. If it had not been your house, I would not have been so surprised and would not have swerved."

"And they stayed there for some time," said Mma Makutsi. "I think they were visiting the people who live there now, whoever they are."

"That could be true," said Mr J.L.B. Matekoni. "The people who live in my house will have friends, no doubt. Perhaps this lady with the Mercedes-Benz is a friend of those people."

Mma Ramotswe agreed that this was a possibility. But the apprentices were always happy to gossip, and if they were mixing socially with Mr J.L.B. Matekoni's tenants they might well have been expected to mention the fact, surely?

Mr J.L.B. Matekoni now shrugged. "It is Charlie's affair," he said. "If he is going round with this woman in his own time, then that is his business. I cannot stop those young men from having girlfriends. That is not my job. My job is to teach them to work on engines, and that is difficult enough. If I had to teach them about looking after themselves once they leave the garage, then . . ." He spread his hands in a gesture of hopelessness.

Mma Ramotswe glanced at Mma Makutsi, who asked, "Who is your tenant, Rra?"

"His name is Ofentse Makola," he said. "I do not know much about him, but he has been paying his rent very regularly every month. He has never been late with it—not once."

Mma Ramotswe caught Mma Makutsi's eye, signalling to her that they should bring this discussion to an end. Mr J.L.B. Matekoni looked a little bit awkward, she thought, and it would be best not to press him at this stage. Besides, she wanted to find out who owned the silver Mercedes, and this would require his co-operation. If he thought that the two of them were up to something, then he might decline to help. So there should be no more talk of Charlie's exploits for the time being.

After Mr J.L.B. Matekoni had returned to work, Mma Ramotswe busied herself with some telephone calls before she turned to Mma Makutsi and asked her directly what she thought they should do.

"Should we bother to find out anything about this woman?" she asked. "Is it really any of our business?"

Mma Makutsi looked thoughtful. "Charlie is a young man," she said. "He is responsible for himself. We cannot tell him what to do."

Mma Ramotswe agreed that this was true, but then, she asked, what should one do if, as an older person, one saw a younger person about to make a bad mistake, or do something wrong. Did one have the right to say anything? Or did one just have to stand by and let matters take their own course?

Mma Makutsi considered this for a moment. "If I was about to do something foolish—really foolish—would you tell me, Mma?"

"I would tell you," said Mma Ramotswe. "I would tell you and hope that you would not do it."

"So should we tell Charlie to be careful? Is that what we should do?"

Mma Ramotswe very much doubted whether Charlie would take advice when it came to the matter of a woman, but thought that perhaps they might try. "We could try talking to him about it," she said. "But we don't really have much to go on, do we? We don't know anything about this woman, other than that she has a Mercedes-Benz. That is not enough to go on. You can't warn somebody if you know only that. You can't say: Have nothing to do with ladies who drive Mercedes-Benzes! You can't say that, can you, Mma?"

"Some people would say that," suggested Mma Makutsi, mischievously.

"But I think we need to know a little bit more," said Mma Ramotswe.

"Then ask him. Isn't that the way we work in the No. 1 Ladies' Detective Agency? Don't we just ask people if we want to find out something?"

Mma Ramotswe had to agree that this was true. If she ever wrote a book like *The Principles of Private Detection,* she would add to what Clovis Andersen had to say. He suggested all sorts of clever ways of finding out facts—following people, looking at what they threw away in the bin, watching the sort of people they mixed with, and so on—but he did not say anything about asking them to their faces. That was often the best way of getting information, and in her book, if she ever wrote it (*Private Detection for Ladies* might be a good title), she would make much of this direct method. After all, this technique had served her well in many of her cases, and perhaps this was another occasion on which it might be used.

She rose from her desk and sauntered into the garage, followed by Mma Makutsi. Mr J.L.B. Matekoni was attending to a car which was parked outside, its owner standing anxiously by. Inside the garage, underneath the hydraulic ramp upon which a large red car was balanced, Charlie and the younger apprentice were peering up at the car's suspension.

"So," said Mma Ramotswe conversationally. "So you are going to fix the suspension of that car. The driver will be very grateful to you. He will not feel so many bumps once you have finished."

Charlie looked away from the car and smiled at Mma Ramotswe. "That is right, Mma. We are going to make this suspension so smooth that the driver will think he is riding along on a cloud."

"You are very clever," said Mma Ramotswe.

"That is right," said Charlie. "I am."

Mma Ramotswe glanced at Mma Makutsi, who bit her lip. It was sometimes very difficult to remain civil when dealing with these boys. It would have been so easy to be sarcastic, but the problem was that they did not understand sarcasm: it was wasted on them.

"We saw you yesterday afternoon," she said airily. "We saw you getting into a very smart car, Charlie. You must have some very smart friends these days."

The apprentice laughed. "Very smart," he said. "Yes. You're right, Mma. I have some very smart friends. Hah! You think I'm nothing, but I have friends who do not think that."

"I have never thought you were nothing," protested Mma Ramotswe. "You have no right to say that."

Charlie looked to the younger apprentice for support, but there was none forthcoming. "All right," he said. "Maybe you do not think that. But I'm telling you, Mma, my life is going to change. It's going to change very soon, and then . . ."

They waited for him to finish speaking, but he did not.

"You are going to get married?" suggested Mma Makutsi. "That is very good news! Marriage is always a big change for people."

"Hah!" said the apprentice. "Who said anything about marriage? No, I am not going to get married."

Mma Ramotswe drew in her breath. The time had come to be direct, and to see what response she could draw. "Is it because that girlfriend of yours, that rich lady, is already married? Is that it, Charlie?"

The moment her question had been posed, she knew that her instinct had been correct. There was no need for Charlie to tell them anything further. The way he had stood up and bumped his head on the bottom of the car made it abundantly clear that the question needed no answer. It was answered already.

THAT EVENING, Mma Ramotswe made sure that she and Mr J.L.B. Matekoni returned to the house on Zebra Drive well before five o'clock, something which seemed to be becoming more and more difficult. Both of them had busy working lives—she as a private detective whose services were increasingly in demand, and he as one of the finest mechanics in all Botswana. Both of these positions had been attained through hard work and a strict adherence to certain principles. For Mma Ramotswe the principle which governed her practice was honesty. Sometimes it was necessary to resort to minor deception—but never anything harmful—in order to get at the truth, but one should never do this with a client. One's duty to a client was never to mislead: if the truth was unpalatable or hurtful, then there were ways of presenting the truth in a gentle way. Often all that one had to do was to get clients to work out conclusions by themselves, merely assisting them by pointing out things that they might have found out for themselves had they been willing to confront them.

Of course there was more to Mma Ramotswe's success than that. Another reason why she was so popular was her sympathetic nature. People said that you could say anything to Mma Ramotswe, anything, and she would not scold you or shake her head in condemnation (as long you did not show an arrogant face; that she would not tolerate). So people could go to see her and tell her frankly of things that they had done wrong—things which had landed them in difficulty—and she would do her best to extricate them from the consequences of their selfishness or their folly. A man could go into Mma Ramotswe's office and confess to adultery, and she would not purse her lips or mutter under her breath, but would say, "I am sure that you are sorry, Rra. I know how difficult it is for you men, with all your weaknesses." This would reassure them, without giving them the impression that she was condoning what they had done. And once the confession was made, then Mma Ramotswe would often prove resourceful in finding a solution, and these solutions usually avoided too much pain. It seemed as if the forgiveness which she was capable of showing was infectious. Competitors and enemies, locked in pointless feuds, would find that Mma Ramotswe would hit upon a solution that preserved dignity and face. "We are all human," she would say. "Men particularly. You must not be ashamed."

And as for Mr J.L.B. Matekoni's reputation, again this was built on that most simple and immediately recognisable of human virtues: decency. Mr J.L.B. Matekoni would never overcharge nor allow shoddy work to go out of the garage (which brought him into frequent conflict with his feckless apprentices and their slipshod ways; "These boys will drive me to an early grave," he said, shaking his head. "Tlokweng Road Late Motors, that will be it: proprietor the late Mr J.L.B. Matekoni").

No less a person than the British High Commissioner, who was driven around in a handsome Range Rover, was amongst those who recognised the merits of Mr J.L.B. Matekoni. He, and his predecessor in office, had entrusted their cars to the care of

Mr J.L.B. Matekoni when other diplomats took theirs to large garages with glittering forecourts. But the first British High Commissioner to use Tlokweng Road Speedy Motors had been a good judge of men and had immediately known that he had made a great discovery when Mr J.L.B. Matekoni, quite unasked, had adjusted something in the vehicle's engine when he had merely stopped to fill the tank. A change in the engine note had alerted Mr J.L.B. Matekoni to the fact that a problem was developing and he had dealt with it on the spot, and without charge. That was the beginning of a long relationship, in which the spotless diplomatic vehicle was routinely serviced by Tlokweng Road Speedy Motors.

And just as Mma Ramotswe was tactful in the breaking of difficult news, so too could Mr J.L.B. Matekoni convey bad news about a car in such a way as to soften the blow to the owner. He had seen some mechanics shake their heads when looking at an engine—even if the car's owner was standing right next to them. Indeed, when he had been an apprentice himself, he had served alongside a German-trained mechanic who would simply point at an engine and shout *Kaput!* This was no way of letting a customer know that all was not well, and Mr J.L.B. Matekoni wondered whether German doctors did the same with their patients and just shook their heads and said *Kaput!* Perhaps they did.

His ways were gentler. If a repair was going to be very expensive, he would sometimes offer the customer a chair before he told them what it would cost. And if there was nothing he could do, he would start off by telling them that there was a limit to the life of everything and this applied to shoes, cars, and even man himself. In this way the passing of a car might be seen by the customer as something inevitable. Mr J.L.B. Matekoni could understand, though, how people might be strongly attached to their cars, as he had found out in his dealings with both Mma Potokwane, the matron at the orphan farm, and with Mma Ramotswe herself. The orphan farm had an old minibus which Mma Potokwane had persuaded him to maintain (free of charge). This van should have been replaced some time ago, just as the water pump at the orphan farm should have been replaced well before it actually was. Mma Potokwane had no particular emotional attachment to the minibus, but was reluctant to spend money if she could possibly avoid it. He had pointed out to her that one day the suspension on the bus would have to be replaced, along with the braking system, the electric wiring, and several of the panels in the floor. He had pointed out the danger if those panels gave way through rust; an orphan could fall out onto the road, he said, and what would people say if that happened? It will not happen, she had replied. You will not let that happen.

In Mma Ramotswe's case, her attachment to the tiny white van was more emotional than financial in origin. She had bought the tiny white van when she first came to live in Gaborone, and it had served her loyally since that day. It was not a fast vehicle, nor a particularly comfortable one; the suspension had been in a bad way for some time, especially on the driver's side, in view of Mma Ramotswe's traditional build, which posed some degree of strain on the system. And the engine had a tendency to go out of tune very shortly after Mr J.L.B. Matekoni had attended to it, which meant that the tiny white van would splutter and jerk from time to time. In Mma Ramotswe's view, though, these were small matters: as long as the tiny white van was capable of getting her around, and as long as it did not break down too often, she proposed holding on to it. She thought of it as a friend, a staunch ally in this world, an ally to whom she owed a strong debt of loyalty.

These professional reputations meant that both Mma Ramotswe and Mr J.L.B. Matekoni were rather busier than they would have liked to be. So it was with some pleasure that Mma Ramotswe managed that evening to secure the hour between five and six as time when the two of them could sit on the verandah, and walk about their garden, and drink a cup of bush tea. She wanted to do this, not only to give Mr J.L.B. Matekoni a chance to unwind (he was, she thought, working far too hard), but also because she wanted to spend some time talking to him, alone, without Mma Makutsi or the apprentices, or even Motholeli and Puso listening in.

They sat together on the verandah, mugs of tea in hand. The sky was of that colour which it assumed at the end of the day— a late afternoon colour of tired blue—and was great and empty. On the leaves of the acacia trees that grew here and there in the garden, the gentle rays of the afternoon sun fell forgivingly, as if the battle between heat and life, between red and green, was temporarily over.

"I am very happy that we can just sit here," said Mma Ramotswe. "All the time these days it is work, work, work. We must be careful or we will work so much that we forget how to sit and talk about things."

"You are right, Mma," said Mr J.L.B. Matekoni. "But it is very hard, isn't it? You can't say to people: go away, we cannot help you. And I can't say to people: I can't fix your car. We cannot do that."

Mma Ramotswe nodded. He was right, of course. Neither of them would want to turn people away, no matter how busy they were. So where did the solution lie? Should they allow the businesses to expand? This was one of the matters that she wished to discuss with him—this, and the difficult issue of Charlie and the older woman.

"I suppose we could make the businesses bigger," she ventured. "You could get another mechanic to help you, and I could take on somebody else."

Mr J.L.B. Matekoni put down his mug and looked at her. "We could not do that," he said. "We are small businesses. If you allow your business to get too big, then you have many headaches. Headaches, headaches—all the time."

"But if you have too much work to do, you end up with a headache too," said Mma Ramotswe mildly. "And what is the point of working so much? We have enough money, I think. We do not need to be rich people. Other people can be rich if they want to. We are happy just as we are."

Mr J.L.B. Matekoni was sure that they were happy, but pointed out that he would not be happy if he had to turn people away, or cut corners in his work.

"I cannot do quick, shoddy work," he said. "That catches up with you sooner or later. The worst thing a mechanic can see is a car he looks after broken down at the edge of the road. Such a mechanic has to hide his face. I could not live like that."

"Well," said Mma Ramotswe. "Perhaps you could take another apprentice. A good one this time. Or you could employ an assistant mechanic—a qualified person."

"How would I know that he would be any good?" asked Mr J.L.B. Matekoni. "I cannot just employ the first person who walks into the garage."

Mma Ramotswe explained that there were ways of preventing this from happening. They could check up on references which the candidate provided, and they could even employ somebody on a temporary basis, on the understanding that they were on approval. Mr J.L.B. Matekoni listened to these suggestions but was noncommittal. Mma Ramotswe changed tack; she had an idea that had occurred to her during the day and which she wanted to put to him.

"Of course," she began, "it might be possible to employ somebody who could do a bit of work for you and a bit of work for me. There might be a person who could be taught some simple garage tasks—changing oil, for instance—and who would at the same time be able to do some enquiry work in the agency. I was not thinking of somebody who was a detective, but of somebody who could take some of the burden off Mma Makutsi and myself. We seem to have too much work these days and it would be useful."

Mr J.L.B. Matekoni said nothing for a moment. He did not appear to be rejecting the idea out of hand, and so Mma Ramotswe continued.

"There is somebody I met who is looking for a job," she said. "I would like to try him out. We could take him for a month maybe, and see how he does. If he is good, then he might be able to help us both."

"Who is this person?" asked Mr J.L.B. Matekoni. "Do you know anything about him?"

"He is a person I happened to bump into," said Mma Ramotswe, and then laughed. "Or I would have bumped into him if he had not swerved on his bicycle."

Mr J.L.B. Matekoni sighed. "You do not have to give him a job just because you almost knocked him over. You do not have to do that."

"I know that. And that is not the reason."

Mr J.L.B. Matekoni lifted up his mug and drained it of the last of his bush tea. "And do you know anything about him?" he asked. "What was his last job? How did he lose it?"

Mma Ramotswe thought carefully. She could not lie to her husband, but she realised that if she revealed that the man had been in prison, then it would be extremely unlikely that he would agree to employ him. They would then be no different from everybody else who was refusing to give him work because of his past. He would never get a job in these circumstances.

"I do not know exactly what happened," she said, truthfully. "But I shall ask him to speak to you himself. Then he could explain what happened."

It was some time before Mr J.L.B. Matekoni replied, but after a period, during which he seemed deep in reflection, he agreed to speak to the man when he came to collect his bicycle. This was all that Mma Ramotswe wanted. Now, with their tea finished, she thought that they might take a short stroll around the garden, in the last of the afternoon light, and discuss the other problem that needed to be resolved—the Charlie problem.

CHAPTER SEVEN

A TEA DISASTER . . . AND WORSE

THERE WAS an unusually large pile of mail awaiting them the next morning at the No. 1 Ladies' Detective Agency. Letters for both businesses were opened in the same office, Mma Ramotswe normally dealing with those addressed to the agency and Mma Makutsi going through the garage mail. It was their policy to reply immediately to everything, and this often took up much of the morning. People wrote to the No. 1 Ladies' Detective Agency about all sorts of things, and with impossible requests. Some of them were under the impression that they were a branch of the police force and made allegations against others, usually anonymously. There was one such letter that morning.

"Dear Mma Ramotswe," it read, "I saw an article about you in the *Botswana Daily News*. It said that you are the only ladies' detective agency in Botswana. Men will not deal with this thing, and so that is why I am writing to you. I want to bring to your notice something that is happening in our village. I have not been able to talk about this thing to anybody here, because there are many people who would not believe me and would only say that I am lying and trying to make trouble. I wish to complain about some teachers at the school. They are always drinking and taking girl pupils to bars where they give them strong drink and make them dance with them. I have seen this thing myself many times, and I think that it is something which the police should deal with. But the police here are also dancing in these bars. So please will you do something about this. I cannot give you my real name and address because I know that they will threaten me if they hear about this. I am one such girl. That is how I know about this. Please do something."

Mma Ramotswe read the letter aloud to Mma Makutsi, who laid aside the spare-parts bill she was dealing with and listened attentively.

"Well, Mma?" said Mma Ramotswe after she had finished. "What do we do about that?"

"Which village is this?" asked Mma Makutsi. "We could pass it on to somebody. Maybe the district police superintendent, or somebody like that."

Mma Ramotswe studied the letter again, and sighed. "There is no address," she said. "This girl has not told us where she is writing from."

"And the postmark?" Mma Makutsi enquired.

"I cannot make it out," said Mma Ramotswe. "It is very indistinct. It could be anywhere. It could be out near Ghanzi for all we know. It could be somewhere very far away. There's nothing we can do. Nothing."

They both stared at the simple, ruled letter which Mma Ramotswe was holding. It was a piece of paper in which a great deal of anxiety had been invested.

"I am sure that this is true," said Mma Ramotswe, as she reluctantly let the letter fall into the wastepaper bin. "I am sure that this thing is really happening. I have heard about the bad behaviour of some teachers these days. They have forgotten what it is to be a teacher. They have forgotten that they should be worthy of respect."

Mma Makutsi agreed with this, but that, she thought, was not the whole story. Teachers may have started behaving badly, like everybody else, but this was not altogether their fault. They now had to put up with children who had not been taught the basics of good behaviour, and it was difficult in such circumstances for the teachers to maintain discipline.

"It is not always the teachers' fault, Mma Ramotswe," she said. "The children are very bad too these days."

They sat in silence for a moment. There had been no alternative but to dispose of the letter, but that did not make it any easier to do. That girl, wherever and whoever she was, would be looking for justice, for the restoration of the balance between right and wrong, and her pleas would continue to go unheard.

Mma Ramotswe looked at the next letter on her desk and picked up her letter knife. "This is sometimes not a very easy job, is it?" she said.

Mma Makutsi spread her hands in a gesture of resignation. "No, it is not easy, Mma."

"But we get by, don't we?" Mma Ramotswe went on, more cheerfully. "Sometimes we are able to do something that helps somebody else. That's the important thing. That makes our job a good one."

"Yes," said Mma Makutsi. "That is it. And you have helped me, Mma. I shall always remember that."

Mma Ramotswe looked surprised. "I don't think I have, Mma. You have helped yourself."

Mma Makutsi shook her head. "No, you are the one who has helped me. You gave me this job and you kept me on even when we were not making any money. Remember that time? Remember how we had very few cases and you said that it didn't matter and I could stay on? I thought that I was going to be out of a job then, but you were kind to me and promoted me. That's what you did."

"You deserved it," said Mma Ramotswe modestly.

"I shall never forget," said Mma Makutsi. "And I shall never forget how kind you were to me when my brother was called."

"You were good to your brother," said Mma Ramotswe gently. "I saw what you did for him. He could not have wished for a better sister. And he is at peace now."

Mma Makutsi said nothing. She looked down at her desk, and then took off her large round spectacles and polished them with the threadbare lace handkerchief that she liked to carry. Mma Ramotswe glanced at her quickly, and then picked up the next letter and began to slit it open.

"This looks like a bill," she said, in a businesslike manner.

WHEN THE TIME CAME for morning tea, they had replied to just about all the letters and sorted out all the bills, both outgoing and incoming.

"This morning's going very quickly," said Mma Ramotswe, as she looked at her watch. "I am ready for tea."

Mma Makutsi agreed. She had a slight tendency to stiffness if she sat at her desk too long, and so she rose to her feet and rocked from side to side for a few moments, stretching her arms up and down as she did so. Then she turned round to get her teapot off the shelf behind her desk.

Mma Ramotswe looked up sharply when she heard the exclamation.

"My new tea-pot!" said Mma Makutsi. "Have you seen my tea-pot?"

"It was on that shelf," said Mma Ramotswe. "Next to the files."

"It is not there any longer," said Mma Makutsi. "Somebody has stolen it."

"But who would steal it?" asked Mma Ramotswe. "Nobody has been in here since we locked up last."

"Well, where is it, then?" retorted her assistant. "Tea-pots don't just walk. If it's not here, then somebody has taken it."

Mma Ramotswe scratched her head. "Maybe Mr J.L.B. Matekoni took it to make himself some tea. He came in very early this morning—before I did. That must be what happened."

Mma Makutsi thought about this. It was just possible that Mr J.L.B. Matekoni had moved the tea-pot, but it seemed unlikely. If he had wanted to make himself tea, then surely he would have used the normal tea-pot which Mma Ramotswe used. And what was more, she could not remember ever seeing him make tea himself, which again made the explanation somewhat un-likely.

Mma Ramotswe had now got up from her chair and was making her way to the door.

"Let's go and ask," she said. "I'm sure that it will turn up. Tea-pots don't just vanish."

Mma Makutsi followed her out into the garage workshop. Mr J.L.B. Matekoni, together with the two apprentices, was standing at the far side. He had in his hand a piece of an engine, and was pointing out something to the two young men, who were peering at the part with interest. As the two women came into the garage, he looked over in their direction.

"Have you seen . . ." Mma Ramotswe began to call out, but then stopped. At the very same instant, she and Mma Makutsi had seen the tea-pot, sitting on top of an upturned oil drum.

Mma Makutsi was smiling with relief. "There it is," she said. "Mr J.L.B. Matekoni must have made tea, as you said."

She walked over to the oil drum and picked up the tea-pot, only immediately to replace it on the surface of the drum. Watching her, Mma Ramotswe instantly knew that something was very wrong. She hurried over to join Mma Makutsi, who was standing in mute dismay, peering into the open top of the tea-pot.

"Diesel oil," Mma Makutsi muttered. "Somebody has filled it with diesel oil."

Mma Ramotswe bent down and sniffed at the tea-pot. The unmistakable smell of diesel was strong in her nostrils.

"Oh!" she exclaimed. "Who has done this? Who has done this?"

She turned and looked at the three men. They stood there, two of them looking puzzled and a third looking sheepishly down at his overalls.

"Charlie!" shouted Mma Ramotswe. "You come over here right now! Right now!"

Charlie sauntered over, accompanied by Mr J.L.B. Matekoni.

"What is all this?" asked Mr J.L.B. Matekoni, wiping his hands on a piece of cotton lint. "What is all this fuss?"

"He's put diesel oil in my new tea-pot," wailed Mma Makutsi. "Why did he do that?"

There was a defensive note in Charlie's voice. "I was draining a tank," he explained. "I had nothing to catch the diesel. So I found that thing in the office and it was empty. I thought I'd use it. Don't worry, I'll wash it."

"Can't you see it's a tea-pot?" snapped Mma Ramotswe. "Can't you see even that?"

"It is not the usual tea-pot," said Charlie defiantly. "The tea-pot we use does not look like that."

"That's because it's my new tea-pot," interjected Mma Makutsi. "You stupid, stupid boy. You are more stupid than a cow."

Charlie bristled at the insult. "Don't you call me stupid, Mma. Just because you got ninety per cent."

"Ninety-*seven* per cent," shouted Mma Makutsi. "You can't even get that right. You are as stupid as a warthog."

"She must not call me a warthog," Charlie protested to Mr J.L.B. Matekoni. "Boss, you cannot let this foolish woman call me a warthog. She is the warthog. A warthog with big round glasses."

Mr J.L.B. Matekoni wagged a finger. "You must not say that, Charlie. You are the one who is in the wrong here. You put diesel oil in Mma Makutsi's new tea-pot. That is not a clever thing to do."

Charlie took a deep breath. His eyes had widened now, and his nostrils were flaring slightly. It was clear that he was very angry.

"I may be stupid," he said. "But I am not stupid enough to stay in this useless garage. That's it, Boss. I quit now. Right now."

Mr J.L.B. Matekoni grasped the apprentice's arm in an attempt to reassure him, but was brushed off. "But what about the apprenticeship?" he said quietly. "You cannot give that up."

"Oh, can't I?" said Charlie. "You'll see. I am not a slave, Boss. I am a free Motswana. I can go when I want. Now I am looked after by a friend. I have a rich friend. I have a Mercedes-Benz—have you not seen me? I do not have to work any more."

He turned away and started to unbutton his overalls. He then ripped these off, and threw them into a puddle of oil on the floor.

"You cannot go," said Mr J.L.B. Matekoni. "We can talk about this."

"No, I am not talking," said Charlie. "I have had enough of being treated like a dog. I am going to have a better life now."

It had all been so sudden and so dramatic that it was difficult to take it all in. But after a few minutes, as they watched Charlie walking quickly away in the direction of the town, they realised that something serious and potentially irremediable had happened. They saw before them the ruins of a career; the wrecking of a life.

MR J.L.B. MATEKONI sat astride the client's chair in the office of the No. 1 Ladies' Detective Agency, his head sunk in his hands, his expression glum.

"I have always tried very hard with that young man," he said to Mma Ramotswe and Mma Makutsi. "I really have. He has been with me now for two years, and I have worked and worked to make him into a good mechanic. And now this has happened."

"It is not your fault, Mr J.L.B. Matekoni," said Mma Ramotswe reassuringly. "We know what you have done. We have seen it, haven't we, Mma Makutsi?"

Mma Makutsi nodded vigorously. She was particularly shocked by the apprentice's outburst and wondered whether in the eyes of Mr J.L.B. Matekoni and Mma Ramotswe she was responsible for his abrupt resignation and departure. It had been wrong of her, perhaps, to lose her temper with Charlie, and she regretted that, but at the same time there was the question of her new tea-pot and its ignominious fate as a receptacle for diesel oil. She doubted whether she would be able to get the smell of fuel out of it now, and tea was such a sensitive substance—the slightest contamination could make it taste peculiar. She had once been served tea out of a flask that had been regularly used for coffee, and she remembered how long the acrid, confusing taste had lingered in her mouth. But she would not have shouted at him like that if she had imagined that it would lead to this—the garage could ill afford the loss of one set of hands, particularly a trained set, if one could call Charlie's hands that.

"I'm very sorry," she said quietly. "I should not have been so cross with him. I'm sorry. I did not think that he would run away like that."

Mma Ramotswe raised a hand to stop her. "You do not need to apologise, Mma," she said firmly. "It was Charlie who called you a warthog. He had no right to say that. I shall not have the

Assistant Detective at the No. 1 Ladies' Detective Agency called a warthog."

She looked at Mr J.L.B. Matekoni, as if to challenge him to defend the indefensible. It was true that Mma Makutsi had initiated the trade of insults, but that was only under the gravest provocation. Had Charlie apologised for ruining the tea-pot, then Mma Makutsi would surely not have spoken in the intemperate way in which she did speak.

Mr J.L.B. Matekoni, it transpired, was of much the same view.

"It is not Mma Makutsi's fault at all," he said simply. "It is just not her fault. That young man has been heading this way for some time. You told me only a little time ago about this woman of his. I was foolish and did not speak to him firmly. Now he has decided that he can give everything up just because his rich lady is running after him in her Mercedes-Benz. Oh dear! Those cars have a lot to answer for."

Mma Ramotswe nodded her head in vigorous agreement. "They do, Rra. They certainly do. They turn people's heads, I think. That is what they do."

"And women turn heads too," continued Mr J.L.B. Matekoni. "Women turn the heads of young men and make them do silly things."

There was a short silence. Mma Makutsi was about to say something, but decided against it. It was arguable, she thought, whether women turned the heads of men any more than men turned the heads of women. She would have thought that responsibility was shared in that respect. But this was not the time to engage in debate on this issue.

"So what do we do now?" asked Mr J.L.B. Matekoni. "Should I go and try to talk to him tonight? Should I see if I can persuade him to come back?"

Mma Ramotswe thought about this suggestion. If Mr J.L.B. Matekoni were to try to persuade the apprentice to return, it might work, but at the same time it could have dire consequences for his future behaviour. It was not right that an employer should run after a subordinate like that; that would mean that the young man could throw his weight around in the future because he would know that ultimately he could get away with anything. It would also give him the impression that he was in the right and Mma Makutsi was in the wrong, and that was simply unfair. No, she thought, if Charlie were to come back, it would have to be at his own request, and preferably accompanied by a proper apology to Mma Makutsi, not only for calling her a warthog but also for spoiling her tea-pot. In fact, he should probably be obliged to buy her a new tea-pot, but they would not press that aspect of the matter in these delicate circumstances. An apology, then, would suffice.

She looked directly at Mr J.L.B. Matekoni. "I don't think that is a good idea," she said. "You are the boss. He is a young man who has run away from work after being rude to a superior. It would not look good, would it, if the boss were to run after the young man and beg him to come back? No, he should be allowed to come back, but only when he has said sorry."

Mr J.L.B. Matekoni looked resigned. "Yes," he said. "You are right. But what are we to do here? What if he does not come back? There is work for three people here at the garage, even if his work has many faults. It will be hard without him."

"I know that, Rra," said Mma Ramotswe. "And that is why we need a plan with two parts. It is always a good idea to have a plan with two parts."

Mma Makutsi and Mr J.L.B. Matekoni looked at her expectantly. This was the Mma Ramotswe they appreciated: the woman with a clear idea of what to do. They had no doubt at all that she would solve this problem, and now all that they wanted was to hear how she was going to do it. A plan with two parts sounded very impressive.

Now it was as if Mma Ramotswe had herself become imbued with the confidence that they had in her. She sat back in her chair and smiled as she laid out the contours of her plan.

"The first part," she said, "is to go immediately to Tlokweng and get the man whose bicycle has been broken. We can offer him work here, as I have discussed with you, Mr J.L.B. Matekoni. This man can then do all the unskilled work in the garage, as if he were an apprentice on the first day of his apprenticeship. I think that he will be a good worker. He will not be a proper apprentice, of course, but Charlie's young friend will imagine that this is just what he is. That means that the news will get back to Charlie straightaway that we have found somebody to replace him. That will give him a big shock, I am sure of it."

On hearing this, Mma Makutsi let out an exclamation of delight. "That will teach him to take off his overalls and throw them in a puddle of oil," she said gleefully.

Mma Ramotswe looked at her disapprovingly and she lowered her eyes.

"The second part of the plan," Mma Ramotswe continued, "is to find out more about this woman of Charlie's and then to see if there is anything we can do to help him come to his senses. I am sure that she is a married lady. Now, if that is so, then there will be a husband somewhere, and it may be that he is paying for that expensive silver Mercedes-Benz. Do you think that men like to pay for cars like that to be driven around in by young men who are seeing their wives? I do not think they do. So all we have to do is to find out where this man is and see to it that he finds out what is going on. Then we let things sort themselves out, and I think that we shall soon have Charlie back, knocking on the door, asking for us to forget what he said about the garage."

"And about me," added Mma Makutsi.

"Yes," said Mma Ramotswe. "About you too."

Mma Makutsi was emboldened. "And would it not help if Mr J.L.B. Matekoni beat him?" she asked. "Just a bit. Would that not help him to behave better in the future?"

They both looked at her, Mma Ramotswe in astonishment, Mr J.L.B. Matekoni in alarm.

"Those days are past," said Mma Ramotswe. "That is no longer possible, Mma."

"Pity," said Mma Makutsi.

CHAPTER EIGHT

AT THE ACADEMY OF DANCE AND MOVEMENT

EVERYBODY'S SPIRITS were considerably lifted by the way in which a credible plan of action had emerged from a shocking and disagreeable row. Mma Makutsi was particularly pleased that she could go home that evening without a burden of worry and guilt over what had happened. For that evening she was due to embark on a new and exciting project—the most important thing that she had done since the founding of the Kalahari Typing School for Men. Unlike the typing school, however, this did not involve work for her, which would be a pleasant change. For as long as she could remember, her life had been a matter of work: as a girl she had worked at home in all the usual tasks of the household, unremittingly; she had walked six miles to school each morning and six miles back to acquire an education; and then, when her great opportunity had presented itself and she had taken up that place at the Botswana Secretarial College, paid for by the scrimping and saving of her entire family, she had worked harder than ever before. Of course she had been rewarded—with that glorious result of ninety-seven per cent—but it had all been such hard work. Now it was time to dance.

She had seen the advertisement in the newspaper and had been immediately intrigued by the name of the person who had placed the advertisement. Who was this Mr Fano Fanope? It was an unusual name, but its musical qualities seemed very suitable for one who offered classes in "dance and movement, and the social skills that go with those things." As to the name, Fano Fanope was a bit like Spokes Spokesi, the famous radio disc jockey. These names had a forward lilt to them; they were the names of people who were *going somewhere*. She reflected on her own name: Grace Makutsi. There was nothing wrong with a name like that—she had certainly encountered stranger names in Botswana, where people seemed to like naming their children in an individual and some-times rather strange way—but it was not a name which suggested much movement or ambition. Indeed, one might even describe it as a safe name, a rather stodgy name, the sort of name that might well be held by the leader of a knitting circle or a Sunday School teacher. Of course, it could have been much worse, and she could have been burdened with one of those names which children then spend the rest of their days in living down. At least she was not called, as one of the teachers at the Botswana Secretarial College had been called, a name which, when translated from Setswana, meant: *This one makes a lot of noise*. That was not a good name to give a child, but her parents still did it.

Now this well-named Fano Fanope was proposing to offer dancing classes (with other skills included) every Friday night. These would take place in a room at the President Hotel, and there would be a small band provided. The advertisement also revealed that instruction would be given in a wide range of ball-room dances, and that Fano Fanope, who had achieved recog-nition in dancing circles in four countries, would personally instruct all those who registered for the class. It would be wise not to wait, the advertisement went on, as there were many people who were keen to improve their social skills in this way and demand would be high.

Mma Makutsi read the advertisement with close interest. There was no doubt in her mind that it would be good to be able to do some of those obscure dances that she had read about—the tango, for one, looked interesting —and there was also no doubt that dancing classes were a good place to meet people. She met people at work, of course, and there were her new neighbours, who were perfectly friendly, but she was looking forward to a rather different sort of meeting. She wanted to meet people who had been places, people who could talk about fascinating things, people whose lives encompassed rather more than the daily round of work and home and children.

And there was no reason why she should not enter into such a world, thought Mma Makutsi. After all, she was an independent woman with a position. She was an assistant detective at the No. 1 Ladies' Detective Agency; she had her own small business in the shape of the part-time Kalahari Typing School for Men; and she had a new house, or part of a house, in a good area of town. She had something behind her now, and it did not matter if she wore very large round glasses and had a difficult complexion; it was her turn to enjoy life a bit more.

She prepared for the evening with care. Mma Makutsi did not have many dresses, but there was one, at least, a red dress with a line of small bows along the hem, that would be ideal for a dancing class. She took this dress out of the cupboard and ironed it carefully. Then she showered, under cold water, as there was no hot water in the house, and spent some time in the other tasks of making herself ready to go out. There was nail varnish to be applied, a very fine pink one that she had bought at ridiculous expense the previous week; there was lipstick; there was powder; there was something to put on her hair. All this took the best part of an hour, and then she had to walk off to the end of the road to catch the minibus into town.

"You're looking smart, Mma," said an older woman in the crowded vehicle. "You must be meeting a man tonight. Be careful! Men are dangerous."

Mma Makutsi smiled. "I am going to a dancing class. It is the first time that I have gone to it."

The woman laughed. "Oh, there will be plenty of men at a dancing class," she said, offering Mma Makutsi a peppermint from a small bag she had extracted from a pocket. "That's why men go to dancing classes. They go to meet pretty girls like you."

Mma Makutsi said nothing, but as she sucked on the peppermint she thought about the prospect of meeting a man. She had not been strictly honest with herself, and she was prepared to admit it, even if only to herself. She would like to learn to dance, and she would like to meet interesting people in general, but what she really wanted to do was to meet an interesting man, and she hoped that this would be her chance. So if what her neighbour in the minibus said was true, then perhaps this was the night that it would happen.

She alighted from the bus at the top of the mall. There were no lights on in the Government buildings behind her, as it was Friday evening and no civil servant would ever work late on a Friday evening, but the mall itself was lit and there were people strolling about, enjoying the cool night air and chatting with friends. There was always so much to talk about, even if nothing much had happened, and now people were going over the events, or non-events perhaps, of the day, catching up on gossip, hearing about things that were happening, or might just happen if one waited long enough.

Outside the President Hotel there was a small knot of young people, mostly in their teens. They were standing about the open staircase that went up to the verandah where Mma Ramotswe liked to have lunch on special occasions. They fell silent as Mma Makutsi approached the stairs.

"Going to learn to dance, Mma?" muttered one of the young men. "I'll teach you how to dance!"

There were titters of laughter.

"I don't dance with little boys," said Mma Makutsi as she went past.

There was silence for a moment, and she added, "When you're big, come and ask me then."

This brought laughter from the rest of the young people, and she turned and smiled at them as she went up the stairs. Her success in this good-natured repartee gave her confidence as she entered the hotel and asked for directions to the room in which the class was to be held. She had felt some trepidation about the outing—what if she failed to remember the steps of the tango, or whatever it was they were going to learn? Would she look stupid? Would she possibly even trip and fall over? And who would be there? Would the people who went to classes like this be much more sophisticated than she was, much richer? It was all very well being the most distinguished graduate of her year from the Botswana Secretarial College, but would that count for much here, in the world of music and elegant dancing and mirrors?

The dancing class was to be held in a room at the back of the hotel, a room which was used for business lunches and cheaper private parties. As Mma Makutsi made her way along the corridor, she heard the sound of an amplified guitar and drums. This was the band which had been promised in the advertisement, and it was a sound which filled her with a feeling of anticipation. And there were voices too, the sound of people talking amongst themselves; there were going to be a lot of people there, it seemed.

At the entrance to the room there was a small table at which a comfortable-looking woman in a red sequinned dress was seated. She smiled at Mma Makutsi and pointed to a small printed notice which gave the cost of the class. It was forty pula, which was not cheap, but then this was a proper dancing class, thought Mma

Makutsi, with a real two-piece band and a room in the President Hotel. She reached into her purse, took out the money, and paid.

"Are you experienced, or are you a beginner?" asked the woman.

Mma Makutsi thought about this. She had danced before, of course, but then so had just about everybody. From the point of view of this woman, with her sequinned dress, though, Mma Makutsi must be very much a novice.

"I have done some dancing," said Mma Makutsi. "Like everybody else. But not very much."

"Beginner," said the woman.

"I suppose so," said Mma Makutsi.

"Yes," said the woman. "If you have not been to a dance academy before, then you are a beginner. But you need not be ashamed. Everybody has to begin somewhere."

The woman smiled at her encouragingly and pointed at the doorway. "Go in. We shall be starting very soon," she said. "Mr Fanope is in the bar, but will come very soon. He is a very famous dancer, you know. Johannesburg. Nairobi. He has danced in all these places."

Mma Makutsi went in. It was a large room, the centre of which had been cleared and the carpet taken up. Chairs had been placed around the sides, and at the far end, on a small platform, the two musicians, the drummer and the guitarist, were perched on stools. The guitarist was fiddling with a lead to his instrument, while the drummer, a thin man wearing a silver-coloured waistcoat, was staring up at the ceiling, tapping his drumsticks against his knee.

Most of the chairs were occupied, and for a moment Mma Makutsi felt awkward as the eyes of those already there fell upon her. She felt that she was being appraised, and she searched quickly for any face that she knew, for any person whom she could approach and greet. But there was nobody, and under the gaze of the sixty or so people present, she crossed the floor to take a seat on one of the few chairs which were still free. Glancing around, she saw, to her relief, that she was dressed in much the same way as the other women, but none, she saw, was wearing glasses. For a moment she thought about taking hers off and putting them away, but the difficulty with doing that was that she really needed them and without them she would not be able to make out what was happening.

A few minutes later Mr Fanope entered the room, followed by the woman in the red sequinned dress. He was a rather small, dapper man, wearing a white evening jacket and a bow tie. Mma Makutsi noticed that he was wearing black patent leather shoes. She had not seen a man in patent leather footwear before and she thought them most becoming. Would Mr J.L.B. Matekoni wear such shoes, she wondered? It was difficult to see him in shoes like that at the garage—the oil would spoil them so quickly—but she could hardly imagine him in shoes like that even in other circumstances. This was definitely not his world, nor the world of Mma Ramotswe, when one came to think about it. Would Mma Ramotswe be a good dancer? Traditionally built women could be rather good at dancing, thought Mma Makutsi, as they have the right bearing, at least for some dances. The tango would hardly suit somebody of Mma Ramotswe's build, but she could certainly imagine her doing a waltz, perhaps, or a sedate jive. Traditional dancing presented no problems, of course, because the whole point about traditional dancing was that everybody could join in. A few weeks previously they had been at the orphan farm for Mma Potokwane's birthday party, and the children's traditional dancing group had performed in the matron's honour, with all the housemothers joining in. Some of them were of a very traditional build—from all that sampling of the good food they cooked for the children—and they had looked very dignified as they had joined in the line of shuffling, singing dancers. But all of that was a long way away from the world of Mr Fanope and his President Hotel dance academy.

"Now then, *bomma* and *borra*," said Mr Fanope into the microphone. "Welcome to the first class of the Academy of Dance and Movement. You have made a very good choice coming here tonight because this is the number-one place to learn ball-room dancing in Botswana. And I am the best teacher for you people. I will make dancers out of all of you, even if you have never danced before. Everybody here has a dancer inside, and I will let that dancer out. That is what I will do."

Somebody clapped at this point, and a number of others followed suit. Mr Fanope acknowledged the applause with a small bow.

"We are going to start this evening with a simple dance. This is a dance that anybody can do, and it is called the quickstep. It goes slow, slow, quick; slow, slow, quick, quick. It is very simple, and Mma Betty and I are going to show you how to do it."

He nodded to the musicians. As they began to play, he moved away from the microphone and turned to the woman in the red sequinned dress. Mma Makutsi watched in fascination as they danced across the floor. They were both extraordinarily light on their feet, and they both moved in such perfect harmony, as if they were one body, moving on strings pulled by a single hand.

"Watch what we do," shouted Mr Fanope, above the music. "Watch us now. Slow, slow, quick, quick."

After a few minutes, he disengaged from Mma Betty and the band stopped playing.

"Choose your partners," he shouted. "Men, you get up and ask the ladies. If anybody is left over, Mma Betty and I will take it in turns to be your partner. Mma Betty will dance with men, and I shall dance with the ladies. Men, get up and choose a lady."

At this signal, the men rose to their feet and crossed the floor or turned to a lady sitting nearby. There was a sudden flurry of activity, and Mma Makutsi caught her breath in the excitement of it all. A man was coming towards her, a tall man with a moustache and a blue shirt. She looked down at her shoes. He would be a good man to dance with, a man who would lead his partner confidently.

But he did not ask her; he approached the woman sitting next to her, who rose up smiling and took his hand. Mma Makutsi waited. Everybody seemed to be finding a partner and moving onto the floor—everybody except her. She lowered her eyes. This was the humiliation she had feared; she should not have come. She would end up being danced with by Mr Fanope, out of charity, and everybody would know that nobody had asked her. It's my glasses, she told herself. It's my glasses, and the fact that I am a plain girl. I am just a plain girl from Bobonong.

She looked up. A man was standing in front of her, bending down to speak to her. In the general hubbub of noise she could not make out exactly what he was saying, but he was clearly a man, and he was clearly asking her to dance.

Mma Makutsi smiled and stood up. "Thank you, Rra," she said. "I am called Grace Makutsi."

He nodded, and pointed back to the dance floor, and they made their way together into the thick of the crowd. Mma Makutsi took a surreptitious glance at her partner. He was slightly older than she was, she thought; not very good-looking, but with a kind face. And he walked in a slightly strange way, as if his shoes did not quite fit him.

"What is your name, Rra?" she asked, as they stood together amongst the other couples, waiting for the music to start.

The man stared at her. It seemed that it was an effort for him to speak.

"I am called Phuti Radiphuti," he said. That is what he said, but it did not come out as directly as that. Called was c . . . c . . . c . . . called and Phuti was ph . . . ph . . . phuti.

It was a bad speech impediment, and Mma Makutsi's heart sank. She was a kind woman, like Mma Ramotswe, but it was typical of her luck, she thought, that she should be the last to be picked and then to be chosen by a man who moved in an odd way and had a very pronounced stutter. But he was still a man, wasn't he, and at least she was dancing with somebody and not sitting unhappily, unwanted. So she smiled encouragingly and asked him whether he had ever danced before.

Phuti Radiphuti opened his mouth to speak, and Mma Makutsi waited for his answer, but no words were formed. He bit his lip, and looked apologetic.

"Don't worry, Rra," said Mma Makutsi lightly. "We don't have to talk now. We can talk a bit later, after we have danced. Don't worry. It is my first time at a dance class too."

Mr Fanope was now organising the couples and was signalling the band to start.

"Take your partners," he called out. "No, do not crush them, gentlemen. A good dancer holds his partner lightly. Like this. See?"

They began to dance, and it became straightaway apparent to Mma Makutsi that her partner had very little sense of rhythm. While she counted slow, slow, quick, quick, as they had been instructed to do by Mr Fanope, he seemed to be counting slow, slow, slow, quick, or even slow, slow, slow, slow. Whatever he was doing, it bore no relation to what Mma Makutsi herself was doing.

After a few minutes of uncoordinated shuffling, Mr Fanope came up to them and tapped Phuti Radiphuti on the shoulder.

"No, Rra," he said, shaking a finger at him. "You are all over the place. This is not football. This is a quickstep. You go slow, slow, quick, quick, like this."

Phuti Radiphuti looked ashamed.

"I am very so . . . so . . . sor . . . sorry," he stuttered. "I am not a good dancer. I am sorry."

"Let me do the counting," said Mma Makutsi. "You just listen to me this time."

They resumed the dance, with Mma Makutsi counting loudly and guiding Phuti Radiphuti in an attempt to bring their movements into unison. It was not easy; Phuti Radiphuti seemed inordinately clumsy, and no matter how clearly she counted he appeared to be following a quite different rhythm.

"It is important to move quickly after I count two," shouted Mma Makutsi above a particularly loud passage of drumming. "That is why the dance is called the quickstep."

Phuti Radiphuti nodded. He looked rather miserable now, as if he was regretting the decision to attend the lesson. Mma Makutsi, for her part, was sure that people were looking at them as they stumbled along. She had changed her mind about whether it would have been better to remain firmly seated, unapproached by any man, than to be subjected to this awkward, bumbling performance. And there, only a few couples away, was somebody she recognised. She stole a glance and then looked away. Yes, it was her, one of the women from her year at the Botswana Secretarial College, one of those fun-loving glamorous girls who ended up getting barely fifty per cent, and there she was, dancing with a confident and attractive man. Mma Makutsi hardly dared look again, but was forced to do so when they found themselves getting closer and closer together.

"So!" shouted the glamorous girl. "So there you are! Grace Makutsi!"

Mma Makutsi affected surprise, smiling at the other girl. She noticed the eyes of the other move quickly to Phuti Radiphuti and then come back to rest on her, amused.

"Who is that?" stuttered Phuti Radiphuti. "Who . . ."

"She is just somebody I know," said Mma Makutsi carelessly. "I have forgotten her name."

"She is a very good dancer," said Phuti Radiphuti, stumbling over each word.

"Dancing is not the only thing," said Mma Makutsi quickly. "There are other things, you know."

THE DANCE CLASS lasted for almost two hours. There were further exhibitions of the quickstep, performed with shimmering fluidity by Mr Fanope and Mma Betty, and then demonstrations of the waltz, which they were then all invited to attempt. Mma Makutsi, who had detached herself from Phuti Radiphuti while the demonstration was being performed, was hoping that somebody else would come and ask her to dance, but was quickly sought out by Phuti Radiphuti, who guided her clumsily back onto the floor.

At the end of the evening, he thanked her and offered to drive her home.

"I have a car outside," he said. "I can take you."

She hesitated. She felt sorry for this man, who seemed harmless enough, but this was not what she had hoped for, nor anticipated, for the evening. She had seen at least four men who looked attractive and interesting, but they had not looked at her, not for so much as an instant. Instead it had been her luck to have the attention of this poor man, decent though he was, with his terrible stutter and his awful clumsiness. So she should say no to his offer, so as not to encourage him, and wait for a minibus, or even walk home. It would take her no more than thirty minutes, and it was perfectly safe at this hour of night.

She looked at him, and noticed that there were dark patches in the armpits of his shirt. We are all human, all creatures of water and salt, all human. And she thought for a moment of her brother, her poor brother Richard, whom she had loved and looked after, and who had suffered from those dreadful fevers that bathed him in sweat at night. She could not hurt this man; she could not say to him, no, I cannot accept your kindness.

She agreed, and they left the room together. At the doorway, Mr Fanope smiled at them and said that he looked forward to seeing them the following Friday.

"You make a very good couple," he said. "You are coming on nicely. You are a good dancer, Mma, and you, Rra, I think you will be good in the future."

Mma Makutsi's heart sank. If she had feared that she might be landed with this man at every class, then this fear had just been confirmed.

"I'm not sure that I shall be able to come here again," she blurted out. "I am very busy."

Mr Fanope shook his head. "You must come, Mma. Your friend here needs you to help him with his dancing, don't you, Rra?"

Phuti Radiphuti beamed with pleasure, wiping his brow with a red handkerchief. "I am very happy dancing with . . ." The words came painfully slowly, and he was interrupted by Mr Fanope before he could finish.

"Good," said the instructor. "We shall see you both then, next Friday. That is very good." He gestured at the other dancers. "Some of these people over there don't really need lessons. But you do."

Outside, they walked in silence to the car park behind the hardware store. Phuti Radiphuti's car was at the far end, a modest white car with a twisted aerial. Yet it was a car, which told Mma Makutsi something about him. As Mma Ramotswe would have pointed out to her, the mere fact that he has a car tells us something, Mma. It means that he has a good job. Now look at his hands, Mma, and his shoes, and see what they say about him. As he started the car, Mma Makutsi looked at his hands, but they told her nothing. Or at least they told her one thing, she thought, with an inward smile. He has all his fingers. He is not a butcher.

She directed him back to her house, where he dropped her, keeping the engine running. She was relieved that he had no expectations beyond that, and she thanked him politely as she alighted.

"I will see you next week," she said, although she had not planned to say this. She had not planned to give any commitment, but she had done it, more out of pity for him than anything else. And she noticed that he appeared to appreciate the gesture, as he smiled and started to say something. But he did not finish. The words were stuck, and he became mute. So she closed the door, and waved to him, and he drew away in his white car, and she watched the red lights of the car disappear down the road, into the darkness.

CHAPTER NINE

MR POLOPETSI STARTS AT THE GARAGE

THE REPAIR of the bicycle had been effected by the younger apprentice. He had managed to straighten the handlebars and attend to a buckle in the wheel, with the result that even if the bicycle was not as good as new, it was possible to ride it safely. Mma Ramotswe had her misgivings about this; she would have liked to be able to say to its owner that it was perfect, indeed that it had been improved upon, but she felt that she could not claim this. Instead she would have to say that they had done their best, and that she hoped that he might be satisfied with the repair. Of course, in view of the offer she was about to make him, he would be unlikely to protest very much.

She had asked him to come to the garage to fetch the bicycle and now he was here, knocking at the door of her office, his hat in his hand. She had bade him enter and he had done so, not boldly as men usually entered, but almost apologetically. Mma Ramotswe noticed this, and thought how this must be the effect of prison, at least its effect on an honest man who had been sent there unjustly. What greater wrong can there be than that, what greater hurt? To know that you were reviled for something that you had not done, or for something for which you did not deserve to be punished; that must be very painful, she thought.

She rose to her feet to greet him.

"You are very welcome, Rra," she said. "You must come in and sit down, and we can talk. Then . . ."

"It is not ready? It is not fixed?"

She smiled to put him at his ease. "Of course it's ready, Rra. We have done our best, or rather the apprentice through there—you might have seen him—has done his best. I hope that it is all right."

His relief was visible. "I am glad of that, Mma. I need that bicycle to look for work."

Mma Ramotswe looked across the room to where Mma Makutsi was sitting at her desk and they exchanged glances.

"Well, Rra," she began. "On that thing I have something to say to you. I can tell you . . ."

As she spoke, Mr Polopetsi suddenly raised a hand to stop her. "No, Mma," he said, his tone becoming firmer. "Please do not tell me. I have had so many people telling me how I can find work. They all tell me that I must look in this place and look in that place. And I do that, and it is no good. It is always the same thing—I tell them about what happened to me and they say thank you, but we cannot help you. That is what they tell me. Every time. So please do not tell me again. I know you are being kind, but I have heard these things so many times."

He stopped, and again there was an apologetic look, as if the courage that his declaration had required had now run out.

Mma Ramotswe stared at him. "I was not going to say that, Rra," she said quietly. "I was not going to give you advice. No, I was going to offer you a job. That is all."

For a few moments Mr Polopetsi said nothing, but looked at her, and then looked over his shoulder at Mma Makutsi, as if for confirmation. Mma Makutsi smiled encouragingly.

"Yes, Rra," she said. "Mma Ramotswe does not say things that she does not mean. She is going to offer you a job."

Mma Ramotswe leaned forward and tapped her desk. "This job is right here in the garage," she said. "And maybe you will do a bit of work for us too. You can help us. It is not a big job."

Mr Polopetsi appeared to be having difficulty in taking in what was being said to him. He opened his mouth to speak, and closed it again. Then he asked a question.

"Is this job for a long time?" he asked. "Or just for a few days?"

Mma Ramotswe looked down at her desk. She had not discussed this matter with Mr J.L.B. Matekoni and now, faced with the hopes of Mr Polopetsi, she had to make a decision.

"It will be for at least a year," she said confidently. "We cannot see what will happen beyond that. But you will be safe for a year."

After she had spoken, she glanced at Mma Makutsi, who raised an eyebrow. Mma Makutsi understood that there was an impulsive side to her employer, just as there sometimes was to Mr J.L.B. Matekoni. Both of them could act in that way when they were being kind, and then find that there were reproaches from the other. There were two fine examples of this that Mma Makutsi knew about. Mma Ramotswe had acted in exactly that way when she had promoted her to Assistant Detective. Mma Makutsi knew that this had been done in times of financial difficulty when sound economic sense should have dictated precisely the opposite course of action. But Mma Ramotswe had been unable to disappoint her and had gone ahead and done what her heart dictated. And then Mr J.L.B. Matekoni had done just the same thing, had he not, when he had adopted the two children from the orphan farm? Everybody knew that Mma Potokwane pushed Mr J.L.B. Matekoni around and must have browbeaten or tricked him into that decision, but the wily matron knew exactly how to play on his good nature. So this decision was nothing unusual, although Mma Ramotswe would at some point have to own up to Mr J.L.B. Matekoni that she had given this assurance.

"Well, Rra?" asked Mma Ramotswe. "Would you like this job?"

Mr Polopetsi nodded his head. "My heart is too full to speak," he said. "My heart is too full, Mma. You are a very kind lady. God was watching when he made you knock me over. That was God's act."

"That is kind of you," said Mma Ramotswe in a businesslike tone. "But I think it was something altogether different. Now I think that we should go through there to speak to Mr J.L.B. Matekoni so that he can start you off."

Mr Polopetsi stood up. "I am very happy," he said. "But I know nothing about cars. I hope that I can do this job."

"For years we have had two young men working here who know nothing about cars," interjected Mma Makutsi. "That did not stop them. So it should not stop you, Rra."

"That is true," said Mma Ramotswe. "But let us talk about that later." She paused before adding, "There is one thing, Rra."

Mr Polopetsi hesitated. "Yes?"

"You have this job now," said Mma Ramotswe, "so you can tell us about what happened to you. Tell us at lunchtime today, right from the beginning, so that we know all about it and will not have to wonder what happened. Tell us so that we no longer have to think about it."

"I can do that," said Mr Polopetsi. "I can tell you everything."

"Good," said Mma Ramotswe. "Now you can start work. There is a lot to do. We are very busy these days and we are very pleased to have another man . . ."

"To order about," interjected Mma Makutsi, and then laughed. "No, Rra, do not worry. I am only joking about that."

MR J.L.B. MATEKONI was busy at lunchtime, taking the remaining apprentice off with him to deal with a breakdown out on the

Molepolole Road. So it was only Mma Ramotswe and Mma Makutsi who sat in the office listening to Mr Polopetsi while he told his story. Mma Makutsi had made sandwiches for them with the bread they kept in the office cupboard—thick slices with generous helpings of jam—and Mma Ramotswe noticed how eagerly Mr Polopetsi tackled the food. He is hungry, she thought, and realised that he had probably been giving what little food there was to his family. She signalled to Mma Makutsi to make more sandwiches, which Mr Polopetsi wolfed down as he spoke.

"I was born in Lobatse," he began. "My father was one of the attendants at the mental hospital there. You will know the place. His job was to help the doctors control the very sick people who struggled when the doctors tried to treat them. There were some very strong patients and they would shout and strike out at everybody. My father was a strong man too, and he had a special jacket that he could put on these people and tie their arms behind them. That would make it easier for the doctors.

"I worked hard at school. I wanted to be a doctor when I grew up, but when the examinations came along I did not do well enough. I knew the answers to the questions, because I had worked so hard, but I became very frightened when the examinations started and I could not write properly. My hand would shake and shake and the examiners must have wondered who was this stupid boy who could not even write neatly. So I never did as well as I should have. If I hadn't shaken like that, then maybe I would have been given a scholarship and gone off to South Africa to study medicine. That happened to one boy at my school, but it did not happen to me.

"But I did not sit and complain about this because I knew that God would find me some other work. And He did. When I was sixteen I was given a job in the hospital where my father worked. There is a pharmacy in the hospital and they needed somebody to wash the bottles and to help carry and lift things. I also had to write notes in the drugs stock book, and I had to count the bottles and the pills. I was very good at that and they made me a pharmacy assistant when I was twenty. That was a very good job. I even took some examinations to do with that work and I found that I was not so frightened this time. I wrote neatly and I passed.

"I worked down there for twelve years before they sent me up to Gaborone. I was very pleased to get this new job because it was more senior and I was given more money. I became a pharmacy assistant at the Princess Marina, which is a very fine hospital. There is a very big pharmacy there and they have many, many shelves of bottles. I worked very hard and did well. Now I could marry a lady whom I had met at my church. She is a very good lady and she has given me two children, two girls, this big and this big, and they are very good children.

"I was a very happy man and a very proud one too. Then one day a very bad thing happened to me, a thing which changed my life forever and which I can never forget. And it was just an ordinary day, the same as any day. When I left my house that morning I did not know what was going to happen to me. I did not know that this was the last day that I would be happy."

Mr Polopetsi paused to bite into the fresh sandwich which Mma Makutsi had passed him. He took a large mouthful, and the two ladies watched him in silence as he chewed on the food. Mma Ramotswe wondered what it was that could have suddenly brought his world to an end. He had said when they had first met them that there had been an accident, but what accident could have resulted in his spending two years in prison? A road accident? Had he driven while drunk and killed somebody? He seemed an unlikely candidate for that.

"We were very busy that morning," continued Mr Polopetsi, wiping crumbs from his mouth with the back of his hand. "Sometimes it was like that. All the wards would run out of medicines at the same time and there would be a whole line of out-patients waiting for their prescriptions. So we would be running this way and that, trying to get things sorted out. There were two pharmacists who were ill that day because there was a lot of flu in the town. So we were very busy.

"We were not allowed to do many things. We were just pharmacy assistants, and so we were not allowed to measure out drugs and things like that. But when it was busy like that they sometimes told us that we could do simple things, like counting out pills and putting them in bottles. So we did that.

"I was doing that sort of thing on that morning. And that is when I made a mistake. I took pills from the wrong place and put them into the bottle which the pharmacist had given me. I put these pills in because I thought that he had pointed to one place and not to another. I misunderstood him.

"The drugs that I put in that bottle were very strong. They killed a lady who took them. It was because of what I did.

"They were very cross when this lady died. They found the bottle with the wrong drugs in it and they asked who had put them in there. The pharmacist said that he had passed the right drugs to me to put in and that I must have disobeyed him. He was very frightened because he thought that they would blame him. He was just a junior person, a foreigner who used to work there, and who has gone now. So he lied. I heard him lying and I shouted out that what he said was not true. So they asked him again and he said that he remembered that morning very well and he remembered giving me the right drugs, and that there were no other pills around at the time. That was not true. There were many containers of pills and he should have realised that I might misunderstand his instructions.

"That evening when I went home I sat at my place and said nothing. I could not speak. My wife tried to comfort me. She said that it was not my fault that somebody had died and that what had happened was a true accident, like a dog running across the road or a plate falling off the table. But I could not even hear her words very well because my heart was cold, cold within me, and I knew that I would lose my job. How would we get anything to eat if I had no job? My father was late now and I could not go back to his place. We would be finished.

"I had no idea then how much worse things would be. It was only a few weeks later, after the police had spoken to me three or four times, that they told me that they were going to charge me with culpable homicide. That's what they called it. They said that it was culpable homicide to do something so careless that another person died. I could not believe that they would blame me so much, but the family of the lady who died were making a very big fuss about this and they kept asking the police when the man who had killed their mother would be punished for what he had done.

"I went to see them. They lived over there in Old Naledi, and I went to their house and begged them to forgive me. I said that I had never intended to harm the mother. Why should I want to harm her? I said that I felt as bad as if I had killed my own mother. I asked them if they would stop asking the police to send me to prison and tell them that I had explained to them what had happened. I went down on my knees to them. But they did not even look at me. They said I was to get out of their house or they would run and fetch the police.

"So I left their place and went home and waited for the day to come when I would have to go to court. I had a lawyer who said that he would work for me if I could pay him. I went to the Post Office and took out almost all the money I had saved and I gave this to the lawyer. He said that he would do his best for me, and I am sure that he did. But the prosecutor said that what I had done was very careless. He said that nobody who was being care-

ful would have done what I did. And the magistrate was looking at me all the time, and I could tell that he thought I was a
very careless man who had gone and killed somebody with his
carelessness.

"When he said that I would have to go to prison for two years,
at first I could not look behind me. My wife was there, and I
could hear her cry out, and so I turned round and saw her there
with my two little girls, and the girls were looking at their daddy
and wondering whether I was coming home with them now, and
I did not know what to do, whether I should wave goodbye to
them, and so I just stood there until the policemen who were
standing on either side of me said that I would have to go. These
policemen were kind to me. They did not push me; they did not
speak unkindly. One of them said, 'I am sorry, Rra. I am sorry
about this thing. You must come now.' And I left, and I did not
look behind me again, and I went away."

He stopped, and there was silence. Mma Ramotswe reached
forward to pick up a pencil from the table top. Then she put it
down again. Mma Makutsi was quite still. Neither of them
spoke, because there was nothing that either of them felt that she
could say.

CHAPTER TEN

THERE IS ALWAYS TIME FOR TEA AND CAKE (IF AVAILABLE)

IT WAS TIME for Mma Ramotswe to visit Mma Silvia Poto-kwane, the redoubtable matron of the orphan farm. There was no particular reason for Mma Ramotswe to pay a visit; she had received no summons from the matron, and there was no request to borrow Mr J.L.B. Matekoni for some maintenance task that needed doing. This was purely a social visit, of the sort that Mma Ramotswe liked to make when she felt that it was time to sit and talk. People did not spend enough time sitting and talking, she thought, and it was important that sitting and talking time be preserved.

The two women had known one another for many years, and had moved into that most comfortable of territories, that of an old friendship that could be picked up and put down at will without damage. Sometimes several months would go by without the two seeing one another, and this would make no difference. A conversation left unfinished at the beginning of the hot season could be resumed after the rains; a question asked in January might be answered in June, or even later, or indeed not at all. There was no need for formality or caution, and the faults of each were known to the other.

What were the faults of Mma Potokwane? Well, Mma Ramotswe might list those quite readily, were she to put her mind to it.

Everybody knew that Mma Potokwane was pushy; she had pushed Mr J.L.B. Matekoni around for years, and he had meekly submitted to such treatment. There had been innumerable requests for help in keeping that water pump alive, well beyond the limits of its natural life, and then there had been the unreliable minibus, which should have been scrapped years before but which was still on the road thanks to the unsurpassed mechanical skills of Mr J.L.B. Matekoni. At least the pump had been disposed of when he had eventually stood up to her and told her that its time had come, but he had yet to make a similar stand over the minibus.

But the worst instance of all had been that business with the sponsored parachute jump, when Mma Potokwane had cajoled Mr J.L.B. Matekoni into agreeing to jump from an aeroplane to raise money for the orphan farm. That had been a dreadful thing to do, and Mma Ramotswe had found herself quite cross over the whole episode. Although she had managed to arrange for Charlie to jump in his employer's stead—and she would never forget how Charlie had landed on a large acacia thorn—the whole matter had caused great anxiety to Mr J.L.B. Matekoni. One had to watch Mma Potokwane, then, so that she did not manoeuvre people into positions in which they felt uncomfortable. This was always the case with pushy people; their pushy schemes were sometimes put into effect without one's being aware of what was going on. And then suddenly one would discover that one had agreed to do something one had no wish to do.

Of course, let she who is without pushiness cast the first stone. Mma Ramotswe would have to admit that she herself was not above the occasional attempt to get people to do things. She would not have called that pushiness; she would rather have described it as . . . Well, it was difficult for her to think of an exact word to express the mixture of psychology and determination which one had to be able to invoke if one was to get anything done. And it should always be borne in mind that even if Mma

Potokwane was pushy, she never pushed for things for herself. She used her undoubted talents in this direction for the benefit of the orphans, and there were many of them who had a great deal to thank her for.

There was that small boy with the club foot, for example. Mma Ramotswe remembered when she had first seen him at the orphan farm four or five years ago. He had been taken in at the age of six, having been sent down from Selibi Pickwe, or somewhere in those parts. Mma Potokwane had explained the background to her, and had told her how the boy had been deserted by his mother, who had gone off with a man and had left him with an aunt who was an alcoholic. This aunt had let a fire get out of control, and the small traditional house in which they lived, with its walls of brushwood, had gone up in flames while the boy was inside it. The aunt had staggered off, and nobody had been aware of the fact that the boy was inside until the fire had died down. He had spent months in hospital and had then been given a home at the orphan farm.

Mma Ramotswe had seen him playing with the other boys, running after a ball with them in one of those strange spontaneous games which boys will make up for themselves. And she had seen his efforts to keep up, in vain because he had to drag his misshapen left foot behind him.

"That is a brave boy, that one," Mma Potokwane had said. "He is always trying to do things. He tries to climb trees, but he cannot because of that foot. And he would like to play football, but he cannot kick the ball. He is a brave boy."

Mma Ramotswe had noticed that look in Mma Potokwane's eyes as she spoke, that look of determination; and it was no surprise to her to hear some months ago that the matron had packed the boy onto a bus with her and had made the long journey to Johannesburg. There she had taken him to the surgery of a doctor she had heard about and had insisted that he see the boy. It was an act of breathtaking bravery. She had later heard, from Mma Potokwane herself, who related the story with frequent chuckles, how she had taken the boy into the waiting room of this doctor, a waiting room in a glittering tall building, and had ignored the protestations of the receptionist that the doctor would never be able to see her.

"The doctor can decide that," Mma Potokwane had announced. "You cannot speak for the doctor. He can look at this boy and then he can tell me, himself, whether he will see him or not."

She had waited and waited, and at last the doctor had poked his head round the door and this had been the signal for Mma Potokwane to leap to her feet and take from her bag a large fruit cake that she had prepared. This was thrust into the astonished man's hands, while the boy, hanging on to Mma Potokwane's skirts, had followed her into the doctor's office.

"He could not say no after that," said Mma Potokwane. "I cut a piece of the cake straightaway and told him that he could eat it while the boy took his shoes and socks off. So he did. He ate the cake and then he could not say that he would not look at the boy. And once he had done that, I asked him when he could do the operation, and while he was trying to think of something to say I cut another piece of fruit cake for him. So that boy had his foot repaired and now it is not too bad at all. He still limps, but not nearly so badly. He can play football. He can even run. That was a very good doctor. And he did not charge anything either. He said that the fruit cake was payment enough."

Achievements like that, Mma Ramotswe thought, were more than enough to make up for the occasional irritation that one might feel over Mma Potokwane's pushiness, and anyway, on this occasion, Mma Ramotswe was not minded to think of her friend's faults. She wanted, rather, to hear her views on several difficult issues with which she was confronted. At least one of these issues was serious—the question of what to do about Charlie—and others merely needed to be aired, to see what insights Mma Potokwane might bring to them.

She spotted the matron on the verandah outside her office, engaged in conversation with one of the groundsmen. These men were important members of the orphan farm staff; they attended to all the minor tasks which cropped up on an orphan farm, problems with blocked drains, or the broken boughs of trees, or the chasing away of a snake or a stray dog.

She waited in the tiny white van until the business between the two appeared to be finished, and then she got out and walked over the dusty car park towards the matron's verandah.

"So, Mma," Mma Potokwane called out. "You have arrived at exactly the time I was thinking that it would be a good time to make some tea. You are very good at that."

Mma Ramotswe laughed, and raised a hand in greeting. "And you always arrive at my office at exactly the same time," she responded. "We are both good at that."

Mma Potokwane called out to a young woman who was standing in the doorway of a neighbouring office, asking her to make tea for both of them, and then she gestured for Mma Ramotswe to follow her inside. Once seated, they looked at one another to see who would begin the conversation.

It was Mma Ramotswe who broke the silence. "I have been very busy, Mma," she began, shaking her head. "We have had a lot of work in the agency, and the garage is always busy, as you know. Mr J.L.B. Matekoni takes on too much."

She had not intended this to be a reference to the fact that some people—principally Mma Makutsi—thought that Mma Potokwane shamelessly added to Mr J.L.B. Matekoni's burdens in this life. Fortunately Mma Potokwane did not appear to interpret her remark in this way.

"He is a good, kind man," said Mma Potokwane. "And such men are often too busy. I have noticed that round here too. That man I was talking to just then—one of our groundsmen—he is like that. He is so kind that everybody asks him to do everything. We had a bad-tempered man working here once and he had nothing to do because nobody, apart from myself, of course, had the courage to ask him to do anything."

Mma Ramotswe agreed that this was the way that people sometimes behaved, and further agreed with Mma Potokwane when she went on to say that people never really changed. It was almost impossible to get a busy man to do less; that was not the way they were made.

"Are you worried about him?" asked Mma Potokwane bluntly. "After that illness he had, maybe you should watch him. Didn't Dr Moffat say that he should not work too hard?"

"He did," said Mma Ramotswe. "But then when Mr J.L.B. Matekoni was told this, he said: 'And what about Dr Moffat himself? He is the hardest worker of them all. I have seen him. He is always rushing off to the hospital and looking after people. If he thinks that I should not work so hard, why is he working so hard himself?' That is what he said, Mma, and I found it difficult to answer that."

Mma Potokwane snorted. "That is no answer," she said. "Doctors are allowed to tell us things which they might not do themselves. They know what the right thing is, but they may not be able to do it themselves. That does not mean that their advice is bad advice."

This was an interesting observation, and Mma Ramotswe thought carefully about it before she replied.

"I must think about what you have said, Mma," she said. "Should we really go around telling other people what not to do?"

The question was asked and hung heavily in the air while the tea tray was brought in and laid on Mma Potokwane's desk. Mma

Ramotswe looked discreetly at its contents; yes, there was cake—two large slices of fruit cake of the sort that she always hoped for when she visited the orphan farm. The absence of cake from the tray could have meant that she was for some reason in disfavour or disgrace; but fortunately that was not the case today.

Mma Potokwane reached forward and placed the larger slice of cake on her friend's plate. Then she placed the other piece on her own plate and began to pour the tea.

"The question you have asked is a very important one, Mma," she pronounced, picking up her slice of cake and taking a bite. "I must think about it. Maybe there are people who would say that I eat too much cake."

"But you do not eat too much, do you?" observed Mma Ramotswe.

Mma Potokwane's response came quickly. "No, I do not. I do not eat too much cake." She paused, and looked wistfully at her now emptying plate. "Sometimes I would like to eat too much cake. That is certainly true. Sometimes I am tempted."

Mma Ramotswe sighed. "We are all tempted, Mma. We are all tempted when it comes to cake."

"That is true," said Mma Potokwane sadly. "There are many temptations in this life, but cake is probably one of the biggest of them."

For a few moments neither of them said anything. Mma Ramotswe looked out of the window, at the tree outside, and beyond that at the sky, which was an empty light blue, endless, endless. A large bird, a buzzard perhaps, was circling on high on a current of air, a tiny, soaring point of black, looking for food, of course, as all of us did, in one way or another.

She looked away from the sky and back towards Mma Potokwane, who was watching her, the faintest of smiles playing about her lips.

"Temptation is very difficult," said Mma Ramotswe quietly. "I do not always resist it. I am not a strong woman in that respect."

"I am glad you said that," said Mma Potokwane. "I am not strong either. For example, right at the moment, I am thinking of cake."

"And so am I," confessed Mma Ramotswe.

Mma Potokwane stood up and shouted to the girl outside. "Two more pieces of cake, please. Two big slices."

THE CAKE FINISHED and the tray tidied away, they settled down with their mugs of tea to continue the conversation. Mma Ramotswe thought that she would begin with the puzzle of the pumpkin, which had been rather forgotten about in all the recent excitement, but which was still something of a mystery. So she told Mma Potokwane about the disturbing experience of finding herself in the house with an intruder, and then the even more alarming discovery that the intruder was under her bed.

Mma Potokwane shrieked with laughter when Mma Ramotswe described how the intruder's trousers had been caught on a bedspring.

"You might have crushed him, Mma," she said. "You could have broken his ribs."

Mma Ramotswe thought that the same might be said of any intruder who was unwise enough to hide under Mma Potokwane's bed, but she did not point this out.

"But then the next morning," she went on, "I found a beautiful pumpkin in front of the house. Somebody had taken the trousers and left a pumpkin in the place of the trousers. What do you make of that, Mma?"

Mma Potokwane frowned. "You have decided that the pumpkin was put there by the person who took the trousers, but are they connected? Might the pumpkin and the trousers be two quite separate matters? You have a pumpkin person, who brings the pumpkin—while the trousers are still there—and then you have a trousers person who takes the trousers and does not touch the pumpkin. That might be what happened."

"But who would bring a pumpkin and leave it there without any explanation?" asked Mma Ramotswe. "Would you do such a thing?"

Mma Potokwane scratched her head. "I do not think that I would leave a pumpkin at somebody's house unless I told them why. You would leave a message with the pumpkin, or you would tell the person later: that was me who left that pumpkin there."

"That is right," said Mma Ramotswe. "That is what most people would do."

"Mind you," said Mma Potokwane, "we have had people leave gifts out here at the gate. Once I found a box of food just sitting there, with no note. Some kind person had left it for the children."

"That is good," said Mma Ramotswe. "But then it is a bit different, isn't it? I am not a charity. Nobody would leave a pumpkin because they felt that I was in need of pumpkins."

Mma Potokwane saw the reason in this and was about to make an observation to this effect when she stopped herself short. Another possibility had occurred to her. Mma Ramotswe was assuming that the pumpkin had been intended for her, but what if somebody had placed it there by mistake? It was possible that somebody had intended the pumpkin for somebody else who lived on Zebra Drive but had delivered it to the wrong house. She was about to suggest this when she was stopped by Mma Ramotswe.

"Does it matter?" mused Mma Ramotswe. "Here we are talking about a pumpkin. There are plenty of pumpkins in this country. Is it sensible to spend one's time talking about pumpkins when there are more important things to talk about?"

Mma Potokwane agreed with this. "You are quite right," she said. "We have talked about this pumpkin for long enough. So let us talk about something more important."

Mma Ramotswe did not waste time. "Well," she said. "We have a very big problem with Charlie. I think that this problem is even bigger than the thorn that he got in the back of his trousers when he did that parachute jump."

"It is to do with a woman?" prompted Mma Potokwane.

"Yes," said Mma Ramotswe. "Now listen to this."

Mma Potokwane settled back in her chair. She had had a soft spot for Charlie since he had done the parachute jump for the benefit of the orphan farm. She considered him something of a character, and the prospect of hearing some juicy bit of information about his amorous entanglements was an interesting one. But then she remembered that there was something that she had meant to mention to Mma Ramotswe. It would be important to bring this up before Mma Ramotswe got into full flow, otherwise she might forget. So she raised a hand to interrupt.

"Before you begin, Mma," she said, "there's something I thought I should tell you about."

Mma Ramotswe looked at her friend expectantly. She wondered whether Mma Potokwane perhaps already knew about Charlie's affair and might even be able to tell her about the woman involved. Mma Potokwane knew so much about what was going on that it would not be at all surprising if she knew exactly who it was who had been at the wheel of that sleek silver Mercedes-Benz.

"You'll never guess who I saw in town the other day," said Mma Potokwane. "I could hardly believe it."

"I cannot guess," said Mma Ramotswe. "Was it somebody well-known?"

"A bit," said Mma Potokwane enigmatically. "Well-known in the jazz world, perhaps."

Mma Ramotswe said nothing, waiting for Mma Potokwane to continue.

"Note," she said simply. "Note Mokoti, your first husband. Remember him?"

CHAPTER ELEVEN

MMA MAKUTSI FINDS OUT MORE ABOUT MR PHUTI RADIPHUTI

WHILE MMA RAMOTSWE was embarking on her second slice of cake with Mma Potokwane, Mma Makutsi was still at the No. 1 Ladies' Detective Agency, tidying up. Mma Ramotswe had given her permission to close early that day since she herself was effectively taking the entire afternoon off. They were still busy with the affairs of a number of clients, but there was nothing that could not wait, and Mma Ramotswe knew that Mma Makutsi would like to have adequate time to get ready for her dancing class, the second one, which would be held that evening.

Mma Makutsi had finished the day's filing—a task which, as had been drummed into her at the Botswana Secretarial College, should never be left to lie over for the following day. This message had come from no less a person than the Principal herself, a tall, imposing woman who had brought the highest standards to the secretarial profession in Botswana.

"Don't let paper lie about, girls," she had admonished them. "Let each paper cross your desk once, and once only. That is a very good rule. Put everything away. Imagine that at night there are big paper rats that will come out and eat all the paper on your desk!"

That had been a very clever way of putting it, thought Mma Makutsi. The idea of the paper rat coming out at night to eat unfiled letters was a vivid one, and she had thought that it was not helpful of those silly, glamorous girls in the back row to laugh like that at what the Principal had said. The trouble with those girls had been that they were not committed secretaries. Everybody knew that most of them came to the Botswana Secretarial College simply because they had worked out that the best way of marrying a man with a good job and a lot of money was to become a secretary to such a man. So they went through the College course looking bored and making very little effort. It would have been different, it occurred to Mma Makutsi, had there been a part of the curriculum entitled: *How to Marry Your Boss*. That would have been very popular with those girls, and they would have paid very close attention to such a course.

In an idle moment, Mma Makutsi had speculated as to the possible contents of a course of this name. Some of the time would be devoted to psychology and this part would include lessons on how men think. That was very important if one was the sort of girl who planned to trap a man. You had to know what attracted men and what frightened them. Mma Makutsi thought about this. What attracted men? Good looks? Certainly if a girl was pretty then she tended to get the attention of men; that was beyond any doubt at all. But it was not just prettiness that mattered, because there were many girls who did not look anything special but who seemed to find no difficulty in making men notice them. These girls dressed in a very careful way; they knew which colours appealed to men (red, and other bright colours; men were like cattle in that respect), and they knew how to walk and sit down in a way which would make men sit up and take notice. The walk was important: it should not be a simple walk, with one leg going forward, to be followed by the other; no, the legs had to bend and twist a bit, almost as if one was thinking of walking in a circle. And then there was the delicate issue of what to do with one's bottom while one was walking. Some people thought that one could just leave one's bottom to follow one when one was walking. Not so. A mere glance at any glamorous girl would show that the bottom had to be more *involved*.

Mma Makutsi thought about all this as she tidied the office that afternoon. It was all very dispiriting. She had been dismayed to see that woman at the dance class—the woman whose name she had forgotten but who had been one of the worst, the very worst, of the glamorous girls at the Botswana Secretarial College. The sight of that woman dancing with such a handsome man, while she, Mma Makutsi, stumbled about the floor with poor Phuti Radiphuti, struggling to make out what he was trying to say; that sight had been immensely depressing. And then there was the question of her glasses, so large that people saw themselves reflected and did not even bother to see the person behind the lenses. What could she do about those? Glasses were very expensive, and although she was better off now, she had so many other costs to meet—higher rent for her new house, new clothes to be bought, and more money needed by those at home in Bobonong.

Her thoughts were interrupted by the arrival at the door of Mr Polopetsi. He had been working at the garage for several days now and had made a very good impression on all of them. Mr J.L.B. Matekoni had been particularly pleased with the way in which he had tidied the store cupboards. Cans of oil had been placed on shelves according to size, and parts had been organised according to make.

"You need a system," Mr Polopetsi had announced. "Then you will know when it is time to order more spark plugs and the like. This is called stock control."

He had also scrubbed the garage floor, removing several large patches of oil which the apprentices had never bothered to do anything about.

"Somebody might slip," said Mr Polopetsi. "You have to be very careful."

Mr J.L.B. Matekoni was delighted with this pronouncement, and drew it to the attention of the remaining apprentice.

"Did you hear that, young man?" he said. "Did you hear what Polopetsi said? Carefulness. Have you heard that word before? Do you know what it means?"

The younger apprentice said nothing, but stared at Mr Polopetsi in a surly way. He had been suspicious of this new employee ever since he had arrived, although Mr Polopetsi had been polite to him and had made every effort to win him over. Observing this, it had been clear to Mr J.L.B. Matekoni that their assumption that Charlie would soon hear that his place had been usurped was perfectly correct. But he was not sure that Charlie would respond in quite the way Mma Ramotswe had anticipated. However, they would see in due course, and for the time being the important thing was that the work in the garage was getting done.

Mr Polopetsi, in fact, had shown considerable talent for the simpler mechanical tasks which Mr J.L.B. Matekoni had given him. Watching the way he changed an air filter, or examined the oil on an engine's dip stick, made Mr J.L.B. Matekoni realise that this man had a feeling for cars, something which some mechanics never developed but which was a necessity if one was to become really good at the job.

"You like engines, don't you?" he said to Mr Polopetsi at the end of his first day. "I can tell that you understand them. Have you worked with them before?"

"Never," admitted Mr Polopetsi. "I do not know the names of all the parts or what they do. This bit here, for example, what does it do?"

Mr J.L.B. Matekoni peered at the engine. "That," he said, "is a very interesting bit. That is the distributor. It is the bit which sends the electric current in the right direction."

"So you would not want any dirt or water to get in there," said Mr Polopetsi.

Mr J.L.B. Matekoni nodded appreciatively. This showed that Mr Polopetsi intuitively understood how engines *felt*. Charlie would never have said anything so perceptive.

Now Mma Makutsi asked Mr Polopetsi whether everything was all right.

"Oh yes," he replied enthusiastically. "Everything is all right. I just thought that I would tell you that I have finished all my work in the garage this afternoon and I wondered if you had anything for me to do."

Mma Makutsi was most impressed. Most people would not ask for more work, but if they had nothing to do would merely pretend to work until five o'clock came and they could go home. In asking for something to do, Mr Polopetsi was proving that Mma Ramotswe had been right in her positive judgement of him.

She looked about the office. It was difficult to see what there was for him to do. She could hardly ask him to do any filing, which had been done anyway, and it would be too much to expect him to be able to type, even if he had been a pharmacy assistant and was therefore an indoor sort of man. So she could not ask him to do any letters; or could she?

Mma Makutsi looked sideways at Mr Polopetsi. "You can't type, can you, Rra?" she asked hesitantly.

Mr Polopetsi was matter of fact in his reply; there was no hint of boasting. "I can type very quickly, Mma. My sister went to the Botswana Secretarial College and she taught me."

Mma Makutsi stared at him. Not only was he a hard and resourceful worker, but he had a sister who was a graduate of the

Botswana Secretarial College! She thought of the name—
Polopetsi. Had she known anybody of that name at the College?

"She has a different name," Mr Polopetsi explained. "She is
my sister by a different father. Her name is Difele. Agnes Difele."

Mma Makutsi clapped her hands together. "She was my
friend," she exclaimed. "She was just before me at the College.
She did very well . . . too."

"Yes," said Mr Polopetsi. "She got eighty per cent in the final
examinations."

Mma Makutsi nodded gravely. That was a good mark, well
above the average. Of course it was not ninety-seven per cent,
but it was perfectly creditable.

"Where is she now?" asked Mma Makutsi.

"She is a secretary in the Standard Bank," said Mr Polopetsi.
"But I do not see her much these days. She was very ashamed
when I was sent to prison and she has not spoken to me since
then. She said that I disgraced her."

Mma Makutsi was silent. It was difficult to imagine somebody disowning her own brother like that. She herself would
never have done that; one's family was one's family whatever happened; surely that was the point of having a family in the first
place. One's family gave one unconditional support, whatever
happened.

"I am sorry to hear that, Rra," she said.

Mr Polopetsi looked away for a moment. "I am not cross with
her. I hope that she will change her mind some day. Then we will
talk again."

Mma Makutsi looked at her desk. There were several letters
which had to be typed, and she had intended to type them the
following day. But here was Mr Polopetsi, with his ability to
type, and it occurred to her that she had never once been in a
position to dictate a letter and have somebody else type it. Now

here she was with letters to be typed and a good typist at her disposal.

"I have some letters to dictate," she said. "You could type them as I dictate. That will save time."

Mr Polopetsi lost no time in setting himself up behind the typewriter at Mma Makutsi's desk, while she installed herself in Mma Ramotswe's chair, several sheets of paper in her hand. This is delicious, she thought. After all these years, I am now sitting in an office chair and dictating *to a man*. This was a very long way from those early days in Bobonong.

MMA MAKUTSI was late in arriving at the dancing class that evening and as she walked along the corridor at the President Hotel she could hear the band in full flow and the sound of numerous feet on the wooden floor. She appeared at the entrance and made her way to a seat at the side, only to be intercepted by Phuti Radiphuti, who had been waiting for her. Her heart sank. She did not wish to be unkind, but she had hoped that perhaps he would not be there and that she might have the chance to dance with somebody else. Now she was trapped, and there would be more stumbling and tripping while every-body else made progress and moved with greater and greater ease.

Phuti Radiphuti beamed with pleasure as he led her onto the floor. The band, which had been augmented by another guitarist, was playing more loudly than the last time, with the result that it was difficult for her to hear what anybody was saying, let alone to understand those with a speech impediment. So Mma Makutsi had to strain to make out her partner's words, and even when she thought she could do so, she was puzzled by their apparent lack of sense.

"This is a waltz," he tried to say, as they started to dance. But Mma Makutsi heard: *This is all false*. She wondered why he would say such a thing. Did he sense that she was only dancing with him out of pity, or a sense of duty? Or did he mean something quite different?

So she decided to seek clarification. "Why?" she asked.

Phuti Radiphuti looked puzzled. Waltzes were waltzes, of course; that was just what they were. He could not answer her question, and instead concentrated on doing the steps correctly, which was difficult for him. One, two, together is what Mr Fanope had said; or had he said that they should count three before they did the side-step?

Sensing her partner's confusion, Mma Makutsi took control. Drawing him to the side of the floor, she showed him how the steps were to be executed and made him repeat them himself while she watched. From the corner of her eye she noticed that the woman she had seen at the first lesson, the one whose name she had forgotten, was watching her in a bemused fashion from the other side of the room. That woman was dancing with the same elegant man who had partnered her before, and she waved at Mma Makutsi over her shoulder as she spun round in his expert arms.

Mma Makutsi pursed her lips. She was determined not to feel put down by this woman with her showy dress and her condescending manner. She knew what she would think of her, that she would be thinking: there's poor Grace Makutsi, who never managed to get any man to pay attention to her, and look what she's landed herself with now! Life has passed her by, of course, in spite of the fact that she graduated top of our class. It's no good getting ninety-whatever per cent if you end up like that.

It did not help to imagine what that woman would be thinking; it would be far better to ignore her, or, better still, to remind herself that it was the other woman who deserved the pity. After all, what did she have in life? She would have no career, that woman, only a life of running around with men. And the problem with that is that as you get older it becomes harder and harder to interest men. There would be a new generation of young women then, women with young faces and flashing teeth, while all the time one's own face sagged with age and one's teeth seemed to get a little less white.

Over the next half hour, they danced in almost complete silence. Mma Makutsi had to acknowledge that Phuti Radiphuti was making an effort and seemed to be improving slightly. He trod on her toes less frequently now, and he seemed to be making some progress with keeping in time. She complimented him on this, and he smiled appreciatively.

"I think I'm getting better," he stuttered.

"We must take a break," said Mma Makutsi. "I'm very thirsty after all this dancing."

They left the dance room and made their way down the corridor and onto the hotel verandah. A waiter appeared and took their orders: a cold beer for Phuti Radiphuti and a large glass of orange juice for Mma Makutsi.

The conversation was slow to begin with, but Mma Makutsi noticed that as he began to relax in her company, Phuti Radiphuti's speech became more confident and clearer. She was now able to understand most of what he had to say, although every now and then he seemed to stumble over a word, and when this happened it could be some time before something intelligible emerged.

There seemed to be a lot to talk about. He explained where he was from (the South) and what he was doing in Gaborone (he had a job in a furniture store in Broadhurst, where he sold chairs and tables). He asked about her; about the school she had gone to in Bobonong, about the Botswana Secretarial College, and about her job at the No. 1 Ladies' Detective Agency. He confessed that he had no idea of what a private detective agency would do and he was interested to find out.

"It's very straightforward," said Mma Makutsi. "Most people think that it is very exciting. But it isn't, it really isn't."

"There are very few exciting jobs," observed Phuti Radiphuti. "Most of us have very dull work to do. I just sell tables and chairs. There is nothing exciting in that."

"But it is important work," Mma Makutsi countered. "Where would we be if we had no chairs and tables?"

"We would be on the floor," said Phuti Radiphuti solemnly.

They thought about this for a moment, and then Mma Makutsi laughed. He had answered her with such gravity, as if the question had been an important one, rather than a mere reflection. She looked at him, and saw him smile in response. Yes, he understood that what he had said was funny. That was important in itself. It was good to be able to share such things with somebody else; the little jokes of life, the little absurdities.

They sat together for a few more minutes, finishing their drinks. Then Mma Makutsi rose to her feet and announced that she was going to the ladies' room and would meet him back in the dance hall for the rest of the class.

She found a door labelled *Powder Room* which bore an outline picture of a woman in a long, flowing skirt. She went in, and immediately regretted it.

"So! There you are, Grace Makutsi!" said the woman standing at the basin.

Mma Makutsi stopped, but the door had closed behind her, and she could hardly pretend that she had come into the wrong room.

She looked at the woman at the basin, and the name came back to her. This was the woman she had seen in the dance class, and her name was Violet Sephotho. She was one of the worst of the glamorous, empty-headed set at the Botswana Secretarial College, and here she was applying powder to her face in the aptly named Powder Room of the President Hotel.

"Violet," said Mma Makutsi. "It is good to see you again."

Violet smiled, closed her powder compact, and leant back against the edge of the basin. She had the air of one who was settling in for a long chat.

"Yes, sure," she said. "I haven't seen you for ages. Ages. Not since we finished the course." She paused, looking Mma Makutsi up and down, as if appraising her dress. "You did well, didn't you? At that college, I mean."

The thrust of the comment was unambiguous. One might do well at college, but this was very different from the real world. And then there was the disdainful reference to *that* college, as if there were better secretarial colleges to be attended.

Mma Makutsi ignored the barb. "And you, Violet? What have you been doing? Did you manage to find a job?"

The implication in this remark was that those who got barely fifty per cent in the final examinations might be expected to experience some difficulty in finding a job. This was not lost on Violet, whose eyes narrowed.

"Find a job?" she retorted. "Mma, I had them lining up to give me a job! I had so many offers that I could think of no way of choosing between them. So you know what I did? You want to know?"

Mma Makutsi nodded. She wanted to be out of this room, and away from this person, but she realised that she had to remain. She would have to stand up for herself if she were not to feel completely belittled by the encounter.

"I looked at the men who were offering the jobs and I chose the best-looking one," she announced. "I knew that that was how they would choose their secretary, so I applied the same rule to them! Hah!"

Mma Makutsi said nothing. She could comment on the stupidity of this, but then that would enable Violet to say something like, "Well that may be stupid in your eyes, but look at the jobs I got." So she said nothing, and held the other woman's challenging glance.

Violet lowered her eyes and inspected her brightly polished nails. "Nice shoes," she said. "Those green shoes of yours. I've never seen anybody wear green shoes before. It's brave of you. I would be frightened that people would laugh at me if I wore shoes like that."

Mma Makutsi bit her lip. What was wrong with green shoes? And how dare this woman, this empty-headed woman, pass comment on her taste in shoes? She looked at Violet's shoes, sleek black shoes with pointed toes and quite unsuitable for dancing. They looked expensive—much more expensive than these shoes which Mma Makutsi had treated herself to and of which she felt so proud.

"But let's not talk about funny shoes," Violet went on breezily. "Let's talk about men. Don't you love talking about men? That man through there. Is that your uncle or something?"

Mma Makutsi closed her eyes and imagined for a moment that Mma Ramotswe was by her side. What would Mma Ramotswe advise in such circumstances? Could Mma Ramotswe provide the words to deal with this woman, or would she say, "No, do not allow yourself to be belittled by her. Do not stoop to her level. You are worth more than that silly girl." And Mma Makutsi saw Mma Ramotswe in her mind's eye, and heard her too, and that is exactly what she said.

"The man you are dancing with is very handsome," said Mma Makutsi. "You are lucky to have such a handsome man to dance with. But then you are a very pretty lady, Mma, and you deserve these handsome men. It is quite right that way."

Violet stared at her for a moment, and then looked away. Nothing more was said, and Mma Makutsi went about her business.

"Well done, Mma," said Mma Ramotswe's voice. "You did just the right thing there. Just the right thing!"

"It was very hard," replied Mma Makutsi.

"It often is," said Mma Ramotswe.

CHAPTER TWELVE

MMA RAMOTSWE REVEALS A PROBLEM
WITHOUT A SOLUTION

MMA POTOKWANE had mentioned it so casually, as if it had been no more than a piece of unimportant gossip. But the news that Note Mokoti had been seen in Gaborone was much more than that, at least to Mma Ramotswe. She had put Note out of her mind and very rarely thought of him, although there were times when he came to her in dreams, taunting her, threatening her, and she would wake up in fright and have to remind herself that he was no longer there. He had gone to South Africa, she understood, and had pursued his musical career in Johannesburg, apparently with some success, as she had seen the occasional magazine photograph featuring him.

I'm a forgiving lady, Mma Ramotswe told herself. I see no point in keeping old arguments alive when it is so simple to lay them to rest. She had made a deliberate attempt to forgive Note, and she thought that it had worked. She remembered the day on which she had done this, when she had gone for a walk in the bush and had looked up at the sky and emptied her heart of its hatred. She had forgiven him on that day: she had forgiven him the physical cruelty, the beatings which she had endured when he had taken drink; she had forgiven him the mental torment which he had inflicted on her when he had promised her something or other and had immediately torn up the promise. And when it came to the money which he had taken from her, she forgave him that too, saying to herself that she did not want it back.

When Mma Potokwane had made her disclosure about having seen Note Mokoti, Mma Ramotswe had not shown much of a reaction. Indeed, Mma Potokwane felt the news was of little importance to her friend, so uninterested did she appear, and so she said nothing more about it. They continued their conversation about Charlie and his worrying behaviour; Mma Potokwane had a great deal to say about this, and made some valuable suggestions, but later, when Mma Ramotswe tried to remember what she had said, she could recall very little. Her mind had been almost completely occupied by the sheer awfulness of the news that had been broken to her so casually. Note was back.

As she drove back from Tlokweng that day, Charlie was far from her mind. If Note Mokoti had been seen in Gaborone, then this could mean that he had returned to live there—and that raised certain very obvious difficulties—or it could mean no more than that he had come back for a visit. If he was on a visit, then he might already have gone back to Johannesburg, and she need worry no more. If, however, he had moved back to Gaborone, then it would be inevitable that she herself would see him sooner or later. The town was bigger these days, and it was possible that two people might live in it without ever seeing one another, but there was a very good chance that their paths would cross. After all, there were not all that many supermarkets and she was always bumping into people at such places. And then there was the mall, the centre of the town, where everybody went sooner or later; what if she were to be walking down the mall and she saw Note walking towards her? Would she turn round and walk in the opposite direction, or would she just walk past him as if he were any other stranger?

She thought about this, as she drove the tiny white van back along the Tlokweng Road. Presumably there were many who felt that they had to avoid somebody or other. People were always having arguments with one another, feuds about land and cattle, family scraps over inheritance—which were rich sources of dispute wherever one went in this world. Some of these people made it up with one another and talked again; others never did this, and kept their anger and resentment alive. Then there were people who split up from a lover or a spouse. If you left your wife for another woman, and your wife failed to see this as a good thing, then what if you were walking down the road with your new woman, holding hands, as those who are newly in love might do, and you saw your old wife coming towards you? This must happen a great deal, thought Mma Ramotswe, and presumably people faced it and coped, as they usually end up doing. People got by in life in spite of all these social pitfalls.

She tried to imagine what she might say to Note if she were to find herself with no alternative but to talk to him. Perhaps it would be best to speak in a very ordinary way and ask him how he was and how life had been treating him. Then she could say something about how she hoped that his music was going well and how she imagined what an exciting life he was leading in Johannesburg. Yes, that would be all. With that she would have shown that she wished him no evil, and even Note, even that unkind man who had treated her so badly, might leave her alone after that.

She turned the tiny white van into Odi Drive to cut through the Village. As she did so, she saw Mrs Moffat walking back along the side of the road, a heavy bag of shopping in her hand. It was not far to the Moffat house, and it would not have taken Mrs Moffat long to walk, but nobody drove past a friend in Botswana, and she drew up alongside and reached over to open the passenger door.

"Your bag looks very heavy," she said. "I will take you back."

Mrs Moffat smiled. "You are very kind, Mma Ramotswe," she said. "And sometimes I feel very lazy. I'm feeling very lazy now."

She climbed into the van and they resumed the short journey back up the road to the Moffat house. Samuel, who worked in the Moffat garden once a week, was standing near the gate, and he opened it for the tiny white van to sweep through.

"Thank you," said Mrs Moffat, turning to her friend. "This bag was getting rather heavy, I'm . . ." She did not finish her sentence, for she had seen the expression on Mma Ramotswe's face.

"Is something wrong, Mma Ramotswe?"

Mma Ramotswe looked away before she gave her reply. "Yes. There is something wrong. I did not want you to know, but there is something wrong."

Mrs Moffat's first thought was of the obvious. Mma Ramotswe and Mr J.L.B. Matekoni had recently married. Their wedding, which she and the doctor had attended, had been a surprise to everybody as they had all decided that Mr J.L.B. Matekoni, fine man though he was, would never make up his mind to get to the altar. Perhaps he had not been ready after all; perhaps the seemingly interminable engagement had been his way of saying that his heart was not really in marriage, and perhaps she was now discovering this. The thought of this appalled her. She knew that Mma Ramotswe had been married before, a long time ago; she had heard a little about this marriage—that it had been one of those awful violent marriages which so many women had to put up with—and it seemed so unfair that things should be going wrong again, if that is what was happening. It would be impossible, though, that they would be going wrong in the same way: Mr J.L.B. Matekoni was incapable of being violent—at least that was certain.

Mrs Moffat reached across and touched Mma Ramotswe lightly on the forearm. "Come," she said. "You can talk to me. We can sit in the garden, or on the verandah if you prefer."

Mma Ramotswe nodded, and turned off the engine. "I do not want to burden you," she said. "It is not a big thing."

"Tell me about it," said Mrs Moffat. "Sometimes it's good just to talk."

They decided to sit on the verandah, where it was cool, and where they could look out over the garden that Mrs Moffat had spent so much time in creating. There was a towering jacaranda tree directly adjacent, and its great canopy of leaves gave shade to the house. It was a good place to sit and reflect.

Mma Ramotswe came straight to the point and told Mrs Moffat about the news which Mma Potokwane had given her. As she spoke, she saw her friend's expression change from one of concern to one of what appeared to be relief.

"So that's all," said Mrs Moffat. "That's all it is."

Mma Ramotswe managed a smile. "I said it was not a big thing."

Mrs Moffat laughed. "It certainly isn't a big thing," she said. "I imagined that there was something wrong with your marriage. I was busy thinking that Mr J.L.B. Matekoni had run away, or something like that. I was wondering what I would be able to say."

"Mr J.L.B. Matekoni would never run away," said Mma Ramotswe. "He is enjoying all the good food that I am putting on the table for him. He would never run away."

"That is a good way to keep a man," said Mrs Moffat. "But, going back to this other man, to Note Mokoti, so what if he's back? You needn't worry about that. Just be polite to him if you see him. You don't have to engage further than that. Tell him you're married . . ."

Mma Ramotswe had been looking at Mrs Moffat as she spoke, but when her friend said *Tell him you're married,* she looked away sharply and Mrs Moffat hesitated. Her words appeared to have upset Mma Ramotswe for some reason and she wondered what it was. Could it be that Mma Ramotswe did not want Note to know this, that for some reason she retained feeling for this man and that she would not want him to know about her marriage to Mr J.L.B. Matekoni?

"You will tell him," she said, "if he shows up, that is. You will tell him that you're married?"

Mma Ramotswe was holding the hem of her dress between her fingers, worrying at it. She looked up and met Mrs Moffat's gaze.

"I am still married to him," she said quietly, her voice barely above a whisper. "I am still married to that man. We did not get a divorce."

In the ensuing moments of silence, a grey African dove moved delicately along a branch of the jacaranda tree, looking down, with quick movements, at the two women below. On a rock just outside the penumbra of shade cast by the tree, a small lizard, tinted blue along its flanks, lifted its head towards the late afternoon sun.

Mrs Moffat said nothing. She was not waiting for Mma Ramotswe to continue; it was just that she had nothing to say.

"So you see, Mma," said Mma Ramotswe. "I am very unhappy. Very unhappy."

Mrs Moffat nodded. "But why did you not get a divorce? He left you, didn't he? You could have got a divorce."

"I was very young," said Mma Ramotswe. "That man frightened me. When he left I just put him out of my mind and tried to forget that we were ever married. I made myself not think about it."

"But surely you remembered later?"

"No," said Mma Ramotswe. "I should have done something about it, but I could not bring myself to face it. I just couldn't. I'm sorry, Mma . . ."

"You don't have to apologise to me!" exclaimed Mrs Moffat. "It's just that this is a bit complicated, isn't it? You're not meant to get married again until you're divorced."

"I know that," said Mma Ramotswe. "I have done a very silly thing, Mma."

They sat together for a short time longer. Mrs Moffat tried to think of something to say, of some advice to give, but she simply could not think of any way out of the situation in which Mma Ramotswe found herself. Friends sometimes behaved in a foolish way—she knew that very well—and this was a good example of that happening. It was not as if Mma Ramotswe had done anything morally reprehensible—it was more a case of being careless about a legal formality. But this was a legal formality which was really rather important, and she simply could not think of any way out of it.

After a few minutes, Mma Ramotswe sighed and stood up. She straightened her blouse and brushed some dust off the side of her skirt, dust more imaginary than real.

"This is my problem, Mma," she said to Mrs Moffat. "I cannot expect you to help me with this. I shall have to do something myself to sort it all out." She paused, before continuing, "Although I cannot think of anything that I can do, Mma. I cannot think of anything at all!"

CHAPTER THIRTEEN

MMA MAKUTSI AND MR J.L.B. MATEKONI
VISIT MR J.L.B. MATEKONI'S HOUSE

MMA MAKUTSI realised the next day that Mma Ramotswe's mind was on other things. Her employer was rarely moody,
but there were occasions when it seemed as if some problem was
preventing her from giving her full attention to the affairs of the
agency. It was usually something domestic—one of the children
might be experiencing difficulty at school or Rose, her maid,
might have told her of the hardship being endured by a relative or
friend. There was so much need, even in a fortunate country
such as Botswana; it seemed as if the reservoirs of suffering were
never empty, and no matter what progress was made there would
always be people for whom there was no job, or no place to live,
or not enough food. And when you became aware of these needs,
especially if they were being felt by those who had a claim on you,
then it was hard to put them out of your mind.

Everybody knew somebody in need. Mma Makutsi herself
had just heard of a young girl whose parents had both died. This
girl, who lived with an aunt, was clever. She had done well in her
examinations, but now there was no money to pay her school fees
and she would have to give up her education if this money were
not found. What could one do? Mma Makutsi could not help her;

although she had a bit of spare money now from the Kalahari Typing School for Men, she had her own people to look after up in Bobonong. So there was nobody to help this child, and she would lose her chance to make something of her life.

Of course you could not allow yourself to think too much about these issues. One had to get on and to attend to the day-to-day business of living. The No. 1 Ladies' Detective Agency was there to solve the problems in people's lives—that's what they did, as Mma Ramotswe often pointed out—but they could not solve all the world's problems. And so you had to turn away from so much that you would like to do something about, and hope that things would work out somehow for those who were in need. That was all you could do.

Mma Makutsi looked at Mma Ramotswe, seated at her desk on the other side of the room, and wondered. She asked herself whether she should say something to her employer, or whether she should remain silent. After a moment's thought, she decided to speak.

"You are looking very worried, Mma Ramotswe," she ventured. "Are you feeling all right?"

For a while Mma Ramotswe said nothing, and Mma Makutsi's question hung awkwardly in the air.

Then Mma Ramotswe spoke. "I am worried about something, Mma," she said. "But I do not wish to burden you with my worries. This is a private thing."

Mma Makutsi looked at her. To describe something as a private thing was a big step. There were very few matters in Botswana which people would treat as a private thing; this was a society in which people knew one another's business. "I do not wish to pry into private things," she said. "But if you are worried about that thing, then you should let me take up your worries about other things. That way I can help you."

Mma Ramotswe sighed. "I do not know which worries I can pass on to you. There are so many . . ."

Mma Makutsi's interjection was brisk. "Well, there's Charlie, for a start. He is a big worry. Let me deal with Charlie. Then you can stop worrying about him."

For a moment Mma Ramotswe thought of ways to decline this offer. Charlie was a garage matter, and his welfare was thus the concern of Mr J.L.B. Matekoni, and of herself, indirectly, as the wife of Mr J.L.B. Matekoni. She and Mr J.L.B. Matekoni had always worried about the apprentices, and it seemed perfectly natural that they should continue to do so. And yet, it was undoubtedly an attractive offer that Mma Makutsi was making. She had no idea what she could do about Charlie—if, indeed she could do anything at all. Mma Makutsi was a resourceful and intelligent lady who was quite capable of sorting out young men. She had taken the apprentices in hand before, with conspicuous success, and so perhaps it was appropriate that she should try to do so again.

"What would you do about Charlie?" she asked. "What can any of us possibly do?"

Mma Makutsi smiled. "I can go and find out just what's going on," she said. "Then I can look at ways of dealing with it."

"But we know perfectly well what's going on," said Mma Ramotswe. "The goings-on are between him and that rich lady with the Mercedes-Benz. Anybody can tell what that's all about. That's what's going on."

Mma Makutsi agreed that this was so. But in her view there was always more beneath the surface, and they had of course seen the lady and the apprentice drive into Mr J.L.B. Matekoni's yard. That remained something of a mystery.

"There are still some things to be looked at," she said to Mma Ramotswe. "I have been thinking that Mr J.L.B. Matekoni and I should have a closer look. That's what I've been thinking."

"You must be careful of Mr J.L.B. Matekoni," cautioned Mma Ramotswe. "He is a very good mechanic, but I do not think that he will be a very good detective. In fact, I am sure he will not be."

"I shall be in charge," said Mma Makutsi. "I shall make sure that Mr J.L.B. Matekoni comes to no harm."

"Good," said Mma Ramotswe. "He is the only husband I . . ." She stopped. She had been about to say that he was the only husband she had, but then she realised, with a feeling of dark foreboding, that this was not strictly true.

WHEN MMA MAKUTSI suggested to Mr J.L.B. Matekoni that they pay a visit to his new tenant, he looked at his watch and scratched his head.

"I have so much to do, Mma," he said. "There is that car over there which has no brake pads left. Then there is that van which is making a noise like a donkey. There are many sick vehicles here, and I cannot leave them."

"They are not dying," said Mma Makutsi firmly. "They will still be here when we come back."

Mr J.L.B. Matekoni sighed. "I do not see why we need to go to the house. They are paying their rent. The house has not been burned down."

"But there is Charlie," pointed out Mma Makutsi. "We should find out why he is going to your house. What if he is being sucked into some sort of criminal activity, with that fancy lady of his and that Mercedes-Benz?"

At the mention of criminal activity, Mr J.L.B. Matekoni grimaced. He had taken those boys on several years ago, and he had imagined their involvement in all sorts of affairs with girls. He did not like to enquire about that, and it was their own business after all. But criminal activity was another matter. What if there were to be an article in the newspapers reporting that an apprentice from Tlokweng Road Speedy Motors had been arrested by the police in connection with some racket? The shame that this would bring on him would be too much to bear. His was a business dedicated to looking after customers and their cars, and doing so honestly. Mr J.L.B. Matekoni had never used cheap, unsuitable spare parts and then charged the customer for expensive, proprietary parts; he had never paid or accepted a bribe. He had done his best to instill this sense of morality—this commercial, or even mechanical, morality—in the boys, but he was not at all sure whether he had succeeded. He sighed again. These women were always pushing him into things against his will. He did not want to interfere with his tenant. He did not want to go back to his old house, now that he was so safely settled in the house at Zebra Drive. But it seemed that he was being given very little alternative, and so he agreed. They could go that evening, he conceded, shortly after five o'clock. Until then he wanted to work on these poor vehicles without interruption.

"I will not disturb you," promised Mma Makutsi. "But at five o'clock I shall be standing here, ready to go."

And at exactly five o'clock she waved goodbye to Mma Ramotswe as her employer drove off homewards in the tiny white van and she went to remind Mr J.L.B. Matekoni that it was time for them to go. He had just finished working on a car, and was in a cheerful mood, as the job had worked out well.

"I hope that we shall not have to be long," he said as he wiped his hands on a piece of lint. "I do not have very much to say to that man who has rented my house. In fact, I have nothing to say to him at all."

"We can say that we have come to see that everything is all right," said Mma Makutsi. "And then we can say something about Charlie. We can ask him if he has seen Charlie."

"I don't see any point in that," said Mr J.L.B. Matekoni. "If he has seen Charlie he will say yes, and if he has not seen him, then he will say no. What is the point of asking him this?"

Mma Makutsi smiled. "You are not a detective, Rra. I can tell that."

"I am certainly not a detective," said Mr J.L.B. Matekoni. "And I do not want to be a detective. I am a mechanic."

"You have married a detective," said Mma Makutsi gently. "People who marry people sometimes pick up a bit about the job. Look at the President's wife. She must know all about opening schools and signing things now."

"But I do not expect Mma Ramotswe to fix cars," objected Mr J.L.B. Matekoni. "So she should not expect me to be a detective."

Mma Makutsi decided not to respond to this remark. Glancing at her watch, she pointed out that they should leave, or they would arrive at a time when the tenant and his family were sitting down to their evening meal, and this would be rude. Reluctantly, Mr J.L.B. Matekoni peeled off his overalls and reached for his hat off its accustomed peg. Then the two of them set off in his truck, to make the short journey along the road that led to his house near the old Botswana Defence Force Club.

As they neared the house, Mr J.L.B. Matekoni began to slow down. Peering over the steering wheel, he remarked to Mma Makutsi, "This feels very strange, Mma. It is always strange coming back to a place where you used to live."

Mma Makutsi nodded. It was true: she had only been back to Bobonong a few times since she had moved to Gaborone, and it had always been an unsettling experience. Everything was so familiar—that was true—but in a curious way it did not seem the same. To begin with, there was the smallness, and the shabbiness. When she had lived in Bobonong the houses seemed perfectly normal to her and the house in which her family lived had seemed quite comfortable. But looking at it with eyes that had seen Gaborone, and the large buildings there, their house had seemed mean and cramped. And as for the shabbiness, she had never noticed when she lived there how Bobonong could have done with a lick of paint, but having been in Gaborone, where things were kept so smart, it was impossible not to notice all the flaking paint and the dirt-scarred walls.

The people too seemed diminished. Her favourite aunt was still her favourite, of course, but whereas she had always been impressed by the wisdom of what her aunt said, now her words seemed no more than trite. And what was worse, she had actually felt embarrassed at some of her pronouncements, thinking that such observations would seem quaint in Gaborone. That had made her feel guilty, and she had tried to smile appreciatively at her aunt's remarks, but somehow the effort seemed too great. She knew this was wrong; she knew that you should never forget what you owed to home, and to family, and to the place that nurtured you, but sometimes it was difficult to put this into practice.

Mma Makutsi had always been impressed by the way in which Mma Ramotswe seemed to be completely at ease with who she was and where she came from. She was clearly very attached to Mochudi, and when she spoke of her childhood there it was always with fondness. This was great good fortune: to love the place in which you were brought up; not everybody could do that. And even greater good fortune would be to have a father like Obed Ramotswe, about whom Mma Makutsi had heard so much from Mma Ramotswe. Mma Makutsi almost felt as if she knew him now, and that at any moment she herself would start quoting things he had said, although of course she had never met him. She could just imagine that happening. She would say to Mma Ramotswe, "As your father used to say, Mma . . ." and Mma Ramotswe would smile and say, "Yes, he always said that, didn't he?"

Of course she would not be the only one to do that sort of thing. Mma Ramotswe was always talking about Seretse Khama and quoting the things that he had said, but Mma Makutsi was a bit suspicious of this. It was not that Seretse Khama had not said a great number of wise things—he had—it was just that she felt that Mma Ramotswe had a slight tendency to express a view— her own view—and then attribute it to Seretse Khama, even if Sir Seretse had never expressed an opinion on the matter in question. There had been an example of this recently when Mma Ramotswe had told her that you should never drive a goat across water and that Seretse Khama himself had said something to that effect. Mma Makutsi was very doubtful about this; Seretse Khama had never said anything about goats, as far as she could remember—and she had studied his speeches when she was at school— and in her view this was merely Mma Ramotswe giving authority to a peculiar view of her own.

"When did he say that?" she had challenged.

Mma Ramotswe had looked vague. "A long time ago, I think," she said. "I read it somewhere or other."

This answer had failed to satisfy Mma Makutsi, and she had been tempted to say to her employer, "Mma Ramotswe, you must remember that you are not Seretse Khama!" But she had not done so, fortunately, because it would have sounded rude, and Mma Ramotswe meant well when she talked about Seretse Khama, even if she did not always get her facts right. The real problem, thought Mma Makutsi, is that Mma Ramotswe did not go to the Botswana Secretarial College. Had she done that, then she would have perhaps been a little bit more careful about some of the things she said. There was no substitute for formal training, Mma Makutsi thought; intuition and experience would get one so far, but you really needed a little bit more than that to round things off. And had Mma Ramotswe been fortunate enough to attend the

Botswana Secretarial College, then what mark, Mma Makutsi wondered, would she have achieved in the final examinations? That was a fascinating question. She would have surely done very well, and might even have finished up with . . . well, with about seventy-five per cent. That was a distinguished result, even if it was some twenty-two per cent below what she herself had achieved. The problem with having got ninety-seven per cent is that it set the bar artificially high for others.

Mma Makutsi's thoughts were interrupted by Mr J.L.B. Matekoni, who tapped her lightly on the shoulder.

"Do you want me to drive up the drive, Mma?"

Mma Makutsi thought for a moment. "It would be best, Rra. Remember that you have nothing to hide here. You are just calling on this man to see that everything is all right."

"And you?" asked Mr J.L.B. Matekoni, as he guided the truck through his familiar gates. "What will they think about you?"

"I could be your niece," said Mma Makutsi. "Many men of your age have nieces who ride with them in their trucks. Have you not seen that, Mr J.L.B. Matekoni?"

Mr J.L.B. Matekoni gave her a strange look. He had never known quite how to take Mma Makutsi, and this sort of ambiguous remark was typical of the sort of thing she said. But he made no reply, and concentrated on positioning the truck next to one of the two cars which had been parked beside the house.

Together they walked round to the front door, where Mr J.L.B. Matekoni knocked loudly, calling out as he did so.

"The yard is not very tidy," Mma Makutsi muttered, discreetly pointing to several up-turned paraffin tins that had been used for some purpose or other and had then just been left where they lay.

"They are busy people, I think," said Mr J.L.B. Matekoni. "Maybe they do not have much time to look after the yard. You cannot blame them for that."

"You can," retorted Mma Makutsi, her voice rather louder now.

"Hush," said Mr J.L.B. Matekoni. "There is somebody coming."

The door was opened by a woman somewhere in her mid-forties, who was wearing a colourful red blouse and a full length green skirt. She looked them up and down, and then gestured for them to come in.

"There aren't many people here," she said before they had the chance to utter a greeting. "But I'll get you something if you go and sit in the back. I've got some rum, or you can just have a beer. What will it be?"

Mr J.L.B. Matekoni half-turned to Mma Makutsi in surprise. He had not expected such a businesslike welcome, and it was rather strange, was it not, to offer somebody a drink like that before anything else had been said? How did this woman, who-ever she was, know who he was? Perhaps she was the tenant's wife: he had dealt only with the tenant himself and had not seen anybody else.

If Mr J.L.B. Matekoni was at a loss to speak, then the same was not true of Mma Makutsi. She smiled at the woman and immediately accepted the offer of a beer for Mr J.L.B. Matekoni. She would have something soft, she said—as long as it was cold. The woman nodded and disappeared into the kitchen, leaving Mr J.L.B. Matekoni and Mma Makutsi to make their way into the room which used to be Mr J.L.B. Matekoni's dining room.

It had been his favourite room when he had lived in the house, as it had a good view of the back yard with its pawpaw trees, and beyond that of a small hill in the distance. Now, as they entered, there was no view, as curtains had been drawn across the window and the only light was provided by two red-shaded lamps that had been placed on a low table in front of the curtains. Mr J.L.B. Matekoni looked about him in astonishment. He knew that people had different tastes, but it seemed extraordinary that somebody would wish to plunge a room into darkness—and waste electricity—when there was perfectly good natural light available outside for nothing.

He turned to Mma Makutsi. Perhaps she had seen this sort of thing before and would be unsurprised. He looked at her for an explanation, but she was just smiling at him in a curious way.

"What have they done to my dining room?" he whispered. "This is very strange."

Mma Makutsi continued to smile. "It is very interesting," she said, her voice lowered. "Of course you know that . . ."

She did not finish what she was saying; the woman in the red blouse had returned with a tray bearing a beer and a glass of cola. She placed the tray on the table and pointed to a large leather-covered sofa at one side of the room.

"You can sit down," she said. "I will put on some music if you would like that."

Mma Makutsi picked up her glass of cola. "You join us, Mma. It has been a hot day and I think that you might like a beer. You can charge it to us. We will buy you a beer."

The woman accepted readily. "That is kind of you, Mma. I will fetch it and come back."

Once she had left the room, Mr J.L.B. Matekoni turned to Mma Makutsi. "Is this . . ." he began.

"Yes," Mma Makutsi interrupted. "This is a shebeen. Your house, Mr J.L.B. Matekoni, has been turned into an illegal bar!"

Mr J.L.B. Matekoni sat down heavily on the sofa. "This is very bad," he said. "Everybody will think that I am involved in it. They will say that man is running a shebeen while he pretends to be a respectable person. And what will Mma Ramotswe think?"

"She'll understand that it has nothing to do with you," said Mma Makutsi. "And I'm sure that other people will think the same."

"I do not like such places," said Mr J.L.B. Matekoni, shaking his head. "They let people run up big bills and spend all their money on drink."

Mma Makutsi agreed. She was amused by the discovery, which she had not expected to make, but she knew that there was nothing very funny about shebeens. Although people could easily go to legitimate bars, there were those who needed to drink on credit, and shebeens exploited such people. They encouraged people to spend too much and then, every month, they would end up taking a larger and larger portion of the drinker's salary. And there were other things too: shebeens were associated with gambling and again in this respect they preyed on human weakness.

The woman returned, an opened bottle of beer in her hand. She raised the bottle in a toast, and Mr J.L.B. Matekoni half-heartedly reciprocated, although Mma Makutsi's response was more convincing.

"So, Mma," said Mma Makutsi brightly, "this is a nice place you have. Very nice!"

The woman laughed. "No, Mma. It is not my place. I am just somebody who works here. There is another woman who runs this place."

Mma Makutsi thought for a moment. Of course: a woman like that, a woman who drove a large Mercedes-Benz, would not go to a shebeen as a mere customer—she was the shebeen queen herself.

"Oh yes," Mma Makutsi said. "I know that woman. She is the one who drives that big Mercedes-Benz and has that young boyfriend, the new one. I think he's called Charlie."

"That is her," said the woman. "Charlie is her boyfriend. He comes here with her sometimes. But there's a husband too. He is in Johannesburg. He's a big man there. He has some bars, I think."

"Yes," said Mma Makutsi. "I know him well." She paused. "Do you think that he knows about Charlie?"

The woman took a swig from her bottle of beer and then wiped her mouth with the back of her hand. "Hah! I think that he will not know about Charlie. And if I were Charlie I'd be very careful. That man comes back to Botswana to see her every few months and then Charlie had better be away for the weekend! Hah! If I were Charlie I'd go right up to Francistown or Maun when that happens. The further away the better."

Mma Makutsi glanced at Mr J.L.B. Matekoni, who was following the conversation closely. Then she looked back at the woman and asked her question. "Does that man, the husband, help to run this place? Does he come here ever?"

"Sometimes," said the woman. "He phones us sometimes to leave messages for her."

Mma Makutsi took a deep breath. Mma Ramotswe had told her that when one asked the important question—the question upon which an entire investigation might turn—one should be careful to sound calm, as if the answer to the question really did not matter all that much. This was the moment for such a question, but Mma Makutsi found that her heart was beating loud within her and she was sure that this woman would hear it.

"So he phones? Well, you wouldn't have his telephone number over there, would you? I'd like to speak to him about a friend we have in Johannesburg who wants to see him about something. I had his number, but . . ."

"It is here," said the woman. "It is through in the kitchen on a piece of paper. I can fetch it for you."

"You are very kind," said Mma Makutsi. "And when you go through to the kitchen, you can get yourself another beer, Mma. Mr J.L.B. Matekoni will pay."

CHAPTER FOURTEEN

REMEMBER ME?

MMA RAMOTSWE had tried very hard to contain the feeling of dread which stalked her now, like a dark shadow. She had tried to put Note Mokoti out of her mind; she had told herself that just because Mma Potokwane had seen him this did not mean that she would do so. But none of this had worked, and she found herself unable to take her mind off her first husband and the meeting that she knew he would seek with her.

Her immediate inclination had been to tell Mr J.L.B. Matekoni what Mma Potokwane had said, but then she found that she simply could not do this. Note Mokoti belonged to her past—to a painful part of that past—and she had never brought herself to speak to Mr J.L.B. Matekoni about this. She had told him, of course, that she had been married before, and that her husband had been a cruel man. But that was all that she had said, and he had sensed that this was something that she did not wish to discuss, and he had respected that. Nor had she discussed it to any great extent with Mma Makutsi, although they had touched upon it once or twice when the subject of men, or husbands in particular, had come up.

But no matter how firmly she had relegated Note to this wished-for oblivion, in real life he was a flesh and blood man who was now back in Gaborone and who would cross her path sooner or later. It happened in the mid-morning, just two days after her meeting with Mma Potokwane, when Mma Ramotswe and Mma Makutsi were working in the office of the No. 1 Ladies' Detective Agency. Mr J.L.B. Matekoni was off fetching spare parts from the motor trades distributor with whom he dealt, and Mr Polopetsi was helping the younger apprentice to fix the suspension on a hearse. It was a very ordinary morning.

Mr Polopetsi made the announcement. Knocking on the door that led from the garage into the agency office, he looked cautiously in and said that there was somebody to see Mma Ramotswe.

"Who is it?" asked Mma Makutsi. They were busy and did not want to be disturbed, but one always had to be ready to receive a client.

"It is a man," said Mr Polopetsi, and with this answer Mma Ramotswe knew that it was Note.

"Who is this man?" asked Mma Makutsi. "Has he given his name?"

Mr Polopetsi shook his head. "He would not give me his name," he said. "He is a man wearing dark glasses, and a brown leather jacket. I did not like him."

Mma Ramotswe rose to her feet. "I will come and see him," she said quietly. "I think I know who this is."

Mma Makutsi looked at her employer quizzically. "Could you not get him to come in here?"

"I will see him outside," said Mma Ramotswe. "I think that he has private business with me."

She made her way out of the office, avoiding Mma Makutsi's gaze. It was bright outside—a day on which the sun cast hard, short shadows; a day on which there was no shelter from the growing heat; a day on which the air seemed heavy and sluggish. As she went out through the wide door of the garage, leaving Mr Polopetsi to return to his labour, she saw the petrol pumps and the acacias and a car driving down the Tlokweng Road, and then, just to the left of the garage, standing under the shade of an acacia tree, looking in her direction, Note Mokoti, thumbs tucked into his belt, standing in that pose that she remembered so well.

She took the few steps that would bring her up to him. She raised her eyes and saw that his face was fleshier, but still cruel, and bore a small scar to the side of his chin. She saw that he had developed a slight paunch, but that this was almost hidden by the leather jacket which he wore in spite of the heat. And she thought, suddenly, how strange it was that one would notice these things when one was frightened of another; that the prisoner facing execution might notice, in those last terrible moments, that the man who was about to take his life had a barber's rash round his throat or that he had hair on the back of his hands.

"Note," she said. "It is you."

The muscles around the mouth slackened, and he smiled. She saw the teeth, so important, he had always said, for a trumpeter, good teeth. And then she heard the voice.

"It is me, yes. Yes, you are right there, Precious. It is me after all these years."

She looked into the lenses of the dark glasses, but could see only the tiny reflection of the acacia tree and the sky.

"Are you well, Note? Have you travelled from Johannesburg?"

"Joeies," he said, laughing as he spoke. "Egoli. Joburg. The place of many names."

She waited for him to say something more. For a few moments there was nothing, then he spoke.

"I've heard all about you," he said. "I've heard that you are the big detective around these parts." He laughed again, as if the suggestion that this should be so was ridiculous. Of course he had thought that about all women: that no woman, in his view, could do a job as well as a man. *How many woman trumpeters do you see?* he had asked her all those years ago, mockingly. She had been too young then to stand up to him, and now, when she could do so, when she had the facts of her success with which to confront him, she felt only the same ancient fear, the fear which had made women through the ages cower before such men.

"I have a good business," she said.

He looked over her shoulder into the garage and then he glanced up at their business sign, the sign which she had proudly displayed over her first office under Kgale Hill and which they had brought with them when they made the move.

"And your father?" he said casually, looking at her now. "How is the old man? Still going on about cattle?"

She felt her heart lurch, and then a rush of emotion that seemed to stifle the very breath within her.

"Well?" he said. "What about him?"

She steadied herself. "My father is late," she said. "It is many years ago now. He is late."

Note shrugged. "There are many people who are dying. You may have noticed."

For a moment Mma Ramotswe could think of nothing, but then she thought of her father, the late Daddy, Obed Ramotswe, who had never said anything unkind or dismissive to this man, although he had known full well what sort of person he was; of Obed Ramotswe who represented all that was fine in Botswana and in the world, whom she still loved, and who was as fresh in her memory as if he had been alive only yesterday.

She turned away and took a few faltering steps back towards the garage.

"Where are you going?" called Note, his voice harsh. "Where are you going, fat lady?"

She paused, still looking away from him. She heard him come towards her, and now he was standing directly behind her, his acrid body odour in her nostrils.

He leaned forward so that his mouth was close to her ear. "Listen," he said. "You have married that man, haven't you? But what about me? Am I not still your husband?"

She looked down at the ground, and at her toes sticking out of the sandals she was wearing.

"Now," said Note. "Now you listen to me. I haven't come back for you—don't worry about that. I never really liked you, you know? I wanted a woman who could have a child, a strong child. You know that? Not a child who wasn't going to last very long. So I haven't come back for you. So you just listen to me. I'm planning a concert here—a big event at the One Hundred Bar. But I need a bit of help with the cost of that, you know? Ten thousand pula. I'll come and collect it in two or three days, from your place. That'll give you time to get the money together. Understand?"

She remained quite immobile, and he moved away suddenly.

"Goodbye," he said. "I'll come for that loan. And if you don't pay, then maybe I can tell somebody—maybe the police, I don't know—that you've married a man before you got rid of the first husband. That's a careless thing to do, Mma. Very careless!"

SHE WENT BACK into the office, where Mma Makutsi was sitting at her desk, immersed in the task of addressing an envelope. The search for the delinquent Zambian financier had brought forth nothing so far. Most of the letters they had written had been ignored by their recipients, although one, which had been sent to a Zambian doctor who was thought to know just about everybody in the local Zambian community, had drawn a hostile reply. "You people are always saying that Zambians are dishonest and that if there is any money missing then you should look in Zambian pockets. This is defamation and we are fed up with such stereotypes. Everybody knows that you should be looking in Nigerian pockets . . ."

Mma Ramotswe made her way to her desk and sat down. She reached for a sheet of paper, folded it, and picked up her pen. Then she put down the pen and opened a drawer, not knowing why she was doing this, but filled with dread and fear. The picking up of a pen, the opening of a drawer, the lifting of the telephone handset—all of these were actions that might be performed in distress by one who did not know what to do, but who hoped that by such movements the fear might be defeated, which of course it never would.

Mma Makutsi watched, and knew that whoever it was who had arrived that morning had upset and frightened her employer.

"You saw that person?" she asked gently. "Was it somebody you knew?"

Mma Ramotswe looked up at her and Mma Makutsi saw the pain in her eyes.

"It was somebody I knew," she said quietly. "It was somebody I knew very well."

Mma Makutsi opened her mouth to ask a question, but stopped herself as Mma Ramotswe raised a hand.

"I do not want to talk about that, Mma," she said. "Please do not ask me about this thing. Please do not ask."

"I will not," said Mma Makutsi. "I will not ask."

Mma Ramotswe looked at her watch and muttered something about being late for a meeting. Again Mma Makutsi was about to ask what meeting this was, as nothing had been said about a meeting, but then she thought better of it and simply watched as Mma Ramotswe gathered her things together and left the office. Mma Makutsi waited for a few minutes, until she heard the engine of the tiny white van start, and then she stood up and looked out of the window to see Mma Ramotswe drive out onto the Tlokweng Road and disappear in the direction of town.

Leaving the office, Mma Makutsi found Mr Polopetsi with the apprentice.

"I need to ask you something, Rra," she said. "That man who came to see Mma Ramotswe—who was he?"

Mr Polopetsi stood up and stretched. It was difficult working on cars in confined spaces, although he was beginning to get used to it. It amused him to think that throughout his education he had worked and worked to get himself a job which would involve no manual labour, and here he was enjoying the rediscovery of his hands. Of course they had said that this job was only temporary, but he had begun to settle in to being a mechanic and perhaps he would ask about becoming a real apprentice. And why not? Botswana needed mechanics—everyone knew that—and there was no reason why older people should be prevented from acquiring such skills.

Mr Polopetsi scratched his head. "I have not seen him before," he said. "He was a Motswana, judging from the way he spoke. But there was something about him that seemed foreign. You know how it is when people are away for a long time. They carry themselves in a different way."

"Johannesburg?" asked Mma Makutsi.

Mr Polopetsi nodded. It was sometimes difficult to put it into words, but there was an unmistakable air about people who came from Johannesburg or who had lived a long time there. There was a way of walking in Johannesburg, a way of holding oneself, that was different from the way in which people did these things in Botswana. Johannesburg was a city of swagger, and that was something which people in Botswana would never do. There were some people who swaggered these days, particularly those who had more money, but it was not really the Botswana way of doing things.

"And what do you think this man wanted from Mma Ramotswe?" asked Mma Makutsi. "Did he bring her bad news, do you think? Did he tell her that somebody is late?"

Mr Polopetsi shook his head. "I have very good hearing, Mma," he said. "I can hear a car when it is far, far away. I can hear an animal before you can see it in the bush. I am like one of those people out in the bush who can tell you everything just by listening to the wind. So I can tell you that he did not tell her that somebody is late."

Mma Makutsi was surprised by this sudden disclosure on the part of Mr Polopetsi. He had seemed such a quiet and inoffensive man, and now he was admitting to the talents of a bush tracker. Such a person could be useful in a detective agency. You were not allowed to tape a person's telephone line, but then there would be no need to do so if you had a Mr Polopetsi. You could just position him on the other side of the street, with his ears pointed in the right direction, and he could report what was said behind closed doors. It would be one of those low technology solutions that people sometimes talked about.

"It must be useful to have hearing like that," said Mma Makutsi. "We must talk about it more some day. But in the meantime, you might wish to tell me what this man said to Mma Ramotswe."

Mr Polopetsi looked Mma Makutsi straight in the eye. "I would not normally tell somebody about Mma Ramotswe's business," he pronounced. "But this is different. I was going to tell you anyway—later on."

"Well?" said Mma Makutsi.

Mr Polopetsi lowered his voice. The apprentice was standing beside the car on which they had been working and was looking at them intently.

"He asked her for money," he whispered. "He asked her for ten thousand pula. Yes, ten thousand!"

"And?"

"And he said that if she didn't pay, then he was going to go to the police and tell them that she is still married to him and that she should not have married Mr J.L.B. Matekoni." He stopped, watching the effect of his words.

For a few moments Mma Makutsi did nothing. Then she reached forward and placed a finger across her lips.

"You must never mention this to anybody," she said. "You must promise me that."

He nodded gravely. "Of course I shall not."

Mma Makutsi turned away and went back into her office, her heart cold within her. You are my mother and my sister, she thought. You gave me my job. You helped me. You held my hand and wept with me when my brother became late. You are the one who made me feel that it was possible for a person from Bobonong to do well and to hold her head up in anybody's company. And now this man is threatening to bring shame upon you. I cannot allow that. I cannot.

She stopped. Mr Polopetsi had been watching her silently, but now he called out. "Mma! Do not worry. I will do something to stop that man. Mma Ramotswe is the woman who gave me a job. She is the one who knocked me down—but then she picked me up again. I will deal with that man."

Mma Makutsi turned round and looked at Mr Polopetsi. It was kind of him to say that, and she was touched by his loyalty. But what could a man like that do? Not very much, she feared.

CHAPTER FIFTEEN

MMA RAMOTSWE AND MR J.L.B. MATEKONI HAVE DINNER IN THEIR HOUSE ON ZEBRA DRIVE

MR J.L.B. MATEKONI was late coming home for dinner that evening. Normally he came back to the house at about six o'clock, which was almost an hour later than Mma Ramotswe. She would leave the office at five, or thereabouts, although she sometimes came back even earlier. If there was nothing particular happening at the agency, she would look at Mma Makutsi and ask her if there was any reason why they should stay in the office. Sometimes she did not even have to say anything, but would give a look that said, "I've had enough; it's a hot afternoon and it would be so much better being at home." And Mma Makutsi would return the look with a look of her own which said, "You're right, as usual, Mma Ramotswe." And with that unspoken exchange, Mma Ramotswe would pick up her bag and close the window that looked out to the side of the garage. Then she would give Mma Makutsi a ride into town, or back to her house in Extension Two, before she went home to Zebra Drive.

One advantage of getting home early was that she would be there for the children when they returned from school. Motholeli always came back a little later than Puso, as her wheelchair had to be pushed all the way from the school. The girls in her class had arranged a rota for this, and took it in turns, week and week about, to wheel their classmate home. The boys had been involved in this too, and had vied with one another for the privilege, but they had, on the whole, been found to be unsatisfactory. Several of the boys—indeed most of them—had been unable to resist the temptation of pushing the wheelchair too fast and there had been an unfortunate incident when one of them had lost control of the chair and Motholeli had careered into a ditch and tumbled out. She had been unharmed by this fall, but the boy had run away in fright and a passer-by, a cook at one of the large houses on Nyerere Drive, had come to her rescue and had helped her back into the chair and pushed her back, at reasonable speed, to the house.

"That boy is very stupid," said the cook.

"He is usually a nice boy," Motholeli replied. "He became frightened. Maybe he thought that he had killed me or something."

"He should not have run away," said the cook. "That is what they call a hit and run. It is very bad."

Puso was too young to be involved in getting his sister home. He could manage the wheelchair, but he had a tendency to be unreliable. He could not be counted upon to come to Motholeli's classroom at the right time, and it was also quite possible that he would lose interest halfway through and run after a lizard or something else that attracted his attention. He was a dreamy boy, moody even, and it was sometimes rather difficult to make out what he was thinking about.

"He thinks differently," observed Mma Ramotswe, not saying, out of delicacy, that the obvious reason for this—in her mind, and in the mind of most, no doubt—was that Puso had in his veins a fair measure of bushman blood. People were funny about that. Some were unkind to such people, but in Mma Ramotswe's opinion there was no need for this. There should be room in our hearts for all the people of this country, she said, and those people are our brothers and sisters too. This is their place as much as it is ours. That seemed clear to her, and she had no time for those who had raised an eyebrow when she and Mr J.L.B. Matekoni had taken on these children from the orphan farm. There were some households where this would not have happened, on the grounds that they were not of pure Tswana blood, but not that house on Zebra Drive.

Yet Mma Ramotswe had to admit that there were aspects about Puso's behaviour that people could well point to and say, "Well, there you are! That is because he is thinking of the Kalahari all the time and wants to be out in the bush. It is just the way his heart works." Well, thought Mma Ramotswe, that might be so; perhaps there stirred within this strange little boy some ancient yearnings which came to him from his people. But even if this were so, then what difference did it make? The important thing was that he should be happy, and in his way he was. He would never be a mechanic, he would never take over the business from Mr J.L.B. Matekoni, but then did that matter all that much? His sister, to the surprise of all, had shown great interest in machinery and had declared her intention of training as a mechanic. So that left it open for him to pursue some quite different career, even if it was difficult to think at the moment what such a career might be. He liked to chase lizards and to sit under trees and look up at the birds. He also liked to make small piles of rocks—they were all over the yard—on which Mma Ramotswe's maid, Rose, sometimes stubbed her toes when she went to hang out the washing. What might such a boy expect to do when he grew up? What clues did such pursuits give to the turn his life would take?

"There are jobs with the game department," Mr J.L.B. Matekoni had pointed out. "They need people who can track animals. Maybe he will be happy out there in the bush, tracking giraffe or whatever it is they do. For some people that is the best job there is."

On that evening, after the awful encounter with Note Mokoti, the children had noticed that there was something wrong with Mma Ramotswe. Puso had asked a question to which she had begun to respond before she had trailed off into silence, as if her thoughts had drifted off elsewhere. He had repeated his question, but this time she had said nothing, and he had gone off in puzzlement. Motholeli, finding her standing in the kitchen staring blankly out of the window, had offered to help her with the preparation of the evening meal, and had received a similar, rather distracted response. She had waited for Mma Ramotswe to say something else, and when nothing further came she had asked her whether there was anything wrong.

"I am thinking of something," said Mma Ramotswe. "I'm sorry if I am not listening to you. I am thinking of something that happened today."

"Was it a bad thing?" asked Motholeli.

"It was," said Mma Ramotswe. "But I cannot talk about it now. I'm sorry. I am feeling sad and I do not want to talk."

The children had left her to herself. Adults were sometimes strange in their behaviour—all children knew that—and the best thing to do in such circumstances was to leave the adult alone. Matters preyed on their mind, matters to which children could never be party; a tactful child understood that very well.

But when Mr J.L.B. Matekoni came home that evening and he too seemed to be preoccupied and distant, they knew that something was very wrong.

"There is something bad happening at the garage," whispered Motholeli to her brother. "They are very unhappy."

He had looked at her anxiously. "Will we have to go back to the orphan farm?" he asked.

"I hope not," she said. "I am happy living here in Zebra Drive. Perhaps they will get over it."

She tried to sound confident, but it was difficult, and her spirits sank even further when they sat down at the table for supper and Mma Ramotswe forgot even to say grace and remained silent for almost the whole meal. Afterwards, wheeling herself into her brother's room, where she found him lying disconsolately on his bed, she told him that whatever happened, he was not to worry about being by himself.

"Even if we go back to Mma Potokwane," she said, "she will make sure that we are kept together. She has always done that."

Puso stared at her miserably. "I do not want to leave. I am very happy here in this house. This is the best food I have ever eaten in my life."

"And they are the best people we have ever met," she said. "There is nobody in Botswana, nobody, as good and kind as Mma Ramotswe and Mr J.L.B. Matekoni. Nobody."

The little boy nodded vigorously. "I know that," he said. "Will they come and see us at the orphan farm?"

"Of course they will come—if we have to go back," she reassured him. But her reassurance could not prevent the tears that he now began to shed, tears for everything that had happened to him, for the loss of the mother whom he could not remember, for the thought that in this large and frightening world there was nobody, other than his sister, to whom he could turn, who might not be taken away from him.

AFTER THE CHILDREN had gone off to their rooms for the night, Mma Ramotswe made herself a cup of bush tea and walked out onto the verandah. She had thought that Mr J.L.B. Matekoni was in the living room, as she had heard the radio on in there and had assumed that he was sitting in his favourite chair brooding over whatever mechanical problem it was that had made him so quiet that night. She imagined that it was a mechanical problem, because that was all that seemed to upset Mr J.L.B. Matekoni; and such problems inevitably solved themselves.

"You are very quiet tonight," she observed.

He looked up at her. "And so are you," he replied.

"Yes," she said. "We are both quiet."

She sat down beside him, balancing her tea cup on her knee. As she did so, she glanced at Mr J.L.B. Matekoni; the thought had occurred to her that he might be feeling depressed—and that was an alarming prospect—but she quickly discounted this. He had behaved very differently when he had been depressed, acting in a listless, vague way. Now, by contrast, he was very obviously thinking of one particular thing.

She looked out into the garden, and the night. It was warm and the moon was almost full, throwing shadows of the acacia, of the mopipi tree, of shrubs that had no name. Mma Ramotswe liked to walk in her garden in the evening, taking care to move slowly and with firm tread; those who crept about at night risked stepping on a snake if they were not careful, as snakes move out of our way only if they feel vibrations in the ground. A light person—a person of non-traditional build, for example—was at far greater risk of being bitten by a snake for that very reason. That was another argument, of course, for maintaining traditional build—consideration for snakes, and safety too.

Mma Ramotswe was well aware of the difficulties now faced by traditionally built people, particularly by traditionally built ladies. There was a time in Botswana when nobody paid much attention to thin people—indeed thin people might sometimes simply not be seen at all, as they could so easily be looked past. If a thin person stood against a background of acacia trees and grass, then might he not either merge into the background or be thought to be a stick or even a shadow? This was never a danger with a traditionally built person; such a person would stand in the landscape with the same prominence and authority as a baobab tree.

There was no doubt in Mma Ramotswe's mind that Botswana had to get back to the values which had always sustained the country and which had made it by far the best country in Africa. There were many of these values, including respect for age—for the grandmothers who knew so much and had seen so much hardship—and respect for those who were traditionally built. It was all very well being a modern society, but the advent of prosperity and the growth of the towns was a poisoned cup from which one should drink with the greatest caution. One might have all the things which the modern world offered, but what was the use of these if they destroyed all that which gave you strength and courage and pride in yourself and your country? Mma Ramotswe was horrified when she read of people being described in the newspapers as consumers. That was a horrible, horrible word, which sounded rather too like cucumber, a vegetable for which she had little time. People were not just greedy consumers, grabbing everything that came their way, nor were they cucumbers for that matter; they were *Batswana,* they were *people!*

But it was not on these matters, grave as they were, that Mma Ramotswe's mind was dwelling; she was thinking, rather, of the meeting with Note and of the threat he had made. He had said that he would come for the money in a few days, and it was the prospect of this visit, rather than the paying over of the money itself, which was unsettling her. She could afford the money—just—but she was dreading the idea that Note would come to the house. It seemed to her that this would be a form of defiling; the house on Zebra Drive was a place of sun and of happiness, and she did not want it to be associated in any way with him. In fact, she had already made her decision, and was now mulling over how to put it into operation. She had written a cheque that afternoon and would take it to him, and the sooner that she did that the better.

Mr J.L.B. Matekoni took a sip of his tea. "You are very worried about something," he said quietly. "Do you want to tell me what it is?"

Mma Ramotswe did not reply. How could she tell him about what Note had said? How could she tell him that they were not married; that the ceremony which the Reverend Trevor Mwamba had conducted was legally meaningless, and that, moreover, it involved the commission of a criminal offence on her part? If there were words for all this, then they were words which she could not bring herself to utter.

The silence that hung so heavy between them was broken by Mr J.L.B. Matekoni. "That man came to see you, didn't he?" he said.

Mma Ramotswe gripped her tea cup. Mma Makutsi must have told him, or perhaps it was Mr Polopetsi. This should not surprise her: there were few secrets in a business that small.

"He did," she said, sighing. "He came and asked me for some money. I am going to give it to him—just to get him to go away."

Mr J.L.B. Matekoni nodded. "It is often like that with such people," he said. "They come back. But you have to be careful. If you give them money, then they might just ask for more and more."

Mma Ramotswe knew that what he said was true. She would tell Note that there would be no more money, and next time, if he came to see her again, she would refuse him. Or would she? What if he were to threaten her again with the police? Surely she would do anything rather than face the shame which that would involve?

"I will give him this money and tell him not to come back," she said. "I do not want to see him again."

"All right," he said. "But you must be careful."

She looked at him. They had not spoken at any length, and she had kept the real truth from him, but even so she felt better after this brief airing of her worry. Now she could ask about him.

"What about you?" she said.

Mr J.L.B. Matekoni groaned. "Oh dear," he said. "I am in a bad mess. I have discovered something about my house."

Mma Ramotswe frowned. She knew that tenants were always a risk. They treated furniture with disrespect; they burned holes in the floor and on the edge of tables with their cigarettes. She had even heard of a farmhouse not far from town which had been rented by python smugglers. Some of the pythons had escaped and taken up residence in the roof even after the tenants had been evicted. One of these had almost succeeded in taking the owners' baby when they returned. The father had gone into the bedroom and had found the python lying on the baby, its jaws opened wide around its feet. He had saved the child, but both of them had been badly bitten by the python's needle-like teeth.

Mr J.L.B. Matekoni was unlikely to have pythons in his house, of course, but it was obviously something troublesome, nonetheless. She looked at him expectantly.

"It's being used as a shebeen," he blurted out. "I did not know this. I would not have allowed it to be a shebeen. But that is what it is."

Mma Ramotswe let out a hoot of laughter. "Your house? A shebeen?"

Mr J.L.B. Matekoni looked at her slightly reproachfully. "I do not think it is funny," he said.

She corrected herself quickly. "Of course not." Her tone became concerned. "You are going to have to do something about that." She paused. Poor Mr J.L.B. Matekoni: he was far too gentle and kind. He would never be able to take on a shebeen queen. She herself would have to sort this out; shebeen queens held no dread for her.

"Would you like me to sort all that out?" she asked. "I can get rid of those people. It's the sort of thing that a detective agency can do quite easily."

Mr J.L.B. Matekoni's gratitude was palpable. "You are very kind," he said. "It is really my problem, but I am not very good at these things. I am happy sorting out cars, but people . . ."

"You are a great mechanic," said Mma Ramotswe, reaching across to pat him on the forearm. "That is enough for one person."

"And you are a very great detective," said Mr J.L.B. Matekoni. This was true, of course, and he meant every word of the compliment, but it was also inadequate. He knew that not only was Mma Ramotswe a great detective, but she was also a great cook, and a great wife, and a great foster-mother for the children. There was nothing that Mma Ramotswe could not do—in his view, at least. She could run Botswana if only they would give her the chance.

Mma Ramotswe drained the last of the tea from her cup and rose to her feet. She looked at her watch. It was only eight o'clock. She would go and seek out Note, hand him the cheque, and have put the whole matter to rest before she turned in that night. Her conversation with Mr J.L.B. Matekoni had filled her with a new resolve. There was no point in waiting. She had a pretty fair idea where Note would be staying—his people lived in a small village about ten miles to the south. It would only take her half an hour at the most to get out there, to pay him off, and to put him out of her life again. Then she could return to Zebra Drive and go to sleep without any dread. He would not be coming there.

CHAPTER SIXTEEN

THE TINY WHITE VAN

MMA RAMOTSWE did not like driving at night. She was not a timid driver, but she knew that there was one danger on the roads at night against which no amount of care could protect one—wandering cattle. Cattle liked to stand on the roadside at night and would suddenly step out into the paths of oncoming cars, almost as if they were curious to find out what lay behind the headlights. Perhaps they thought that the headlights were torches, held by their owners, and came out to see if they brought food; perhaps they were looking for warmth and thought the lights were the sun. Perhaps they thought nothing in particular, which was always possible with cattle, and with some people too, for that matter.

Mma Ramotswe's friend Barbara Mooketsi was just one of the many people Mma Ramotswe knew who had collided with a cow at night. She had been driving down from Francistown late one evening and had hit a cow north of Mahalapye. The unfortunate animal, which was black, and therefore almost completely invisible at night, had been scooped up by the collision and had entered the car through the windscreen. One of its horns had scraped Mma Mooketsi's shoulder and would have killed her had she been sitting in a slightly different position. Mma Ramotswe had visited her in her hospital bed and had seen the myriad of cuts on her face and arms from the shattered glass. This was the danger of driving at night, and it had been enough to put her off. Of course, in the town it was different. There were no cattle wandering about, although sometimes they drifted into the outlying parts of Gaborone and caused accidents there.

Now, leaving the edge of the town and peering into the darkness ahead of her, she searched the road for obstacles. It was not much of a road—a track ploughed out of the red earth and eroded into tiny canyons by the rains. Note's people lived in the village at the end of this track, along with some twenty other families. It was the sort of place that was halfway between town and country. The young people here would work in Gaborone and walk out along this track to the main road each morning to catch a minibus into town. Others would live in town and come out for weekends, when they would slip back into the role of village people, looking after cattle and ploughing a few meagre fields.

Mma Ramotswe hoped that she would remember the house where Note's people lived. It was late now for village people, and there was a chance that there would be no light on in the house and she would have to turn round and go back home. It was also possible that Note would not be there—that he would be staying somewhere in the town. As she thought of these possibilities it occurred to her that the whole idea of coming out here was ridiculous. Here she was coming in search of a man who had ruined years of her life, planning to give him hard-earned money so that he could pursue some absurd plan, and all of this being done out of fear. She was a strong woman, a resourceful woman who had built up a business from scratch, and who had shown on numerous occasions in her professional life that she was prepared to take men on head to head. But not this man. This man was different; he made her feel inadequate, and had always done so. It was a curious experience, to feel so young again, and as uncertain and in awe as she had been so long ago.

She reached the first of the houses, a brown block caught in the tiny white van's wavering headlights. If her memory served her correctly, the Mokoti place was three houses down; and there it was, just as she remembered it—a whitewashed building of four rooms joined together, with a lean-to shed to one side and an old granary at the edge of the front yard. And there was a light on in the front room.

She stopped the van. There was time to go back if she wished, to turn round and drive home. There was time to tear up the cheque which she had written out—the cash cheque, payable to bearer, for ten thousand pula. There was time to stand up to Note and to dare him to go to the police, after which she could go and make a clean breast of things to Mr J.L.B. Matekoni, who would surely understand. He was a kind man and he knew that people sometimes forgot to do important things, such as getting a divorce before they remarried.

She closed her eyes and took a deep breath. She knew what she should do now, but something deep within her, that part of her which had survived from all those years ago, that part which just could not stand up to Note, which drew her to him like a light draws in a moth—that part propelled her to the gate and to the door beyond the gate.

They were slow to open the door to her knocking, and when it was opened it was done in such a way that it could be quickly slammed shut. She saw a figure within which at first she could not make out, and then she recognised her mother-in-law, and she caught her breath. She was aged now, and stooped, but it was the same woman whom she had not seen for many years, and who recognised her too, after a moment's hesitation.

For a while neither woman spoke. There was so much that could be said, and Mma Ramotswe might have wept in the saying of it, but that was not what she had come for, and this woman did not deserve that. She had always sided with Note, of course, and had turned a blind eye to what was going on, but then what mother would admit to others, or to herself, that her own son was capable of such cruelty?

After a minute or so, the older woman moved slowly to one side and nodded. "You should come inside, Mma," she said.

Mma Ramotswe stepped into the house, noticing the smell as she did so. This was the odour of poverty, of life on the edge of making do; the smell of carefully husbanded cooking fuel, of clothes that were not washed frequently enough—for lack of soap. She glanced around. They were in a room which served as a living room and kitchen. A naked bulb burned weakly above a table on which a half-empty jar of jam stood flanked by a couple of knives and a folded cloth. On a shelf at the other end of the room was stacked a small number of tin plates and several steel cooking pots. A picture, cut out of a magazine, had been pinned to the wall beside the shelves.

She had been in this house many times before. That had been a long time ago, and she was now feeling the usual effect of memory, which was to diminish places, to make them more cramped and shabbier than they had once appeared. It was as though one was looking at the world from a long way away, and it was smaller. She tried to remember exactly when it was that she had last been here, but it was too many years ago, and the painful memories had been obliterated.

"I am sorry that I have come to your house so late at night," said Mma Ramotswe. She spoke respectfully, because this was an old woman she was addressing, and it did not matter that she was the mother of Note Mokoti—she was an old Motswana lady and that was enough.

The woman looked down at her hands. "He is not here," she said. "Note is not here."

Mma Ramotswe did not say anything. On the other side of the room two doors led off into the rest of the house, the bedrooms. These were both closed.

Mma Mokoti saw her look at the doors. "No," she said. "There is only my husband in one room and in the other there is a lodger, a young woman who works in a Government office. She pays us to stay here. That is all."

Mma Ramotswe felt embarrassed that Note's mother had sensed her doubts. "I believe you, Mma," she said. "Can you tell me where I can find him?"

The old woman pointed vaguely in the direction of the town, and then dropped her hand. "Somewhere in town. He is staying somewhere in town."

"But you don't know where?"

Mma Mokoti sighed. "I do not know. He has come to see us, and he will come again. But I do not know when." She muttered something else that Mma Ramotswe did not catch, and then looked up at her visitor, and Mma Ramotswe saw the clouded eyes, with their brown irises and their muddy, milky whites. They were not the eyes of a malevolent person, but the eyes of one who had seen a great deal and had done her best to make something of a hard life. They were the eyes of the sort that one could see anywhere, at any time, of people who had a life of difficulty and who still managed to keep their human dignity in the face of suffering and want.

She had no idea why she should say it—certainly she had not planned it—but Mma Ramotswe suddenly spoke. "I want you to know, Mma," she began. "I want you to know that I do not think ill of you, or of Note. What happened was a long time ago. It was not your fault. And there are things about your son of which you can be proud. Yes. His music. That is a great gift and it makes people happy. You can be proud."

There was a silence. Mma Mokoti was staring at her hands again. Then she turned away and looked at the shelf with the pots. "I did not want him to marry you, you know," she said quietly. "I argued with him. I told him that you were a young girl and that you were not ready for the life that he was leading. And there was another girl he was seeing. You didn't know about that, did you? There was another girl, who had a baby. She was already there when he met you. He had already married that girl."

Mma Ramotswe stood quite still. From within one of the rooms a man coughed. She had suspected, all those years ago, that Note was seeing other women, but she had never thought that he had been married. Did this change anything, she wondered? What should I feel about this? It was another of his lies, of his concealments, but she should not feel any surprise about that. Everything he had said to her was a lie, it seemed; there was simply no truth in him.

"Do you know who this other girl was?" she asked. She did not think about the question, nor whether she really wanted to know the answer. But she felt that she had to say something.

Mma Mokoti turned back to face her. "I think that she is late, now," she said. "And I never saw that baby. He is my grandchild, but I have never seen him. I feel very sad about that."

Mma Ramotswe took a step forward and put her arm gently about the old woman. The shoulder was hard and bony. "You must not feel too sad, Mma," she said. "You have worked hard. You have made this home for your husband. You must not feel sad about any of that. The other things are not so important, are they?"

The old woman said nothing for a moment, and Mma Ramotswe kept her arm about her shoulder. It was a strange feeling, she had always thought; feeling the breathing of another, a reminder of how we all share the same air, and of how fragile we are. At least there was enough air in the world for everybody to breathe; at least people did not fight with one another over that. And it would be difficult, would it not, for the rich people to take all the air away from the poor people, even if they could take so many other things? Black people, white people: same air.

The old woman looked up at her quite suddenly. "Your father," she said. "I remember him from the wedding. He was a good man, wasn't he?"

Mma Ramotswe smiled. "He was a very good man. He is late now, as perhaps you know. But I still go to his grave, out there at Mochudi. And I think of him every day."

The old woman nodded. "That is good."

Mma Ramotswe took her arm away, gently. "I must go now," she said. "I must get back to my place."

She said goodbye to Mma Mokoti, who saw her to the door, and then she went out into the night to where the tiny white van was parked. The engine started first time, as it always did, now that it was being regularly looked after by Mr J.L.B. Matekoni, and she was soon negotiating her way back up the rough dirt track, the undelivered cheque still firmly in her pocket. It will remain undelivered, she thought, because of the conversation which she had had with Mma Mokoti. So Note had been married before he met her. Well, if that were the case, then one might well ask the question: *Did he get divorced?*

SHE HAD ALMOST REACHED the end of the track when the tiny white van died. The end came suddenly, just as the end may come to those who suffer a stroke or a heart attack, without notice, when they are least expecting it. Certainly Mma Ramotswe was not thinking of the possibility of mechanical failure; her thoughts, rather, were on the conversation she had had with Mma Mokoti. It had been a painful visit for her, at least at the beginning. It had been hard to go back to that house, which had actually been the scene of one of Note's assaults on her, one weekend all those years ago when they had been the only people there and he had been drunk and had turned on her with vicious suddenness. But she was glad that she had gone now, and had been able to talk to Note's mother. Even if she had not revealed that information about her son, it had done both of them good, she thought, to talk. For the mother, it would perhaps be easier for her to know that she, Precious Ramotswe, did not hold anything against her, and had forgiven her son. That would be one less thing in a life which she suspected had been full of things to worry about. And for her part, saying to the mother what she had said had cost her very little, and had made her feel much better anyway. And then there had been the massive relief of realising that perhaps she had not committed bigamy after all. If Note had still been married when he had married her, then there was no marriage in the first place. That meant that her marriage to Mr J.L.B. Matekoni was perfectly legal.

It was while she was thinking of this that the tiny white van suddenly lost all power. She was not going at all fast when it happened, barely ten miles an hour on that pitted surface, but the drawing to a halt happened very quickly and the engine stopped.

Mma Ramotswe's first thought was that she had run out of fuel. She had filled the tank only a few days ago, and when she looked down, it showed that it was still half full. So that possibility was excluded. Nor had there been electrical failure, as the lights were still illuminating the track ahead. So the problem, she felt, was in the engine itself.

With sinking heart, she switched off the ignition and then tried to turn it on again. There was the sound of the starter turning over, but nothing else happened. She tried again, with the same result.

Mma Ramotswe switched off the headlights and opened the door of the van. There was some moonlight, if not very much, and for a moment she stood there, looking up at the sky, humbled by its sheer immensity and by the quiet of the bush. The tiny white van had been a cocoon of safety in the darkness; now it was just her, an African lady, under this great sky and with a long walk ahead of her. She would be able to reach the main road, she thought, in twenty minutes or so, and then they were about ten miles from the town. She could walk that far, of course, if she had to, but how long would that take? She knew that an average person could cover four miles in an hour, as long as there were no hills. She was not an average person, she feared; the rate for traditionally built people was probably three miles an hour. So that would mean a walk of about three hours, just to reach the outskirts of town. From there it would be at least half an hour—probably rather more—to Zebra Drive.

Of course there was the chance that she would be able to flag down a minibus, if there was one on the prowl. The driver would probably take advantage of her need and charge much more than was normal, but she would readily pay whatever it cost to get home before midnight. Or she might be able to persuade a passing driver to stop and pick her up as an act of charity. There had been a time when people would do that, and indeed Mma Ramotswe would still let people ride in the back of the van when she went up to Mochudi. But she doubted whether people would stop at night out here to pick up a woman who for no apparent reason was standing by the roadside.

She locked the door of the tiny white van and was about to start her walk when she heard a sound. There were many sounds in the bush at night—the screeching of insects, the scurrying of small creatures. This sound, though, was not one of those; it was the sound of liquid dripping. She stood where she was and strained her ears. For a few moments there was only silence, but then it came again and this time it was clear that it emanated from under the van itself.

Unlike Mma Makutsi, and indeed unlike Motholeli, Mma Ramotswe was no mechanic. But it was difficult to be married to a mechanic and not to pick up some knowledge of engines, and one thing that she did know was that if an engine lost its oil it would seize up. The dripping sound which she heard from under the van must be oil, and then she remembered. Coming down the track she had certainly felt a bad bump when she hit one of the rocks which protruded from the dirt surface. She had not thought much about it, but now she realised just what it could have done. The rock could have damaged the sump and the oil simply drained out of the van. If the crack in the sump were not too large it would have taken some time, but once it had occurred, then the engine would simply stop, just as hers had done that night. And Mma Ramotswe further knew that when an engine seized, awful damage was done. She and Mma Makutsi could survive for long periods without tea, but engines, alas, were different.

She turned away with a heavy heart and began to trudge up the track. She was closer to the main road than she had thought and in less than fifteen minutes she was at the junction. The road to Lobatse was relatively busy, and it was not long before a set of headlights swung into view over the brow of the hill. She watched as a truck sped by, the wind from its passing brushing against her face. That had been going in the wrong direction, down towards Lobatse, but there would be vehicles going the other way. She began to walk.

It was easy walking along the road, along the well-used tar. This was a properly maintained road, with a smooth surface, and walking along it one might make good progress. But it still felt strange to her to be so utterly isolated in the night, with darkness stretching out on either side of the road. How far away, she wondered, was the nearest creature that might wish to eat her? There were no lions this close to Gaborone, but if one went forty miles to the east, then that might be different. And what would happen if a lion decided to wander? Forty miles for a lion was nothing, and after having covered forty miles a lion might be hungry and in just the right mood to find a traditionally built meal . . .

It did not help to think about lions, and so Mma Ramotswe moved on to something different. She began to think, for some reason, of Mr Polopetsi, and of how well he had fitted into his new job at the garage. She had not discussed the situation with Mr J.L.B. Matekoni, but she was going to propose to him that their new employee be taken on permanently and be trained for the job. There was simply too much work to be handled at the garage, and she was beginning to get concerned over how much Mr J.L.B. Matekoni had to do. The apprentices had always been a worry for him, and when they finished their apprenticeship—if they ever did—then he should encourage them to go elsewhere. That would leave him without an assistant, unless Mr Polopetsi stayed. And there was another reason why he was so suitable. Mma Makutsi had already used him for some secretarial work and had spoken highly of his abilities. He could be attached to the detective agency in some vague, unspecified capacity. Yes, he was certainly the best choice, and it had been a happy accident when she had made him fall off his bicycle. Life was full of these happy accidents, if one came to think of it. Had she not taken her tiny white van to Tlokweng Road Speedy Motors—and she could quite easily have gone to another garage—then she would not have met Mr J.L.B. Matekoni and she would never then have found herself marrying him. And had Mma Makutsi not been looking for a job just at the time that she was setting up the

No.1 Ladies' Detective Agency, then she would never have got to know her and Mma Makutsi would never have become an assistant private detective. That was a fortunate coincidence, and for a few minutes she thought of what might have happened had she employed one of those useless secretaries about whom Mma Makutsi had told her, one of those girls who got barely fifty per cent in the final examinations of the Botswana Secretarial College. That hardly bore thinking about.

This train of thought, speculative though it was, might have sustained her for a good part of her walk, but it was interrupted by the sound of a vehicle approaching from behind her and by the sudden appearance of lights. Mma Ramotswe stopped where she was and stood in such a position that the driver of the vehicle would see her face-on.

The car came up quickly, and Mma Ramotswe took a step backwards as the lights came towards her. But she still waved her arm up and down, in the recognised way of one pleading for a lift. The car shot past, which was just what she had feared it would do. But then, once it had gone past her, and she had turned round in disappointment, its rear lights glowed red and it drew to a halt. Mma Ramotswe, hardly believing her good fortune, ran up to the side of the vehicle.

A man looked out at her from the driver's window, a face in the darkness that she could not see.

"Where are you going, Mma?"

"I am going into town, Rra," she said. "My van has broken down back there."

"You can get in the back. We are going that way."

She opened the door gratefully and slipped into the back seat. She saw now that there was another person in the car, a woman, who turned to her and greeted her. Mma Ramotswe could just make out the face, which seemed vaguely familiar even if she could not say who it was.

"It is very bad when your car breaks down," said the woman. "That would have been a long walk back into town."

"It would," said Mma Ramotswe. "I used to be able to walk for long distances, years ago, before I had a van. But now . . ."

"It is easy to forget how to walk," the woman agreed. "Children used to walk ten miles to school. Remember that?"

"Some children still do," said Mma Ramotswe.

They continued the conversation for a while, agreeing with one another on a variety of subjects. Now the lights of Gaborone were visible in the distance, a glow that lit up the sky, even at that late hour. Soon they would be home.

CHAPTER SEVENTEEN

MMA RAMOTSWE, MR J.L.B. MATEKONI, AND MR POLOPETSI GET AN UNPLEASANT SURPRISE

MR J.L.B. MATEKONI was sound asleep by the time that Mma Ramotswe arrived home from her visit to the Mokoti house. When he awoke the next morning, Mma Ramotswe was already out of bed and walking in the garden, nursing a cup of bush tea in her hands. Mr J.L.B. Matekoni got up, washed and dressed, and went out to find her standing sunk in thought in front of the mopipi tree.

"It is a fine morning again," he said, as he walked up to her.

She turned to him and smiled. "I am always happiest in the early morning," she said. "Standing here in the garden watching the plants wake up. It is very good."

Mr J.L.B. Matekoni agreed. He found it difficult to get out of bed quite as early as she did, but he knew that the first few hours of light was the best part of the day, a time of freshness and optimism. He particularly liked it when he was in at the garage early enough to feel the first rays of the sun on the back of his neck as he worked on an engine. That was perfection itself—a state of bliss for a mechanic—to be warm (but not too warm) and comfortable while he worked on a challenging engine. Of course it depended to a great extent on the engine. There were some engines that made one despair—engines with inaccessible corners and parts that were difficult to reorder—but an engine that was *co-operative* was a delight to work on.

Mma Ramotswe's tiny white van was a case in point. He had spent a great deal of time on that van and felt that he knew it quite well now. Its engine was not a difficult one to deal with, as all the essential parts could be got at without too much trouble, but it could not be kept going forever and he was not sure whether Mma Ramotswe understood that. He had the same problem with Mma Potokwane and the old minibus that she used to transport the orphans. It was a miracle that that vehicle was still going—or rather it was down to the constant nursing by Mr J.L.B. Matekoni. Sooner or later, though, one had to face reality with an old vehicle and accept that it had come to the end of its life. Mr J.L.B. Matekoni understood the attachment that people developed to a car or a truck, but sentiment had got to be kept in its place. If we are prepared to throw away old clothes, then why not throw away old vehicles once they had had their day? He had noted that Mma Ramotswe had been ready to throw out his clothes, and it was only after a spirited defence on his part that he had succeeded in keeping some of the jackets and trousers which had served him well and which—in his opinion at least—still had a great deal to offer. But his opposition had not prevented her from getting rid of several pairs of trousers (which still had a lot of wear in them and which had only one or two patches), a favourite pair of old brown veldschoens, and a jacket which he had bought at OK Bazaars over the border in Mafikeng with his first pay cheque as a qualified mechanic. He had wanted to ask her how she would feel if he had gone through her wardrobe and thrown out some of her dresses, but he had refrained from doing so. It was an entirely hypothetical question anyway; it would never have occurred to him to do such a thing. And he readily admitted that he knew nothing about women's clothing, as most men would have to admit; and yet women always claimed to know what clothes were right for a man. There was some injustice here, thought Mr J.L.B. Matekoni, although he was not quite sure how one might pursue the point.

Standing beside Mma Ramotswe, Mr J.L.B. Matekoni took a lungful of the early morning air.

"And how did it go?" he asked, as he breathed out. "Did you find him?"

"He was not there," said Mma Ramotswe. "But I spoke to his mother and that was useful. I learned something important."

"And what was this important thing?" asked Mr J.L.B. Matekoni, closing his eyes and breathing in deeply again.

Mma Ramotswe did not answer his question. She should not have said anything about it, she realised, even if she wanted to share the overwhelming sense of relief that the visit had brought her.

"Well?" said Mr J.L.B. Matekoni, opening his eyes and looking around the yard. "The important thing. Why is it . . ." He stopped. Then, frowning, asked, "Where is the white van?"

Mma Ramotswe sighed. "It broke down on the way back. It is sitting out over there." She waved a hand in the general direction of the south, the direction of Lobatse, the Cape, and the oceans to the south of the Cape. "It is down there."

"Broke down?" asked Mr J.L.B. Matekoni sharply. "What happened?"

Mma Ramotswe told him of how the engine had suddenly lost power and then stopped. She told him that there had been no warning, but that it had all happened rather quickly, just before she reached the main road. Then she mentioned the oil and her suspicions that it had something to do with the cracking of the sump on a rock.

Mr J.L.B. Matekoni grimaced. "You are probably right," he said reproachfully. "Those rocks can do a lot of damage. You really shouldn't take a small van like that on those roads. They're not built for that sort of work."

Mma Ramotswe took the rebuke quietly. "And if the engine has seized? What then?"

Mr J.L.B. Matekoni shook his head. "It is very bad news. You'll need a new engine block. I don't think it would be worth it."

"So I would need a new van?"

"Yes, you would."

Mma Ramotswe thought for a moment. "I have had that van for a long time," she said. "I am very fond of it. They do not make vans like that any more."

Mr J.L.B. Matekoni looked at her and was suddenly filled with a great sense of pride. There were some women who would be only too eager to get hold of a new van or car and who would willingly scrap a faithful vehicle for the sake of something flashier and smarter. It made him feel proud to know that Mma Ramotswe was not like that. Such a woman would never want to trade in an old and useless husband for a newer, smarter man. That was very reassuring.

"We'll take a look at it," he said. "You must never say that a van is finished until you've had a good look. We can go out in my truck and collect it. I'll tow you back."

THERE WAS NOTHING very much happening at the No. 1 Ladies' Detective Agency that morning. Mma Makutsi was planning to go out, with a view to pursuing, without any real hope of success, the elusive Zambian financier, and with her correspondence up to date, there was little for Mma Ramotswe to do. Mr J.L.B. Matekoni had a car to service, but it was an uncomplicated job and could safely be left to the remaining apprentice. As for Mr Polopetsi, he never liked to be idle, and would fill any spare minutes tidying the garage, sweeping the floor, or even polishing the cars of customers. On several occasions a client of the agency had come out of a meeting with Mma Ramotswe to discover that his car had been washed and waxed while he was consulting the agency. This was often very much appreciated, and was another point in favour of Mr Polopetsi.

"Just imagine if everybody in Botswana was like that," Mma Ramotswe had remarked to Mma Makutsi. "Imagine how successful this country would be. We would be so rich we wouldn't know what to do."

"Can you ever be that rich?" asked Mma Makutsi. "Surely there is always something to spend your money on. More shoes, for example."

Mma Ramotswe had laughed. "You can only wear one pair of shoes at a time," she said. "Rich people are like the rest of us—two feet, ten toes. We are all the same that way."

Mma Makutsi was not sure about this. One might not be able to wear more than one pair of shoes at a time, but that did not mean that one could not wear a different pair each day, or even one pair in the morning and another in the afternoon. Did rich people do that sort of thing, she wondered. She only had two pairs of shoes at the moment, although she was planning to acquire another pair before too long. She had her ordinary working shoes, which were brown and had been resoled and repaired rather more times than she would care to remember; and then there was her special pair of shoes, green on the outside and with sky-blue linings—the pair of shoes which she had bought with the first profits of the Kalahari Typing School for Men and of which she was so inordinately proud. She wore these shoes to work from time to time, but it seemed a pity to waste them on such mundane use and so she usually reserved them now for occasions such as the dancing class. What she needed now was to buy a smarter pair of shoes for use in the office, and she had in fact identified just such a pair in one of the stores. The shoes were red, and although they had no special coloured lining, they had two large gold ornamental buckles which gave them an air of authority which her other shoes did not have. These were bold shoes, and she would wear them when confronting difficult men, as she occasionally had to do. Men would be mesmerised by the buckles, and this would give her just the advantage that one needed when dealing with men like that.

Although she was reluctant to raise the issue, Mma Makutsi had long been wanting to say something to Mma Ramotswe about the sort of shoes which the older woman wore. Mma Ramotswe was not a flashy dresser, preferring good, reliable skirts and loose blouses, but she nonetheless had a good eye for colour and always looked smart. But when it came to shoes, then it seemed that her dress sense let her down, as she was usually to be seen in a pair of rather shapeless brown shoes with bulges on both sides reflecting the shape of her toes. These shoes were in no sense elegant, and it seemed to Mma Makutsi that they should be replaced by something rather more in keeping with Mma Ramotswe's position as Botswana's senior lady private detective.

Mma Ramotswe's shoes had been touched upon in conversation once before, and the outcome had not been satisfactory. Mma Makutsi had mentioned that there was a shoe sale at one of the shops at the Game Centre, and that in her view there were bargains to be had.

"Perhaps people who have been wearing the same shoes for a long time would be able to find something suitable there," she remarked casually.

Mma Ramotswe had looked at her. "You mean somebody like me?" she said.

Mma Makutsi had laughed to cover her embarrassment. "No, I was not just thinking of you. But maybe you would like to get yourself some new shoes. You can afford them."

"But what's wrong with the shoes I have?" asked Mma Ramotswe. "I have very wide feet. These are very wide shoes and they suit my feet. What would my feet say if I bought a thin pair of fashionable shoes? Surely they would think that something was wrong."

Mma Makutsi decided to stand her ground. "But you can get wide shoes which look very good," she said. "They have something for everybody."

"I am very happy in these shoes," said Mma Ramotswe. "They never give me any trouble."

"You might buy some for Mr J.L.B. Matekoni, then," suggested Mma Makutsi.

"And what is wrong with Mr J.L.B. Matekoni's shoes?"

Mma Makutsi was beginning to regret raising the subject. There was a great deal wrong with Mr J.L.B. Matekoni's shoes in her opinion. To begin with, they were covered in oil stains and she had seen the beginnings of a hole in the toe cap of one of them. Like Mma Ramotswe, he had a position in society as the proprietor of Tlokweng Road Speedy Motors, and shoes in good order were expected of such a person.

When Mma Makutsi did not provide an answer to her question, Mma Ramotswe went on to explain that new shoes would be wasted on Mr J.L.B. Matekoni. "There is no point in buying men new shoes," she said. "They are wasted on them. Men are not interested in shoes. That is very well known. If a man is always thinking about shoes, then there is something wrong with that man."

"And what do men think about?" asked Mma Makutsi. "If they cannot think about shoes, what can they think about?"

Mma Ramotswe raised an eyebrow. "Men think about ladies a great deal of the time," she said. "They think about ladies in a disrespectful way. That is because men are made that way, and there is nothing that can be done to change them. Then if they are not thinking about ladies, they are thinking about cattle and cars. And some men think a lot about football too. These are all things that men like to think about."

On that morning, though, the main topic of conversation was not shoes, nor the foibles of men, but the drama of the tiny white van. Mr Polopetsi had been dismayed to hear about the break-down of the van, to which he felt he owed a debt of gratitude as it was the van that had brought him into contact with Mma Ramotswe and given him his new job. When Mma Ramotswe said that she and Mr J.L.B. Matekoni would shortly be going to retrieve the van and tow it back into Gaborone, he asked whether he could accompany them. Mma Ramotswe agreed, and once Mr J.L.B. Matekoni had explained to the apprentice what needed to be done to the car which had been brought in for servicing, the three of them set off in the truck, leaving Mma Makutsi alone in the office.

The morning had remained fine, and as they drove down past Kgale Hill the sun seemed to paint with gold the trees and rocks on the hillside. Above them the sky was quite empty, apart from a few soaring birds of prey, circling high in the currents of rising warm air; ahead of them the road was clear and straight, a ribbon of black making its way through the grey-green acacia scrub. It was a morning which made one happy to be alive, and to be in that place.

Mr Polopetsi was in a talkative mood, and gave them his views on a speech which Chief Linchwe had recently given in Gaborone and which had given rise to a lot of discussion in the papers. Was Chief Linchwe right in what he had said? Mr Polopetsi thought he was. He had a lot of respect for Chief Linchwe, he said, and he thought that more attention should be paid to his views. Then he moved on to the issue of what should be done about people who dropped litter. There had been some talk about this out at Tlokweng, where he lived, and some people had suggested that those who abandoned litter should be made to go on litter picking-up squads. Either that, or they should be obliged to wear large signs on their backs saying DIRTY PERSON. That would soon stop littering, in Mr Polopetsi's view.

Mma Ramotswe was not sure about that. "Shame can be a very strong way of encouraging people to behave well," she said. "Yes, I can see that. But you couldn't put signs on people saying DIRTY PERSON because that would make others think that those people did not wash. But they might wash quite a lot."

"I think that signs are a good idea," said Mr J.L.B. Matekoni. "You could put signs on cars too. DANGEROUS DRIVER, for example, or SPEEDER. That would make people drive more safely, I think."

"But it would look a bit silly, wouldn't it?" said Mma Ramotswe. "Everybody would eventually have some sort of sign. I would have a sign saying MMA RAMOTSWE on my back, or DETECTIVE perhaps. That would be silly." And then she thought, but did not say it: *And Mma Makutsi would have a sign on her back which said 97 per cent.*

"I did not suggest that," said Mr Polopetsi, rather peevishly. "All I said was that people who drop litter could have a sign. That is all."

It was Mr J.L.B. Matekoni who brought the discussion to an end. "We are almost there," he said. "Is this not the turning that you said you took?"

They slowed down, and Mr J.L.B. Matekoni cautiously headed the truck down the track. By daylight the potholes and rifts in the ground looked far worse than they had at night. It was no surprise to Mma Ramotswe that the tiny white van had been damaged in these conditions; stones, exposed by the movement of soil, reared up in jagged points and at places there jutted onto the track the fallen limbs of trees, plastered now in dried red mud by energetic white ants. Beside the track, watching the truck with mournful eyes, was a small herd of cattle, standing listlessly under the shade of a tree.

"Those cattle are not in good condition," said Mr J.L.B. Matekoni. "Look at the ribs on that one."

Mma Ramotswe cast an expert eye over the light grey beast and agreed. "It is ill," she said. "My father would have known what to do about that."

"Yes, he knew about cattle," said Mr J.L.B. Matekoni. He had never met Obed Ramotswe, of course, but he knew of his reputation as a fine judge of cattle. Mr J.L.B. Matekoni was always prepared to listen to stories about Obed Ramotswe, although he had heard them all from Mma Ramotswe many times over. He had heard the story of how Obed Ramotswe had met Seretse Khama once when he had come to Mochudi, and had shaken the great man's hand. He had heard the story of his hat, and how it had once been left near the kgotla and carefully placed on a wall where he might find it again. He had also heard about how the hat had been blown off his head once in a dust storm and had ended up in a tree. There were many such stories, and he understood just how important they were, and listened with patience and with respect. A life without stories would be no life at all. And stories bound us, did they not, one to another, the living to the dead, people to animals, people to the land?

They drove slowly down the track. After a while, Mr J.L.B. Matekoni turned to Mma Ramotswe. "You said that it happened very close to the turn-off," he said. "But it must have been further than you thought."

Mma Ramotswe cast an anxious glance over her shoulder. She was sure that it was about there, at that bend, where the track went off in a different direction. Yes, it must have been that spot, but there was no sign of the van.

She looked at Mr J.L.B. Matekoni. "We must stop here," she said. "I am very sure that it was here."

Mr Polopetsi, who was sitting between Mr J.L.B. Matekoni and Mma Ramotswe, now leaned forward in his seat. "It has been stolen!" he exclaimed. "Your van has been stolen!"

"We'll see," said Mma Ramotswe. She feared that he was right, even though she felt cross with him for saying it. If her van had been stolen, then it was for her to make the announcement, not Mr Polopetsi.

They alighted from the truck and Mma Ramotswe walked over the edge of the track, a few yards behind the place where they had stopped. Looking down at the ground, she saw what she had been looking for, a patch of oil in the sand. The patch measured only six inches or so across, but it was dark and obvious, and there was now no doubt in her mind. She was looking at the place where she had had her last sight of the tiny white van, and it was undoubtedly no longer there.

Mr J.L.B. Matekoni joined her and followed her gaze, down towards the sand. "Ah!" he said, and then, turning to face her, "Ah!" again.

"It has been taken," she said, her voice cracking. "My van. It is gone now."

Mr Polopetsi now came to stand beside them. "Somebody must have fixed it and driven it away."

"Very strange," said Mr J.L.B. Matekoni. "But that means that your engine can't have seized. It must have been something else. They would not have been able to drive it away if it had seized."

Mma Ramotswe shook her head. "We will have to go to the police and report it. That is all we can do. They will have driven it far away by now."

"I'm afraid that you're right," said Mr J.L.B. Matekoni gently. "When a vehicle is stolen, it disappears very quickly. Just like that. It's gone."

Mma Ramotswe turned away and began to walk back to the truck, followed by Mr J.L.B. Matekoni. Mr Polopetsi, though, stood where he was.

"We must get back," called Mr J.L.B. Matekoni over his shoulder.

Mr Polopetsi looked down at the place where the van had been, and then out into the bush beside the track, through the trees and the shrubs and the termite mounds, as if he might see something other than the brown of the grass and the red, red earth and the thorn trees; as if he might hear something other than the screech of the cicadas and the call of birds.

"Leave me here," he said. "I want to look for clues. You go back to town. I'll get a minibus from the main road later on. You leave me here."

Mma Ramotswe turned and stared at him. "There will be no clues," she said. "They have come and gone. That is all."

"Just let me try," said Mr Polopetsi.

"If he wants to," said Mr J.L.B. Matekoni. "There is no harm. There is not much for him to do at the garage this morning."

They climbed into the truck and Mr J.L.B. Matekoni manoeuvred it back to face up the track. As they drove slowly past him, Mr Polopetsi raised a hand in farewell. Mma Ramotswe noticed that he looked excited, and remarked on this a little later to Mr J.L.B. Matekoni.

"He is playing the detective," she said. "But there is no harm in that. He is very keen to do some detective work."

Mr J.L.B. Matekoni laughed. "He is a good man," he said. "And you did the right thing when you asked him to join us."

The compliment pleased Mma Ramotswe, and she touched him gently on the forearm. "You have been good to him too," she said.

They travelled on in silence. A few minutes later, Mr J.L.B.

Matekoni glanced at Mma Ramotswe, and he saw that she was crying, silently, but there were tears on her cheeks.

"I am sorry," she said. "I am sorry. My white van. I loved it very much. It had been my friend for many years."

Mr J.L.B. Matekoni shifted in his seat. He found it difficult when women became emotional; he was a mechanic, after all, and these things were awkward for mechanics.

"I will find a new one for you," he said gently. "I will find you a good van."

Mma Ramotswe said nothing. It was kind of him, she knew, but the finding of a new van was not the point. She wanted only that tiny white van that had driven her all over Botswana. That was all she wanted.

CHAPTER EIGHTEEN

THE DOUBLE COMFORT FURNITURE STORE

I T WAS THAT MORNING, while Mma Ramotswe was finding out about the loss of the tiny white van, that Mma Makutsi made a discovery of her own. The matter of the missing Zambian financier was proving frustrating. Letters had been sent out to no avail, and telephone calls had taken them no further. Mma Ramotswe had suggested a few personal calls on prominent members of the Zambian community in Gaborone, and that was what she was proposing to do. They had three names—a dentist with a long list of patients, many of them Zambians, a minister of religion, and a businessman who ran a thriving import-export agency. Looking at the list that morning, she had decided not to try to speak to the dentist, as she knew that dentists were usually very busy and she would be unlikely to get past the receptionist. Of course she could make an appointment to see him—she had not had her teeth checked for some time and it might be a good idea to have that done—but it would be difficult to ask questions while one's mouth was full of dental equipment. It was for this reason, perhaps, that conversations with dentists were often somewhat one-sided.

She had telephoned the minister of religion but had been spoken to by his answering machine. *I am not in, but you may leave a message,* a careful voice had announced, *and in the meantime, my prayers are with you.* Mma Makutsi had been momentarily taken by surprise when she heard this message, and she put down the receiver without saying anything. How could his prayers be with her if he did not even know who it was who had called? It would be different, she thought, if he had said that his prayers would be with her in the future, once he had heard that she had called. That, at least, would have been honest. Of course, he was only trying to be kind—she understood that—but it was important, she felt, that one should always speak the truth, and ministers of religion, more than others, should understand that.

Mma Makutsi thought about this for a few minutes, and the more she pondered it, the crosser she became. Eventually, picking up the telephone she dialled the number again and listened, with irritation, to the insincere message. Then, after hearing the tone which indicated that she could leave a message, she spoke. "This is Grace Makutsi of the No. 1 Ladies' Detective Agency here. I am calling you about some important matters. But how can your prayers be with me until you have heard who I am? Should you not say that you will pray for people after you find out who they are? Shouldn't you do that? Thank you very much, Reverend, and goodbye."

She felt better for having struck a blow for truth-telling and accuracy. She would tell Mma Ramotswe about that when she came back with the van; she would approve of it, she imagined, as she was a very truthful woman and did not like people who made false claims. She would certainly approve of this . . . or would she? Suddenly Mma Makutsi was visited by doubts. It occurred to her now that Mma Ramotswe might think it rather unkind to give a lecture of this sort—and a recorded lecture to boot—to a minister of religion who was only trying to be helpful to the people who telephoned him. Might not Mma Ramotswe say something like, "Well, Mma, many of the people who call that man will be troubled in some way. Maybe they will have somebody who is late and they will be phoning him about that. Maybe that is why he is trying to make them feel better."

Mma Makutsi thought a little longer and then picked up the telephone and dialled the number again. She had decided to leave another message saying that she had not quite meant what she had said, but this time the telephone was answered by the minister.

For a few moments, Mma Makutsi was unsure what to say, and even considered putting down the receiver, like a child who is caught playing with the telephone.

But better judgement prevailed. "It is Mma Makutsi," she said. "I left a message a few minutes ago and . . ."

"I have listened to your message, Mma," the minister interrupted her. "And you are right. I was not thinking when I said 'in the meantime.' I shall re-record the message and say, 'When I hear your message, I shall put you in my prayers.' That is what I shall say."

Mma Makutsi felt a flush of shame. "I did not mean to be rude," she said hurriedly.

"I know that," said the minister. "And you did not sound at all rude. You were very polite about it."

A short silence ensued before the minister continued. "But you said that you had something to say to me. May I ask what that was?"

Mma Makutsi told him of her business with him, and when she had finished, he said, "What exactly are you asking of me, Mma? Are you asking me to tell you whether any such person, any businessman from Zambia, has spoken to me? Is that what you are asking?"

"Yes," said Mma Makutsi. "You will know many of your countrymen down here. They come to ask you for help. I thought that perhaps this man had done that too."

The minister was silent. At the other end of the line, sitting at her desk in the No. 1 Ladies' Detective Agency, Mma Makutsi watched a small white gecko climb expertly and effortlessly up a wall. The creature's head moved from side to side as it made its journey, watchful for predators and prey.

Then the minister cleared his throat. "I cannot speak about these things, Mma," he said, his tone now reproachful. "When people come to me in their sorrow and their difficulties, they do not expect me to talk to other people about that. They do not think that I shall discuss their affairs with the first private detective who telephones."

Mma Makutsi felt her embarrassment increase at the rebuke. What would he think of her? Not only had she left an unsolicited lecture on his answering machine, but now she had quite improperly asked him to disclose a confidence. She would have to apologise and bring the conversation to an end before the reputation, in his eyes, of the No. 1 Ladies' Detective Agency suffered even further.

"I am very sorry, Reverend," she began. "I did not mean . . ."

"People think," interrupted the minister, "people think that ministers sit in judgement on them. They think that we sit here and think, now that's a very bad thing to do, or that's a very wicked person. But we do not do that, you know. We recognise that all of us are weak and that we all do things that we should not. There is not one of us who is not a sinner, you know. Not one. And so when this poor man came to see me with his troubled soul, I did not sit here and think you should not have taken that money. I did not think that. Nor did I tell him that he should not go running off to Johannesburg, to his cousin, who works in a big hotel there, as he was intending to do. I did not do that. But I did tell him that he could speak to me in complete confidence and that I would not go to the police. And I have not gone to the

police, because that would be to break the secrecy of the conversation that a minister has with one of his flock, whoever he might
be. So, you see, Mma, I cannot talk to you about this man. I just
cannot do that."

Mma Makutsi sat bolt upright at her desk. In front of her, on
a small piece of paper, she had written the words: *Gone to Johannesburg. Cousin. Hotel.*

She smiled to herself. "You have been very kind," she said to
the minister. "I am sorry for asking about these private matters."

"And I am sorry that I cannot help you," said the minister.

"But you have been most helpful," said Mma Makutsi. And
with that, the conversation came to an end, as did the case of the
missing Zambian financier. The problem could now be passed on
to somebody else, but passed on in a useful way, and with some
positive information attached to it. Their quarry was now in
Johannesburg, which was a very large place, of course, but there
were not all that many big hotels there, and now those who were
after this man would know precisely where to start looking.

They had enough information now to report back to the attor-
neys, and to do so with their heads held high. Their report would
be well worth their fee, she thought; and from her point of view,
she was eagerly awaiting the chance to tell Mma Ramotswe
about what she had discovered. It was always satisfying to be able
to make a positive report.

When she heard the truck come back, she got up from her
desk and went outside. She had expected, of course, to see Mma
Ramotswe's van ignominiously tied to the truck with a tow-rope,
and was dismayed when she saw only the truck and a disconsolate-
looking Mma Ramotswe getting out of the passenger seat.

Mma Ramotswe told her what had happened, and Mma
Makutsi let out a wail of sorrow, for a moment quite forgetting the
good news with which she had intended to welcome her back.

"Ow, Mma!" she cried. "Your van! They have stolen your van! Ow!"

Mr J.L.B. Matekoni stood back from the two women, looking miserable. He tried to calm them, saying, "We will find another van. There are many vans . . . ," only to be hushed by Mma Makutsi, who felt that this was not the moment for sensible male advice.

Later, when she and Mma Ramotswe were sitting down together in their office for a quickly brewed cup of bush tea— which Mma Makutsi had now decided that she liked—it was Mma Ramotswe who set out to calm her assistant.

"I suppose that it had to go sometime," she said. "Mr J.L.B. Matekoni has often said that cars and vans do not last forever. We have to face that. And he's right, isn't he?"

Mma Makutsi had to admit that this was so. But that did not make this monstrous misfortune any easier to bear. "You are being very calm about it. I would be very angry if this had happened to me."

"Well," said Mma Ramotswe, "I have felt that anger. I felt it when I saw that the van had gone. I felt it a bit in the truck on the way back. But what is the point of anger now, Mma? I don't think that anger will help us."

Mma Makutsi sighed. "You are right about anger," she said. "There is no point in it."

"So tell me what has been happening here," said Mma Ramotswe.

At this invitation, Mma Makutsi sat up in her chair and grinned. At least here was something to make up, even in small part, for the news of the van. "I have solved a case," she said modestly. "That Zambian . . ."

Mma Ramotswe let out a cry of delight. "You've found him? Where is he?"

Mma Makutsi held up a hand. "Not exactly found him," she said. "But I've found out that he's no longer here. He's in Johannesburg."

She explained to Mma Ramotswe about the telephone call to the minister and about his inadvertent disclosure of the whereabouts of their quarry.

"You assume that it was inadvertent," corrected Mma Ramotswe. "But I rather think that the minister may have known exactly what he was saying. He did know that you were looking for somebody who had probably stolen a very large amount of other people's money? He did know that?"

"He did," said Mma Makutsi. "He knew all about that."

"Well," said Mma Ramotswe, "I think that this minister is not as stupid as you think he is. It sounds to me as if he was looking for a way of telling you something without running up problems with his own conscience. He knew that he should not break any confidences, but if he could do it indirectly, as he obviously has done, then perhaps he would not feel so bad about it."

"But is that the way that ministers think?" asked Mma Makutsi.

"It certainly is," said Mma Ramotswe. "One thing I have learned in this job is that everybody, even ministers, find ways of telling you things that they feel they should not tell you directly. And in the case of this minister, he probably thinks that it would be a very good thing for somebody to catch up with this man. So he has told you all that he knew, but he has done it in a special, roundabout way."

Mma Makutsi was thoughtful. "So, what should we do now, Mma? Is that enough?"

"What would Clovis Andersen suggest?" asked Mma Ramotswe.

Mma Makutsi looked at the well-thumbed copy of *The Principles of Private Detection.* She had never actually read the book from cover to cover, although she knew that one day she should do this.

"He would say that you should always remember when to stop asking questions," she ventured. "I think he says that, doesn't he?"

"Exactly!" exclaimed Mma Ramotswe, adding, "I don't think we even need that book any more. I think we know enough to start writing our own book, Mma. Do you agree?"

"I do," said Mma Makutsi. "*Private Detection for Ladies* by Precious Ramotswe and Grace Makutsi. I can see that book already."

"So can I," said Mma Ramotswe, taking a further sip of her tea. "It will be a very good book, Mma. I am sure of that."

TO REWARD MMA MAKUTSI for her success, Mma Ramotswe gave her the rest of the day off.

"You have worked very hard," she said to her assistant. "Now you can go and spend the bonus I am going to give you."

Mma Makutsi could not hide her surprise. No mention had ever been made of bonuses, but she had heard people who worked for large companies talk about them.

"Yes," said Mma Ramotswe, smiling, and reaching for the cash box which she kept in the top drawer of her desk. "We shall get a very good fee for this Zambian work. I think that it will be about ten thousand pula altogether." She paused, watching the effect of her words on Mma Makutsi. "So your bonus will be twenty-five per cent of that, which is . . ."

"Two thousand five hundred pula," said Mma Makutsi quickly.

"That much?" said Mma Ramotswe absent-mindedly. "Well, yes, I suppose it will be two thousand five hundred pula. Of course you'll have to wait until we're paid before you get all of that, but here is five hundred pula to be going on with."

Mma Makutsi accepted the notes gratefully and tucked them into the top of her blouse. She had already decided what she would do with her bonus, or this portion of it, and it seemed to her that this was exactly the time to do it. She looked down at her shoes, her work shoes, and shook a finger at them.

"More new shoes?" asked Mma Ramotswe, smiling.

"Yes," said Mma Makutsi. "New shoes and some new handkerchiefs."

Mma Ramotswe nodded her approval. The tiny white van had crossed her mind again, and the thought threatened to darken the mood of joy. But she said nothing to Mma Makutsi, who was now preparing to leave the office and catch a minibus to the shops. She deserves this happiness, thought Mma Ramotswe. She has had so many years in which there has been little for her. Now with her typing school and her new house, and this bonus of course, her life must be taking a marked turn for the better. Perhaps she would find a man too, although that might be too much to ask for at the moment. Still, it would be good for her to find a nice man, if there were any left, which was a matter about which Mma Ramotswe was beginning to feel some doubt. The tiny white van would not have been stolen by a woman, would it? That would have been a man. And this dishonest Zambian financier—he was a man too, was he not? Men had a lot to answer for, she thought; except for Mr J.L.B. Matekoni, of course, and Mr Polopetsi, and her late father. So there were good men around, if one looked hard enough. But where, she wondered, were these good men when one was looking for a husband? Where could Mma Makutsi find a good man at her age, with her large spectacles and her difficult complexion? It would not be easy, thought Mma Ramotswe, and there really was very little that she, or anybody else, could do to help.

THE BUYING OF THE NEW SHOES took remarkably little time. She had already seen the pair that she wanted—the red shoes with the gold buckles—and to her delight they were still prominently displayed in the shop window when she reached it. There was a moment of anxiety while the assistant searched for her size, but the shoes were soon produced and they fitted perfectly.

"You look very good in those," said the assistant admiringly. "Those buckles, Mma! They will dazzle the men all right!"

Mma Makutsi looked at her anxiously. "I am not always trying to dazzle men, you know."

"Oh, I can tell that," the assistant corrected herself. "Those shoes would be good for work too. They are very good shoes for all sorts of things."

Mma Makutsi decided to wear the shoes immediately, and as she walked along the pavement she felt that extraordinary pleasure that comes from having fresh leather soles beneath your feet. It was a feeling of satisfaction, of security, and in this case it was compounded by the flashing of the buckles in the sunlight. This is what it must feel like to be a rich person, she thought. And rich people would feel like this all the time, as they walked about in their fine clothes and their new shoes. Well, at least she had a bit of that feeling, as long as the shoes were new and the leather unscuffed.

She decided to walk a bit further down the line of shops. Not only would this give her the chance to wear in her new shoes, but she had a bit of money left over from the purchase of the shoes and she might find something else which would take her fancy. So she set off, walking past a small radio shop of no interest, and a shop that sold garden equipment. None of this seemed at all promising, and she wondered whether she should catch a mini-bus that would take her to the shopping centre where Mma Ramotswe liked to sit and have tea. There were shops there that might have something tempting.

Mma Makutsi stopped. She was in front of a shop which sold furniture, the Double Comfort Furniture Shop, and standing inside the shop, looking out at her through the plateglass window, was Phuti Radiphuti.

Mma Makutsi smiled and waved. Yes, of course: he worked in a furniture store, and here he was, selling furniture. Well, it would be interesting to see his shop, even if she had not been planning to buy any furniture.

Phuti Radiphuti waved back and moved towards the door to open it for her. As she went in, he greeted her warmly, stumbling over the words, but making his pleasure at seeing her clear enough.

"And look at your sh . . . sh . . . sh . . . shoes," he said. "They are very pr . . . pr . . ."

"Thank you," said Mma Makutsi. "Yes, they are very pretty. I have just bought them with my bonus."

Phuti Radiphuti smiled and wrung his hands together.

"This is my shop," he said. "This is where I work."

Mma Makutsi looked around. It was a large furniture shop, with all sorts of inviting-looking sofas and chairs. There were also tables and desks, set out in serried ranks.

"It is a very big place," she said. "Are there many people who work here?"

"I have about ten people working here," he said, the words now coming more easily. She had noticed that his stammer was most pronounced when he started a conversation and that it became less marked when he got into his stride.

She thought for a moment. He had said that he had ten people working here; this sounded rather as if he was the manager, which seemed a little bit unlikely.

"Are you the manager then?" she asked jokingly.

"Yes," he said. "My father owns the store and I am the manager. He is mostly retired these days. He likes to spend his time with his cattle, you know, but he still comes here. He is in the office back there now."

For a few moments Mma Makutsi said nothing. The knowledge that Phuti Radiphuti effectively owned a store should have made no difference to how she viewed him, but it did. He was no longer the inept dancer, the likeable, but rather vulnerable man with whom she danced at the dance academy. Here he was an important man, a man of wealth. The money did not matter. It did not matter.

The silence was broken by Phuti Radiphuti. "You must meet my father," he said. "Come to the office and meet him."

They walked to the back of the showroom, past the tables and chairs and into a large room with a blue carpet and a couple of cluttered desks. As they entered, an elderly man who had been sitting behind one of the desks looked up from behind a pile of invoices. Mma Makutsi moved forward to greet him, using the traditional and respectful greeting appropriate for an older man.

"This is my friend from the dancing class," said Phuti Radiphuti. There was pride in his voice, and Mma Makutsi noticed it.

The old man looked up at Mma Makutsi and rose slowly to his feet. He grimaced as he did so, as if he was in pain.

"It is very good to see you, Mma," said Mr Radiphuti. Then, turning to his son, he told him that he could see a customer in the showroom waiting for attention. He should not be kept waiting, he said.

With Phuti Radiphuti out of the room, the old man gestured for Mma Makutsi to sit down on a chair beside his desk.

"You have been very kind to dance with my son," he said quietly. "He is a shy boy. He does not have many friends."

"He is a good person," said Mma Makutsi. "And his dancing is getting better. It was not so good to begin with, but now it is getting better."

The old man nodded. "He speaks more clearly too, when he is with people he knows," he said. "I am sure that you have helped him in that way too."

Mma Makutsi smiled. "Yes, he is less shy now." She looked down at her new shoes, wondering what this old man would make of them. Would he think her flashy to be wearing shoes with such large buckles?

Mr Radiphuti did not seem to notice her shoes. "What do you do, Mma? Do you have a job? My son has spoken about you many times, but he has not told me what you do."

"I work at the No. 1 Ladies' Detective Agency," said Mma Makutsi. "I am an assistant there. There is a lady . . ."

"Called Mma Ramotswe," said Mr Radiphuti.

"You know her?"

"Of course I do," said the old man. "And I knew her father too. He was called Obed Ramotswe and he was a very good man. I bought cattle from him, you know, and I still have some of the descendants of those cattle down on my farm near Lobatse. They are fine beasts." He paused. "So you work with Precious Ramotswe. Well, that is very interesting. Do you solve many cases?"

"I solved one today," said Mma Makutsi lightly. "I almost found a man who had taken a lot of money."

"Almost? Did he get away?"

Mma Makutsi laughed, and explained about the information that she had obtained which would enable people in Johannesburg to track him down. The old man listened carefully and smiled with pleasure.

"I can tell that you are very clever," he said. "That is good."

Mma Makutsi did not know how to take this remark. Why was it good that she was clever? Why would it make any difference to this old man? For a brief moment she wondered whether she should tell him about her ninety-seven per cent at the

Botswana Secretarial College, but eventually decided against it: one should not speak too often about these things.

They talked for a few minutes more, mostly about the shop and the furniture which it sold. Then Phuti Radiphuti returned with a tray on which three cups of tea were balanced, and they drank this before he offered to run her back to her house in his car, and she accepted. It would be good, she thought, not to have to walk too far in these new red shoes, which were beginning to pinch a little bit on the right foot—not a great deal, but noticeable nonetheless.

When they arrived at her house, Phuti Radiphuti stopped the engine of his car. Then he reached into the back and took out a large parcel, which he gave to Mma Makutsi.

"This is a present for you, Mma," he said. "I hope that you like it."

Mma Makutsi looked at the carefully wrapped gift. "May I open it now?" she asked.

Phuti Radiphuti nodded proudly. "It is from the shop," he said.

Mma Makutsi tore open the paper. Inside was a cushion, an ornate gold velvet cushion. It was the most beautiful thing she had seen for a good while, and she struggled with her tears. He was a fine man this, a good man, who liked her enough to give her this beautiful cushion.

She looked at him and smiled. "You are very kind to me," she said. "You are very kind."

Phuti Radiphuti looked at the steering wheel. He could not speak.

CHAPTER NINETEEN

DOING THE DONKEY WORK

MR POLOPETSI stood under the empty sky, beside the track and a half-dead acacia tree. His excitement was making itself felt physically: a pulse that was becoming more rapid and a prickling in his skin at the back of his neck. He had watched Mr J.L.B. Matekoni's truck make its bumpy way up the track in the direction of the main road, a small cloud of dust being thrown up behind it as the heavily treaded tyres engaged with the surface dirt. Now it had disappeared and he was alone in the middle of the bush, looking down at the stain on the ground where Mma Ramotswe's van had bled its final drops of oil. He smiled. If his father could see him now, how proud he would be. He would never have dreamed, of course, that the skills which he had taught his son would be put to this use, nor would he have dreamed that his son would end up in prison, nor work as a mechanic at Tlokweng Road Speedy Motors, nor be, if he dared to think of it, an assistant private detective at the No. 1 Ladies' Detective Agency. He could not really claim that last title, of course, but if only they gave him the chance to prove himself then there was surely no reason why he should not be every bit as good as Mma Makutsi. He would not aspire to become another

Mma Ramotswe—nobody could do that—but at least he might be able to do the things that Mma Makutsi did, ninety-seven per cent or no ninety-seven per cent.

Mr Polopetsi's father, Ernest Polopetsi, had been a small-scale farmer who had enjoyed hunting in his spare time. He had rarely shot any game, as he had no rifle and relied on others for that, but he had been adept at following animal spoor and had taught his son how to do it too. He had shown him the prints made by the different animals—by civet cats, by duiker, by rock rabbits—and he had shown him how to tell how long ago an animal had passed by. There was the wind, which blew small grains of sand into the indentations made by the animal hoof or pads; there was rain, which washed everything away; there was the sun which dried out freshly turned soil. Then there was the bending of the grass, which could spring back, but slowly and in a time that could be read as a person might read the hands of a clock. This knowledge had been passed on to Mr Polopetsi as a boy and now, so unexpectedly, he was presented with the chance to use it.

He looked down at the ground and began his examination. There were prints which he could rule out at the outset: his own, to begin with; the marks of Mr J.L.B. Matekoni's veldschoens—a flat footprint reflecting soft rubber soles; then there were Mma Ramotswe's footprints, one set more recent than the other, because she had walked around the van the night before, immediately after it had broken down. Then there were other prints—a pair of boots that had walked along a path that joined the track from the right. The boots had been accompanied by a set of bare feet, small in size and therefore the feet of a child, perhaps, or of a small woman. That pair of boots had walked round and round in a circle and had then stopped and done something near the oil stain. After that, the boots had gone off and, yes, they had come back with another set of prints. Mr Polopetsi bent down and looked at the confusion of spoor: boots, tyres (small tyre prints—the prints of the tiny white van itself), and then, quite unmistakably, the prints of donkey hoofs. Yes! thought Mr Polopetsi. And then, yes! again.

He stood up and stretched. It was uncomfortable bending down like that, but it was the only thing to do when one was tracking. One had to get down to that level, to see the world from the point of view of the grains of sand and the blades of grass. It was another world down there, a world of ants and tiny crusts of earth, like miniature mountain ridges, but it was a world that could tell you a great deal about the world of a few feet up; all you had to do was ask it.

He stooped down again and began to move off, following the donkey spoor. This went up the road a short way and then turned off to the right, in the same direction as the path down which the pair of boots had walked. Now, in the ground between the shrubs, the picture was becoming much clearer. There had been much activity on the track itself; now the donkeys, inspanned to the tiny white van, had pulled their burden across undisturbed ground and the tracks were tell-tale. The donkeys—and there had been four of them, concluded Mr Polopetsi—had been led, whipped no doubt, by the man in boots and behind them, moving over at least some of the donkey tracks and obliterating them—had come the tiny white van itself. There must have been somebody else sitting at the wheel and steering the van as it was pulled along. Of course that was the pair of bare feet—a boy no doubt. Yes, the boy had steered while his father drove the donkeys. That is what had happened.

It was easy from there. Mr Polopetsi followed the tracks across the virgin ground for about half a mile before he saw the small cluster of single-room traditional houses and the stock pen made from brushwood. He paused. He was sure that the tiny white van would be there, concealed, perhaps, under a covering of sticks and leaves, but there nonetheless. What should he do? One possibility would be to run back to the track and make his way up the main road. He could be back in Gaborone within a couple of hours and he could tell the police about it, but by that time the van might well have vanished altogether. He stood and thought, and as he stood there he noticed a boy looking at him from the doorway of one of the houses. That decided it for him. He could not leave now as his presence would be reported and action would be taken to get rid of the van.

Mr Polopetsi walked towards the nearest of the four buildings and, as he did so, he saw the tiny white van. It was parked behind the house he was approaching, half covered with an old tarpaulin. The sight filled him with indignation. He had never been able to understand dishonesty, and here was a blatant example of the most bare-faced thievery. Did these people—these useless people—know what sort of person's van they had stolen? The worst in Botswana had stolen from the finest in Botswana; it was as straightforward as that.

As he came closer to the house, a man came out. This man, clad in khaki shirt and trousers, now walked towards Mr Polopetsi and greeted him.

"Are you lost, Rra?" the man asked. His tone was neutral.

Mr Polopetsi felt his heart thumping within him. "I am not lost," he said. "I have come to fetch my employer's van." He gestured towards the half-concealed van, and the man's eye followed him.

"You are the owner of that van?" asked the man.

"No," said Mr Polopetsi. "As I told you, it is owned by my boss. I have come to get it back."

The man looked away. Mr Polopetsi watched him, and realised that the man was thinking. It would be difficult for him to explain its presence, half hidden, behind his house.

Mr Polopetsi decided to be direct. "You have stolen that van," he challenged. "You had no right to take it."

The man looked at him, his eyes narrowed. "I did not steal it, Rra. Watch what you say. I merely brought it here for safe-keeping. You cannot leave vans out in the bush, you know."

Mr Polopetsi drew in his breath. The sheer effrontery of this man's explanation astonished him. Did this man think that he was quite that gullible?

"But how would we have found out that you were looking after this van for us?" he asked sarcastically. "Perhaps you left a note that we missed?"

The man shrugged. "I do not want to discuss this with you," he said. "Please take that van away. It is cluttering up our yard."

Mr Polopetsi stared at the other man, struggling with his indignation. "Now listen to me, Rra," he said. "You listen very carefully. You have made a very bad mistake in taking that van. A very bad mistake."

The man laughed. "Oh yes?" he said. "Let me think now. Does it belong to the President? Or maybe it belongs to Ian Khama or the Chief Justice or somebody just as important! What a bad mistake I have made!"

Mr Polopetsi shook his head. "That van belongs to nobody like that," he said quietly. "That van belongs to Mma Ramotswe, who is a senior detective in Gaborone. You have heard of the CID, Rra? You know about detectives? Detectives are plain-clothes senior policemen. You do know that, Rra?"

Mr Polopetsi saw that his words were having the desired effect. The attitude of the other man now changed, and he was no longer off-hand.

"I'm telling the truth, Rra," he whined. "I was just trying to look after that van. I am not a thief. Believe me, Rra. It is true."

Mr Polopetsi knew that it was not in the slightest bit true, but now he changed tack.

"I am prepared to forget all about this," he said. "You just return this van to the main road up there—you get your donkeys out—and then we shall arrange for a tow truck to come out."

The man frowned. "All the way up to the main road? That will take a long time."

"I'm sure that you have plenty of time," said Mr Polopetsi. "That is, unless you want to spend some of that time in prison."

The man said nothing. Then he turned round and called out to the boy who had been watching from afar. "Get the donkeys," he shouted. "The van is going up to the main road."

Mr Polopetsi smiled. "And there's another thing," he said. "The detective—the chief detective, I should call her—has had her time wasted by having to come out to look for her van and then finding it gone. I see that you have grown some very good pumpkins down here. I suggest that you put four of your best pumpkins into the back of the van. That will make up for her wasted time."

The man opened his mouth to protest, but thought better of it, and sulkily went off to fetch the pumpkins. Then, with its fine cargo of yellow vegetables stacked in the back, the tiny white van was connected to the team of donkeys, and the journey began. Mr Polopetsi began to walk alongside, but thought better of it and decided to make the rest of the journey in the van, with the pumpkins. It was comfortable there, resting on some old sacking, watching the sky above and thinking with some satisfaction of the pleasure which Mma Ramotswe would experience when he told her that the tiny white van was safe, rescued from captivity vile, ready to resume duties—after some necessary repairs, of course.

CHAPTER TWENTY

NOTE

THE DAY AFTER the return of the tiny white van—which had been fetched by Mr J.L.B. Matekoni from the side of the main Lobatse road and towed back with the apprentice at the wheel— was a day of taking stock. Mr J.L.B. Matekoni had to decide what to do about the van, the engine of which had seized up, just as he had feared. His instinct was to scrap it, and to explain to Mma Ramotswe that it was hardly worth pouring money into such an old vehicle, but he knew what reaction such an opinion would bring, and so he devoted some time to looking at just what needed to be done and how long it would take to do it. Mr Polopetsi felt justly proud of himself. He had explained to an attentive audience of Mma Ramotswe and Mma Makutsi how he had followed the tracks through the bush and how he had intimidated the thief with references to senior detectives. Mma Ramotswe had smiled at that. "I suppose I am a senior detective," she said. "In one sense at least. I suppose that strictly speaking you told no lies."

For Mma Ramotswe, it seemed that things were improving rapidly. Only recently, her situation had seemed rather bleak, with the loss of the van, the absence of any progress on the Zambian case, and Note's demands hanging over her. Now the van was back, and in the expert hands of Mr J.L.B. Matekoni; they could claim something of a victory in the Zambian case; and she was positively looking forward to seeing Note and confronting him with the information she had received from his mother.

She now no longer cared whether Note came to the house or to the office. She had nothing to hide from Mr J.L.B. Matekoni—she had not been married before, and the marriage which Trevor Mwamba had performed for them under the tree at the orphan farm was perfectly valid. She also realised that if Note had already been married at the time of her marriage to him, then her marriage to him was null and void, and this meant that Note had never been her husband at any point. That was a liberating thought for her, and it had a curious effect on her feelings for him. She was not afraid now. He had never been her husband. She felt free of him, quite free.

Note chose that afternoon to come to the garage, and she was ready for him. It was Mr J.L.B. Matekoni who spoke to him first, and he came through to the office to let her know that he had arrived.

"Do you want me to get rid of him?" he whispered. "I can tell him to go away. Do you want me to do that?"

Mma Makutsi watched from her desk, pretending not to be too interested, but excited nonetheless. She would be happy to tell Note to go away too; they had only to ask her and she would deal with him in a most decisive manner.

Mma Ramotswe rose from her chair. "No," she said. "I want to speak to him. I want to say something to him."

"Do you want me to be there?" asked Mr J.L.B. Matekoni.

Mma Ramotswe shook her head. "This is something that I wish to do for myself," she said. And Mr J.L.B. Matekoni knew, from her tone, that she was resolved. Note would have to be a strong man to stand up to Mma Ramotswe in this mood. He glanced at Mma Makutsi, who raised an eyebrow, and made a slow cutting movement across her throat. She too realised what a risk Note was running.

Mma Ramotswe walked out of the office and saw Note standing next to a customer's car, running a hand across the highly polished bodywork.

"Nice car," he said. "There are some rich people in this town these days. Lots of cars like this."

"Don't put your finger-marks on it, please," said Mma Ramotswe. "The apprentice has spent hours polishing that car."

Note looked at her in astonishment. He opened his mouth to speak, but before he could say anything Mma Ramotswe launched into her attack.

"I went to see your mother," she said. "I went to your place the other night. Did she tell you?"

Note shook his head. "I have not been down there over the last few days."

"Poor woman," said Mma Ramotswe. "She must be very ashamed of you."

Note's eyes widened. "You mind your own business," he spat out. "You keep away from her."

"Oh, I have no plans to go there again," retorted Mma Ramotswe. "And I don't want to see you again, either."

Note sneered. "You're getting a bit cheeky, aren't you? You know what I do to cheeky women?"

Mma Ramotswe closed her eyes, but only briefly. She remembered the violence, yes, but now it seemed less frightening.

"You listen to me," she said. "If you've come for money from me, the answer is that I do not have to give you a single thebe, not one. Because I was never your wife in the first place, and I owe you nothing. Nothing."

Note moved slowly towards her. "You say you were not my wife? Why do you say that?"

"Because you were still married when you married me," she said. "That makes you the bigamist, not me. I am not the one who could be reported to the police. You are. You were married to another girl and you had a child by her, didn't you? I know that now."

Note stopped in his advance. She saw his lip quiver, and she saw his fingers move in that strange way, as if he were practising the trumpet. She wondered for a moment whether he would strike her, as he had struck her before those many years ago, but decided that he would not. Behind her she could hear Mr J.L.B. Matekoni cough, and drop a spanner loudly—his way of signalling that he was at hand, that he would intervene should it be necessary. And there was Mr Polopetsi too, standing at the entrance to the garage, pretending to sweep the floor, but watching closely. Her two friends, those two good men who were so different from Note: her husband—her real husband—and that kind and helpful Mr Polopetsi were there at hand, ready to come to her aid. Note was no threat while they stood there; cruelty was a thing of shadows and hidden places, not a thing that flourished under the eyes of such men as those.

Note looked at her, a look of pure hate, and for a moment Mma Ramotswe was afraid again, but then she stopped herself and taking a deep breath, she stepped towards him. Now they were face to face, and when she spoke she did not have to speak loudly.

"I loved you," she said, making sure that he should hear each word. "You were not good to me. Now that is all over. I do not hate you, Note Mokoti, and I am . . ."—she paused. It was hard to say this, but she knew that she had to. "I want you to go in peace. That is all." And she spoke in Setswana those two simple words that mean Go in Peace, Go Slowly.

Then she reached into the pocket of her skirt and took out a small envelope. Inside there was some money—not ten thousand pula by any means, but some money to help him.

"I do not hate you, Note Mokoti," she repeated. "This is a gift from me. It is to help you. Please go now."

Note looked at the envelope which was being held out to him. For a moment he hesitated, but then he reached forward and took it. He looked at her.

"Thank you," he said, and then he turned and began to walk away. But he stopped after a few paces, and turned round to face her again. She thought that he was going to say something, and there were things that she wished he might have said; but he did not speak, but left her standing there outside the garage, with the afternoon sun on her face. She turned back, to see Mr J.L.B. Matekoni coming towards her slowly, wiping his hands on a piece of greasy rag; and Mr Polopetsi with his broom, quite still, all pretence of work abandoned. And she wanted to cry, but somehow there were no tears, for they had been shed many years ago, and now she was beyond tears for that part of her life and for that particular suffering. She might weep for her tiny white van, yes, and for its travails, but she could no longer weep for the man to whom she had now said a final farewell.

"THERE," said Mma Ramotswe as she raised a cup of bush tea to her lips. "That has settled that. No more Note Mokoti. No more searching for our friend from Zambia. Everything is settled. Except for one thing."

"And what is that thing, Mma?" asked Mma Makutsi.

"Charlie," said Mma Ramotswe. "What are we going to do about Charlie?"

Mma Makutsi picked up her cup and looked at Mma Ramotswe over the rim. "What makes you think that has not yet been settled?" she asked.

"Well, he's not here," said Mma Ramotswe. "He hasn't come back to work. Presumably he is still with that woman."

Mma Makutsi put her cup down and examined her nails.

"Charlie will be back very soon," she said. "Either tomorrow, or early next week. I dealt with that matter myself, as I thought you had enough on your plate at the moment."

Mma Ramotswe frowned. Mma Makutsi's methods were sometimes rather unconventional, and she wondered what measures she had resorted to in order to deal with Charlie.

"Don't worry," said Mma Makutsi, sensing her employer's concern. "I handled it very tactfully. And I think he will be coming back just as soon as he leaves that flashy lady, which I think will be very soon."

Mma Ramotswe laughed. "And how do you know that he's going to leave her? Are you sure that you are not just hoping that he will come to his senses?"

"That boy has very few senses," said Mma Makutsi. "No, I think that he will very soon be persuaded by that lady's husband to come back. I telephoned him, you see. I managed to get his number from the shebeen queen who is living in Mr J.L.B. Matekoni's house. Then I telephoned the husband in Johannesburg and said that I thought that he should know that his wife was carrying on with a young man. He said that he would come over to Gaborone and sort out that young man. I said that he should not harm Charlie, but should just warn him off and tell him to get back to his job. He was unwilling to agree to this, of course, but then I said that if he did not, then he would have to look for another wife. I said that if he would promise not to harm Charlie, then I would see to it that Charlie stopped carrying on with his wife."

Mma Ramotswe looked puzzled.

"Yes," Mma Makutsi went on. "I told him that this wife of his was ready to run away with this young man. The only way of stopping that would be to get the young man to leave her of his own accord."

"And how could that be done?" asked Mma Ramotswe. She had seen how headstrong Charlie could be, and she could not imagine him yielding to advice from Mma Makutsi, or anybody else for that matter.

"I then got hold of Charlie and told him that I had heard that the woman's husband was coming to deal with him," she said. "He looked very frightened and asked me how I knew this thing. That's the point at which I had to tell a small lie, although it was a lie for Charlie's benefit. I told him that I had a cousin in the police who had told me that this man was suspected of disposing of another of his wife's boyfriends. They had not been able to prove it, but they said that he had done it."

"That was not a very big lie," observed Mma Ramotswe. "It may even be true."

"It could be," said Mma Makutsi. "That man certainly talked about Charlie in a very threatening way."

"So Charlie is now scared off?" asked Mma Ramotswe.

"Yes," said Mma Makutsi. "And he asked me whether Mr J.L.B. Matekoni would take him back. I said that I thought that he might, provided that he promised to work very hard and not to spend all his time looking at girls."

"And what did he say to that?"

"He said that he had always been hard-working and, anyway, he was getting a bit tired of women. Apparently this lady with the

Mercedes-Benz is a bit demanding. She wants him to pay a lot of attention to her."

"I have always thought that about people who drive around in expensive cars," said Mma Ramotswe. "But I have never thought that about ladies who drive vans."

They laughed at this, and each of them poured another cup of tea.

CHAPTER TWENTY-ONE

A VISIT FROM MR PHUTI RADIPHUTI'S
FATHER, THE ELDER MR RADIPHUTI

I N THE DAYS and weeks that followed, life returned to normal at the No. 1 Ladies' Detective Agency and at Tlokweng Road Speedy Motors.

"I have had quite enough excitement," observed Mma Ramotswe to Mma Makutsi. "There was that bad business with Note. There was the terrible thing that happened to the tiny white van. And then there was the row over Charlie. I do not think that I could have taken much more."

"You are right, Mma," said Mma Makutsi. "We have never had so much happen all at the same time. It is better for things to happen separately. I have always said that." She paused to think for a moment before continuing. "At the Botswana Secretarial College they taught us to do one thing at a time. That is what they said we should do. One thing at a time."

Mma Ramotswe nodded. "That is very true," she said. She was not sure that everything that Mma Makutsi attributed to the Botswana Secretarial College could really have been taught there; after all, surely they had much more to teach than aphorisms. And for her part, of course, Mma Makutsi had those doubts about Mma Ramotswe's attribution of sayings and views to Seretse Khama. But neither expressed their doubts very much, which was what civility required.

It was true that rather too much had happened. Now both Mma Ramotswe and Mma Makutsi were looking forward to a period of stability and peace. That is not to say that they were averse to the appearance of an interesting client with a challenging problem; such clients were always welcome—indeed they were necessary—but it would be helpful if such a person did not cross their threshold for a week or two.

Mma Ramotswe was sure that Mr J.L.B. Matekoni would share her views on this. He had busied himself with the repair of the tiny white van—a task that had taken him several days—but now that was finished and she was once again at the wheel of the vehicle she loved so much.

"That van will not last forever," Mr J.L.B. Matekoni had warned her. "You know that, don't you?"

Mma Ramotswe had admitted this, as she had done on many occasions, "A few more years will be enough," she said. "Five, six years maybe. Then I shall say goodbye to it."

"Five or six years?" Mr J.L.B. Matekoni had repeated. "Oh, no. No. That is too long. You cannot hope for that. A machine is like a person. It gets tired."

"We shall see," said Mma Ramotswe. "You never know. There are some very old cars that are still working. I have seen some that are older than my van."

They had left the subject there, as there were other things for Mr J.L.B. Matekoni to do. Charlie had returned, as had been anticipated by Mr Polopetsi, and had asked for his job back. Mma Makutsi had witnessed the scene from the office doorway, standing just far back enough not to be seen by the chastened apprentice, but in a good position to listen to what was said. Later she told Mma Ramotswe with considerable satisfaction about the exchange.

"You should have seen his face, Mma," she said, smiling at the memory. "He looked like this." She turned down the corners of her mouth and gazed glumly at the floor.

Mma Ramotswe smiled. She took no pleasure in the young man's humiliation, but there were lessons he had to learn and there was a certain justice in what had happened.

"He shifted his weight from foot to foot," went on Mma Makutsi. "Like this. And Mr J.L.B. Matekoni stood like this, with his hands on his hips, like a teacher speaking to a naughty boy."

"What did he say?" asked Mma Ramotswe.

"I heard it all," said Mma Makutsi. "Charlie said, 'I am back here now, Boss. I have been away for a few days. I have taken a little holiday. Now I am back.'

"Mr J.L.B. Matekoni said, 'A holiday? I thought you said that you were quitting the job. I thought you said that you didn't need to work any more? Did you not say that?'

"And then Charlie said that this was a mistake. He said that he had not been serious when he said that he was not going to work any more. He said that he had meant to say that he was going on a holiday."

Mma Ramotswe sighed. "That young man has not learned anything yet," she said. "Did he really expect Mr J.L.B. Matekoni to believe that nonsense?"

"I think he did," said Mma Makutsi. "But then, you know what Charlie is like. He is not a boy with first-class brains. He is a forty-two per cent boy, at the most. That is the sort of result he would get in an exam. Forty-two per cent. I am pretty sure of that, Mma."

Mma Ramotswe's eyes wandered up for a moment to the certificate on the wall behind Mma Makutsi's head. It was the certificate from the Botswana Secretarial College, proudly framed, with the motto of the College in bold letters under the College title: *Be Accurate*. And under that, the remarkable result, inscribed in a hand that must have marvelled at the figures it was obliged to pen: 97 *per cent*.

"Anyway," went on Mma Makutsi, "Mr J.L.B. Matekoni listened to all this, and then he leaned forward and he shook a finger at Charlie, just as he did when Charlie shouted at me that day and called me the rude name."

A warthog, thought Mma Ramotswe. Yes, he called you a warthog, and I think you called him one too, if I remember correctly. She thought this and tried not to smile as for a brief moment an image of a warthog in big round glasses crossed her mind. Big round glasses and green shoes with blue linings.

"Mr J.L.B. Matekoni told him that he was a very silly young man," continued Mma Makutsi. "He said that young men should not run off with ladies who were much older than they were. He said that it was asking for trouble. He also told him that he should act more responsibly and find a nice girl of his own age whom he could marry. He said that this was what the Government was saying men should do, and that Charlie should listen to what the Government had to say on this subject.

"And all the time Charlie was looking down at the ground and wringing his hands, like this. I almost felt sorry for him. In fact, maybe I did feel a little bit sorry for him, although he had asked for all of it and only had himself to blame.

"And then I heard him promise Mr J.L.B. Matekoni to behave better in the future and I heard him say that he knew that he had been very stupid and that he would not be stupid again. Those were his very words, Mma, and I wrote them down on a piece of paper which we can keep in the office here and take out and wave at him some time in the future if we need to do so."

Mma Ramotswe looked at the piece of paper which Mma Makutsi had produced. Yes, it might be useful, but they should remember, she said, that Charlie was still a young man and that young men were apt to do foolish things, and that they probably all had to learn by their mistakes. Mma Makutsi was more grudging about it, but eventually agreed that he had probably suffered enough and should be given another chance. Perhaps he would meet a nice girl now, and all would change, although she had to admit to some reservations about that.

"But Charlie said something else," added Mma Makutsi. "He said something about a pumpkin."

Mma Ramotswe looked up sharply. "A pumpkin?"

"Yes," said Mma Makutsi. "He said that Mr J.L.B. Matekoni should not think that he was all bad. He said that he should remember that he had given you a pumpkin."

"I see," said Mma Ramotswe, and then, again, "I see."

She gazed out of the window. So it was Charlie who had brought that pumpkin, which meant that the man under the bed was not the person who had brought it, and this in turn meant that she still did not know the identity of the intruder. It was certainly not Charlie, because she would have recognised him, so . . . She stopped. An idea came to her, and it was an icy one. Perhaps it had been Note Mokoti under her bed. But she put that out of her mind, as there was no point in scaring herself after the event.

"Well, just think of that," said Mma Ramotswe to Mma Makutsi. "Charlie brought me a pumpkin! Don't young men do strange things, Mma Makutsi?" And everybody might be kind, she thought to herself—even a young man like Charlie, with his thoughts of women and his vanity and all the rest.

"They do," agreed Mma Makutsi. "Especially that young man." She would not mention her tea-pot again, but she had not forgotten.

Of course, Charlie's return had raised issues about Mr Polopetsi's future. Mr Polopetsi himself had been silent when Charlie had been re-engaged. He had continued to work conscientiously, but he had noticed Charlie's hostile glances and seen the two apprentices whispering to one another and looking in his direction. He had assumed that the return of the apprentice would mean the end of his job, and there was a resignation about his manner that day and the next. At last, waiting for a quiet moment, he had slipped into the office and spoken to Mma Ramotswe.

"I have come to thank you, Mma," he blurted out. "Now that my job is over, I am coming to thank you for what you did for me. I have been happy here. You have been kind to me."

Mma Ramotswe looked up from her desk. "I do not know what you are talking about, Rra," she said. "What is over? What are you talking about?"

"My job," he said. "The apprentice has come back. Now there will be no more work for me."

Mma Ramotswe, who had been adding up garage receipts, put down her pen and looked at Mr Polopetsi.

"I do not think your job is finished," she said. "Has Mr J.L.B. Matekoni said anything to you?"

Mr Polopetsi shook his head. "He is a very kind man," he said. "I do not think that he wants to tell me. But I think that this thing has happened anyway. I think that I shall have to go soon. Maybe tomorrow. I do not know."

Mma Ramotswe rose to her feet. "We will go and speak to him," she said. "You come with me, Rra."

Mr Polopetsi raised a hand. "No, Mma. Please, no. I do not want to make a fuss."

But Mma Ramotswe had brushed aside his objections and had ushered him out of the office and into the garage, where Mr J.L.B. Matekoni was standing over a handsome red car, deep in thought, contemplating its exposed engine.

"These people who make these cars are trying to make our lives difficult," he said. "They put in all these computers and what are we to do when they go wrong? They are trying to make cars into space ships, that is what they are doing. But we do not need space ships here in Botswana. We need good cars with engines that do not mind the dust. That is what we need."

"You should write to the people who make these cars," said Mma Ramotswe. "You could tell them."

"They would not listen to me," said Mr J.L.B. Matekoni. "I am just one man. I am just Mr J.L.B. Matekoni of Tlokweng Road Speedy Motors. They would look at my letter in Japan or America and say, 'Who is this Mr J.L.B. Matekoni? Do we know him? What is he writing to us about?' And then they will throw my letter in the bin. That is what would happen. I am not important."

"You are," said Mma Ramotswe. "You are very important. You are the best mechanic in Botswana."

"Yes," said Mr Polopetsi. "That is true, Rra. You are the very best mechanic. I have been proud to work with you."

Mr J.L.B. Matekoni turned and looked at them, first at Mma Ramotswe, and then at Mr Polopetsi.

"You are a good mechanic too, Rra," he said to Mr Polopetsi. "I have seen the way you handle an engine. You respect machinery. That comes from having worked in the hospital. You are like a doctor dealing with a patient."

Mma Ramotswe glanced at Mr Polopetsi, and then she addressed Mr J.L.B. Matekoni. "And he is a good detective too," she said. "He is the one who followed the tracks of the van. That was a fine piece of detective work. We could use him from time to time, as a sort of assistant. Maybe he could be an assistant-assistant detective to Mma Makutsi. She would like that."

Mr J.L.B. Matekoni looked thoughtful. "Yes," he said. "That would be a good idea." He paused, and frowned. "You did not think that your job was over, did you, Rra? Just because Charlie has come back?"

Mr Polopetsi nodded. "I did think that, Rra. And it is all right with me. I cannot expect you to give a job to everyone."

Mr J.L.B. Matekoni laughed. "But I never thought that you should go, Rra. I should have told you. I never thought that you should go. What is going to happen to this place once those boys finish their apprenticeship—if they ever finish it? Where would I be then if I did not have somebody like you to help me? And now you have heard what Mma Ramotswe says about your doing some work for her from time to time. You are going to be a very busy man, Rra."

THAT AFTERNOON, just as Mma Ramotswe was on the point of suggesting that they close the agency an hour earlier than normal, as she needed to go to the butcher to collect some meat for that evening's meal, Mr Polopetsi came into the office to announce that there was a man who was asking to see her. He was an elderly man, he said, who had arrived in a car driven by a driver, and he did not wish to come inside. Could Mma Ramotswe speak to him outside, under the tree?

Mma Ramotswe smiled. This was what an elderly person, a traditional person, might feel comfortable doing: talking under a tree, as people had always done. She went outside, and saw that her visitor was already standing under the tree, his hat in his hand. He looked so like her father, she thought, with a pang of regret; he had enjoyed talking to people while standing or sitting under a tree, watching the cattle grazing, or simply looking at the sky and the hills of the country that he had loved so much.

"Dumela, Mma Ramotswe, you remember me, do you not?"

She reached forward and they shook hands.

"I remember you well, Rra. You were a friend of my father. I have not seen you for a long time, but of course I remember you. You are well, Rra?"

He tapped his head lightly with a forefinger. "My head is getting very old now," he said, smiling as he spoke. "And that means that I forget many things. But I have not forgotten Obed Ramotswe. We were boys together. You do not forget that."

She nodded. "You were his good friend," she said.

"And he was a good man, your father."

There was a silence. She wondered whether she should invite him into the office for tea, but decided that this was not what he wanted. But what then did he want? Sometimes old people just liked to talk about the past, that was all, and perhaps that was why he had come to see her.

But no, there was something else. "I have a son," he said. "I have a son who is called Phuti. He is a very good man, but he has not found a wife. That is because he is a very shy man, and has always been like that. He cannot speak properly, and his words come out very slowly. That makes him very shy with women. I think that maybe the girls used to laugh at him when he was younger."

"People can be very cruel," said Mma Ramotswe.

"Yes," said Mr Radiphuti. "But now he has met a very nice lady."

Ah, thought Mma Ramotswe. This is why he has come to see me. He has come to ask me to find out something about this lady. She had been asked many times to do that sort of thing—to investigate a prospective marriage partner. It was a common thing for detectives to do, and indeed there was a whole section in Clovis Andersen's book about how to approach such a task.

"Who is this lady?" asked Mma Ramotswe. "If you give me her name, then I shall see if I can find out anything about her for you. I can find out whether she would make a good wife for your son."

Mr Radiphuti fingered his hat awkwardly. "Oh, I am sure that she would make a very good wife for him," he said. "And I think that you would know that thing already."

Mma Ramotswe looked at him in incomprehension, and he broke into a smile. "You see, Mma," Mr Radiphuti went on, "the lady works in that office over there, just behind you. So you will know her very well."

For a few moments Mma Ramotswe did not say anything. Then, very quietly, she said, "I see." Then she paused, and said again, "I see."

"Yes," said Mr Radiphuti. "My son has been seeing your assistant. She has been very kind to him and has made his dancing much better. She has also helped his speaking, because she has given him confidence. I am very happy about that. But there is a problem."

Mma Ramotswe's heart sank. She had allowed herself to hope, on Mma Makutsi's behalf, but now it seemed that there was some difficulty. It would be a familiar story of disappointment for Mma Makutsi. That seemed inevitable now.

Mr Radiphuti slowly drew breath before proceeding—a thick, wheezy sound. "I know that my son would like to marry this lady, I am sure of that. But I am also sure that he will never get round to asking her. He is too shy. In fact, he has told me that he cannot ask her because he would just stutter and stutter and no words would come. So he does not feel that he can ask her this important question."

He stopped, and looked imploringly at Mma Ramotswe.

"So what can we do, Mma?" he went on. "You are a clever lady. Maybe you can do something."

Mma Ramotswe looked up at the sky through the branches of the acacia tree. The sun was lower now, which always seemed to make the sky seem emptier. It was a time of day that made her feel a bit sad; a time of thinness and soft light.

"It is a very strange thing," she said. "But it seems to me that there is no reason that I know of why one person should not act as the messenger for another person in a matter like this. Have you seen those love messages that Zulu women used to make in beads and send to others? Those messages might contain a proposal of marriage. So why should we not use a messenger in a case like this? I see no reason."

Mr Radiphuti's gnarled fingers worked more anxiously on the brim of his hat. "Do you mean that I should ask her, Mma? Is that what you want me to do? Do you think . . ."

She raised a hand to stop him. "No, Rra. Do not worry. A woman is the best messenger in a case like this. But I must first ask you: Are you sure that your son wishes to marry this lady? Are you one hundred per cent sure?"

"I am," he said. "He told me that. And, what is more, he knows that I was coming to talk to you about it."

Mma Ramotswe listened carefully to his reply. Then, telling him to wait where he was, she made her way back into the office, where her assistant was sorting a pile of papers on her desk. Mma Makutsi looked up as Mma Ramotswe entered the room.

"What did he want?" she asked casually. "Is it a client?"

Mma Ramotswe said nothing, but stood there, smiling.

"Is it something funny?" asked Mma Makutsi. "You look as if you have heard something amusing."

"No," said Mma Ramotswe. "It is not funny. It is very important."

Mma Makutsi put down a piece of paper and looked quizzically at her employer. There were times when Mma Ramotswe was opaque in her manner, when she seemed to want Mma Makutsi to work something out for herself, and this seemed to be one of those occasions.

"I cannot guess, Mma," she said. "I just cannot guess. You are going to have to tell me what it is."

Mma Ramotswe took a deep breath. "Would you like to get married some day, Mma?" she asked.

Mma Makutsi looked down at her shoes. "Yes," she said. "I would like to get married one day. But I do not know if that will happen."

"There is a man who wishes to marry you," said Mma Ramotswe. "I understand that he is a good man. But he is too shy to ask you himself because he is very worried about his stammer . . ."

She tailed off. Mma Makutsi was staring at her now, and her eyes were wide with astonishment.

"He has sent his father to ask you whether you will marry him," Mma Ramotswe continued. "And I have come as the messenger from the father. All you have to do is think very carefully. Do you like this man? Do you love him enough to marry him? Is that what you want? Do not say yes unless you are sure. Be very careful, Mma. This is a very important decision."

As she finished her sentence, it seemed to her as if Mma Makutsi was unable to speak. She opened her mouth, but then she closed it again. Mma Ramotswe waited. A fly had landed on her shoulder and was tickling her, but she did not brush it off.

Mma Makutsi suddenly stood up, and looked at Mma Ramotswe. Then she sat down again, heavily, almost missing her chair. She took off her glasses, those large round glasses, and polished them quickly with her threadbare lace handkerchief, the handkerchief that she had treasured for so long and which, like the tiny white van, was near to the end of its life.

When she spoke, her voice was distant, almost a whisper. But Mma Ramotswe heard what she said, which was, "I will marry him, Mma. You can tell the father that. I will marry Phuti Radiphuti. My answer is yes."

Mma Ramotswe clapped her hands in delight. "Oh, I am happy, Mma Makutsi," she shrieked. "I am happy, happy, happy. His father said that Phuti was one hundred per cent certain that he wanted to marry you. One hundred per cent, Mma. Not ninety-seven per cent—one hundred per cent!"

They went outside together, to the place where Mr Radiphuti was standing. He looked at them anxiously, but could tell from their expressions what answer they were bringing him. Then the three of them spoke together for a short time, but only a short time, as Mr Radiphuti was keen to get back to his son to tell him what Mma Makutsi's response was.

Back in the office, Mma Ramotswe tactfully said nothing. Mma Makutsi gathered her thoughts, standing before the window, looking out to the trees in the distance and the evening sun on the grey-green hills beyond the trees. She had so much to think about: her past, and the place from where she had come; her family, who would be so pleased with this news, up there in Bobonong; and her late brother, Richard, who would never know about this, unless, of course, he was watching from somewhere, which he might be, for all she knew. She loved this country, which was a good place, and she loved those with whom she lived and worked. She had so much love to give—she had always felt that—and now there was somebody to whom she could give this love, and that, she knew, was good; for that is what redeems us, that is what makes our pain and sorrow bearable—this giving of love to others, this sharing of the heart.

africa
africa africa
africa africa africa
africa africa
africa

ALEXANDER McCALL SMITH

JOIN THE FAN CLUB TODAY!

Photo © Chris Watt

WWW.ALEXANDERMCCALLSMITH.COM

Membership to the Alexander McCall Smith Fan Club is absolutely FREE!
You can register online at **www.alexandermccallsmith.com** or simply complete the form
below and mail it to: **Alexander McCall Smith Fan Club, c/o Anchor Books, 1745 Broadway,
New York, NY 10019.** As a member, you will receive a quarterly newsletter covering all of
Alexander McCall Smith's beloved series, his latest work and travels, and details about
where you can see him on tour. Additionally, members will have exclusive opportunities
to hear from the author, participate in contests, and receive excerpts of McCall Smith's
titles before the books are available in stores. Don't miss this chance to have a greater
connection to one of your favorite authors!

NAME: _____

ADDRESS: _____

CITY: _____ STATE: _____ ZIP: _____

E-MAIL: _____

WHERE DO YOU BUY BOOKS? _____

MORE FROM THE NO. 1 LADIES' DETECTIVE AGENCY

THE NO. 1 LADIES' DETECTIVE AGENCY

Millions of readers have fallen in love with the witty, wise Mma Ramotswe and her Botswana adventures. Share the magic of Alexander McCall Smith's No. 1 Ladies' Detective Agency series in three alternate editions:

1-4000-3477-9 (pbk)
1-4000-9688-X (mm)
0-375-42387-7 (hc)

TEARS OF THE GIRAFFE

The No. 1 Ladies' Detective Agency is growing, and in the midst of solving her usual cases—from an unscrupulous maid to a missing American—eminently sensible and cunning detective Mma Ramotswe ponders her impending marriage, promotes her talented secretary, and finds her family suddenly and unexpectedly increased by two.
Volume 2
1-4000-3135-4 (pbk)

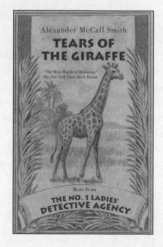

MORALITY FOR BEAUTIFUL GIRLS

While trying to resolve some financial problems for her business, Mma Ramotswe finds herself investigating the alleged poisoning of a government official as well as the moral character of the four finalists of the Miss Beauty and Integrity contest. Other difficulties arise at her fiancé's Tlokweng Road Speedy Motors, as Mma Ramotswe discovers he is more complicated than he seems.

Volume 3
1-4000-3136-2 (pbk)

The mysteries are "smart and sassy . . . [with] the power to amuse or shock or touch the heart, sometimes all at once."
—*Los Angeles Times*

THE KALAHARI TYPING SCHOOL FOR MEN

Mma Precious Ramotswe is content. But, as always, there are troubles. Mr J.L.B. Matekoni has not set the date for their wedding, her assistant Mma Makutsi wants a husband, and worst of all, a rival detective agency has opened up in town. Of course, Precious will manage these things, as she always does, with her uncanny insight and good heart.

Volume 4
1-4000-3180-X (pbk)
0-375-42217-X (hc)

THE FULL CUPBOARD OF LIFE

Mma Ramotswe has weighty matters on her mind. She has been approached by a wealthy lady to check up on several suitors. Are these men interested in her or just her money? This may be difficult to find out, but it's just the kind of case Mma Ramotswe likes.

Volume 5
1-4000-3181-8 (pbk)
0-375-42218-8 (hc)

IN THE COMPANY OF CHEERFUL LADIES

Precious Ramotswe is busier than usual at the No. 1 Ladies' Detective Agency when the appearance of a strange intruder in her house and a mysterious pumpkin in her yard add to her concerns. But what finally rattles Mma Ramotswe's normally unshakable composure is the visitor who forces her to confront a painful secret from her past.

Volume 6
1-4000-7570-X (pbk)
0-375-42271-4 (hc)

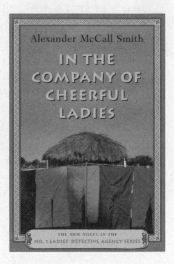

THE LATEST IN THE
NO. 1 LADIES' DETECTIVE AGENCY SERIES

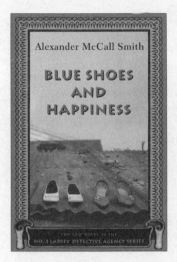

BLUE SHOES AND HAPPINESS

Mma Ramotswe and her inestimable assistant, Grace Makutsi, have their hands full with finding a cobra in their office and investigating the medical clinic and the local advice columnist. But the most troubling situation of all is the question of Mma Makutsi's impending marriage to a wealthy man. Her family is demanding an extra-large bride price, and while his money may buy her the new shoes she wants, Mma Ramotswe promises she'll find more contentment in simpler things.

Volume 7
0-375-42272-2
Hardcover available April 2006

THE SUNDAY PHILOSOPHY CLUB

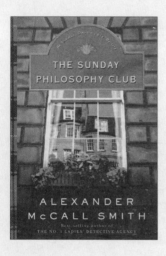

THE SUNDAY PHILOSOPHY CLUB

Isabel Dalhousie is fond of problems, and sometimes she becomes interested in problems that are, quite frankly, none of her business— including some that are best left to the police. Filled with endearingly thorny characters and a Scottish atmosphere as thick as a highland mist, *The Sunday Philosophy Club* is an irresistible pleasure.

Volume 1
1-4000-7709-5 (pbk)
0-375-42298-6 (hc)

FRIENDS, LOVERS, CHOCOLATE

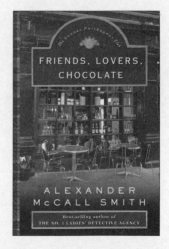

While taking care of her niece Cat's delicatessen, Isabel meets a heart transplant patient who has had some strange experiences in the wake of surgery. Against the advice of her housekeeper, Isabel is intent on investigating. Matters are further complicated when Cat returns from vacation with a new boyfriend, and Isabel's fondness for him lands her in another muddle.

Volume 2
0-375-42299-4 (hc)
Paperback available Fall 2006

ANCHOR BOOKS
ORIGINAL TRADE PAPERBACKS

44 SCOTLAND STREET

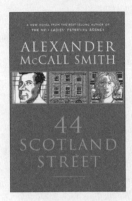

44 SCOTLAND STREET
All of Alexander McCall Smith's trademark warmth and wit come into play in this novel chronicling the lives of the residents of an Edinburgh boardinghouse. Complete with colorful characters, love triangles, and even a mysterious art caper, this is an unforgettable portrait of Edinburgh society.

Volume 1
1-4000-7944-6

ESPRESSO TALES
The eccentric denizens of a converted Georgian townhouse in Edinburgh are back, and McCall Smith fans will delight in their latest misadventures. From the talented six-year-old Bertie, who is forced to arrive in pink overalls for his first day of class, to the self-absorbed Bruce, who contemplates a change of career in between admiring glances in the mirror, there is much in store as fall settles on 44 Scotland Street.

Volume 2
0-307-27597-3
Paperback available Summer 2006

ANCHOR BOOKS
ORIGINAL TRADE PAPERBACKS

THREE NOVELLAS
INTRODUCING THE ECCENTRIC AND EVER-LIKABLE
PROFESSOR DR VON IGELFELD

Welcome to the insane and rarified world of Professor Dr
Moritz-Maria von Igelfeld of the Institute of Romance Philology.
Von Igelfeld is engaged in a never-ending quest to win the
respect he feels certain is due him—a quest which has a way
of going hilariously astray.

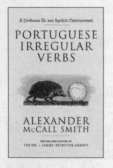 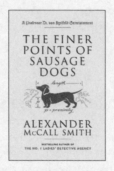 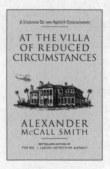

1-4000-7708-7   1-4000-9508-5   1-4000-9509-3

Available at your local bookstore, or call toll-free to order:
1-800-793-2665 (credit cards only).

The Official Home of Alexander McCall Smith on the Web

WWW.ALEXANDERMCCALLSMITH.COM

A comprehensive Web site for new readers and longtime fans alike, with five exclusive content areas:

- **THE NO. 1 LADIES' DETECTIVE AGENCY**
The original site for McCall Smith's bestselling series. Explore Precious Ramotswe's Botswana through book descriptions, a photo gallery, advice from Mma Ramotswe, and more.

- **THE SUNDAY PHILOSOPHY CLUB**
Enter a Scottish atmosphere as thick as a highland mist, complete with a photo tour of Isabel Dalhousie's Edinburgh.

- **PROFESSOR DR VON IGELFELD ENTERTAINMENTS**
Three original paperback novellas introducing the eccentric and ever-likable Professor Dr von Igelfeld, his colleagues, and their comic adventures.

- **ABOUT THE AUTHOR**
Read about Alexander McCall Smith and get updates on tour events and other author activities.

- **JOIN THE COMMUNITY**
Share the world of Alexander McCall Smith with friends, family, and fellow book club members. Print our free Reading Group Guides and sign up for the Alexander McCall Smith Fan Club and e-Newsletter.